GIRLS ON CAMPUS

Visit us at www.boldstrokesbooks.com

GIRLS ON CAMPUS

edited by

Sandy Lowe and Stacia Seaman

A Division of Bold Strokes Books

2016

GIRLS ON CAMPUS

ISBN 13: 978-1-62639-733-0

"Guise and Dolls" by Allison Wonderland appeared in *Wild Girls, Wild Nights* (Cleis Press, June 2013)

This Trade Paperback Original Is Published By
Bold Strokes Books, Inc.
P.O. Box 249
Valley Falls, NY 12185

First Edition: May 2016

Credits
Editors: Sandy Lowe and Stacia Seaman
Production Design: Stacia Seaman
Cover Design by Melody Pond

GIRLS ON CAMPUS

PLEDGE NIGHT

Radclyffe

A re you sure you want to do this?" I asked Kari for probably the hundredth time in the last hour. The whole thing had seemed like such a good idea until I really thought about what it meant for a straight girl to pledge a lesbian sorority, even though the sorority made a point of being open to all. If that was true, why was the initiation so secret? I mean, like cloak-and-dagger secret. Tonight was the official pledge night, and we didn't know where we were going, who would be there, or what would happen. We'd already sworn oaths of secrecy just to get this far. What if Kari hated whatever it was that was coming? No pun intended.

Kari slammed her hands on her size 1 gymnast hips and gave me the evil eye. Her coffee-and-cream complexion always flushed to a lovely cocoa color when she was pissed. She looked ready for whipped cream and chocolate shavings right about now. "How many times do I have to tell you, I'll be fine. It's not like I don't know what you get up to in bed. You've been telling me since we were fifteen."

Well, yeah, okay. That's what best friends did, right, shared the highs and lows of high school dating, including the sex and broken hearts? Besides, Kari knew about the first girl I ever had a crush on—her. We'd gotten as far as kissing a few times before she let me down easy.

"You're a great kisser," she'd told me when we were lying on top of my covers fully clothed one night after soccer practice.

We'd been practicing kissing for a couple of weeks, and I spent a lot of time fantasizing about what happened next. I hadn't gotten to try any of the scenarios I'd fantasized about yet, but Kari had always been able to read me really well and knew what I was picturing. "But you know," she said, "I don't think I want you to be my girlfriend."

My heart felt like applesauce in my chest, crushed and pulpy. I didn't say anything because if I opened my mouth I'd probably make embarrassing whimpering sounds.

She kissed me again, gently, sweetly. "You're my best friend, and I bet if we had sex, it would be amazing. I'm pretty sure I'm bi for you, but the rest of the time, not so much, and you know—I kind of like the wanting part best."

Weirdly, that seemed to make it okay. She wanted me, and I knew she'd always love me. Ditto for me, and here we were. Best friends and still hot for each other.

I studied her annoyed and totally gorgeous face. She had almond-shaped dark eyes, high slanted cheekbones, and a wide sensuous mouth. She was movie-star beautiful, at least I'd always thought so. "You're not just pledging because you love me?"

She tried to keep looking mad, but she burst out laughing. "I think it'll be a trip for us to be in that sorority together. Everybody knows it's a cool place to be. And yeah, I *do* like being where you are." She gave me a little hip bump. "You're such a dork, and I don't trust you by yourself."

I laughed. She knew all about my romantic foibles and failures and near disasters over the years. But hey, now I was almost nineteen and experienced. Mature. Totally unprepared for whatever was coming. I took her hand and mumbled, "I think I'd be scared out of my pants to do this without you."

She gave my hand a little tug and sent me a pretend kiss. "Honey, you're going to be out of your pants one way or the other tonight."

My throat was dry. "Yeah, I think that might be what I'm afraid of."

"Well, you're the lesbian. You ought to know what it's all about."

"That's the whole point of the initiation. No one knows what it's all about—at least no one who will talk about it. All I know is, we have to go through this step in order to finalize our pledge."

"Right," Kari said, "it's like a hazing, but they don't call it that. It's a rite of passage. They probably make us..." She frowned, the tiniest of wrinkles appearing between her perfectly plucked, arched eyebrows.

"You know," she said with a questioning lilt in her voice, "I don't actually have any idea what they might do."

"Or have us do," I muttered.

"I guess we'll find out soon." Kari glanced at her watch. "Because they're supposed to pick us up right about—"

On cue, a knock sounded at the door of the dorm room we shared.

I opened it and two women, one dark and one light, one brown eyed, one blue, stood shoulder to shoulder filling the frame. The blonde's slightly curly hair was down to her shoulders, and she wore an aqua blue dress that hugged her curvy body, plunged between her breasts, and ended just barely south of her ass. The brunette, taller and slimmer than the bombshell blonde, looked dangerously debonair in a black tuxedo shirt, black belt, and tailored black silk trousers. Our ushers for the evening.

The blonde smiled at me, her blue eyes frankly appraising. "Larson?"

I nodded, found my voice. "Yes."

"I'm Shar."

Kari came up beside me and, like she often did, rested her hand on the small of my back, answering sweetly to save me further humiliation. "Hi. I'm Kari."

The brunette took Kari's free hand, raised it to her mouth, and kissed her knuckles. "Hello." Her voice was buttery smooth, rich and deep. "I'm Paulie. I'll be your guide tonight."

I waited for Kari's response. She could still back out. I

wouldn't blame her. The whole idea was probably crazy to begin with.

Kari hooked her fingers around Paulie's forearm and stepped up beside her. "I can't wait to get started."

❖

We followed Shar and Paulie into the elevator and rode silently down to the lobby and out into the parking lot. The night had turned cold, but fortunately their car was nearby and we didn't have to walk very far. Shar opened the rear door of a dark sedan and gestured inside. "You'll find blindfolds on the seat. Please put them on and keep them on until we reach our destination. It shouldn't be long."

I glanced to Kari, who shrugged.

We buckled up, slid on the blindfolds, which were actually those kind of blackout masks you get on airplanes, and someone started the engine. I'm pretty good with time, and I estimated we didn't ride more than fifteen minutes and might've been going around in circles. When we'd parked and Shar told us we could remove the blindfolds and step outside, I realized we were at one of the boathouses situated on the large lake that bordered our campus. Rowing was a big intramural activity. No lights showed inside, but since this was supposed to be secret, that didn't surprise me.

"Let's go, lovelies," Shar said.

Kari and I followed the two sorority sisters down the ramp to the rear dock and into the boathouse. The windows had been covered with some kind of dark fabric, and where the boats were usually stored had been artfully turned into a giant sitting area with multiple sofas and overstuffed chairs. I wondered where they kept them when the boathouse was in use, but I certainly wasn't going to ask. I was surprised to see at least a dozen other women, some of whom I knew by name, others only by sight, already gathered in a loose group in the center of the big space.

I recognized six of the senior sorority sisters in addition to our ushers. I counted the pledges again. There were sixteen of us. A 2-to-1 ratio. I wondered if that meant anything.

Sorority president Rainer McDaniels stepped to the center of the room, and the low murmur of conversation between the sorority sisters abruptly stopped. The rest of us had been silent, probably too scared to speak, and a hush fell over the room. Rainer was legendary on campus. A senior now, she was some kind of musical prodigy and could have had a career in classical music, but had decided to pursue a high-level tech engineering degree, the details of which I could barely understand. Apparently she was highly sought after by several big Silicon Valley companies. She'd never had a girlfriend that anyone knew of. Pale and lean, dark-haired and black-eyed, she was the epitome of a brooding genius.

"Tonight," Rainer pronounced, "we finalize our list of pledges and offer you the opportunity to join us in solidarity and seduction for the remainder of your time. I'll remind you that everyone has signed an oath of secrecy, and even those of you who will not become one of us are sworn to uphold that vow." She didn't smile even though her tone was soft and seductive. "Just remember this. If you ever decide to share what happens here tonight," she glanced around, and it seemed as if she made eye contact with each of the pledges, "we'll know. We'll know, and we will uphold the honor of the oath. Do you all understand?"

"Yes," we answered in one voice. I glanced out of the corner of my eye at Kari. She was staring, an odd expression on her face. If I had to put a name to it, I'd say she was fascinated. Maybe she really would enjoy what was coming.

"Good." Rainer smiled. "We want tonight to be pleasurable for all of you, even those of you who will be eliminated."

I registered the shock on everyone's face and was sure my expression echoed it. What did that mean, elimination?

"We've invited twice as many participants as we plan to accept as new pledges. All of you show the kind of personality and passion we seek, but we can only make a final decision after we see how you put that potential into practice." Someone pushed a large green fabric chair into the circle and Rainer sat down, resting her hands on the broad wooden arms and crossing one ankle over the other. The other sorority members came to stand on either side of her. I was viewing the queen, or in this case, the king, and the royal court.

Two sorority members brought maroon velvet-covered footstools, placed them on either side of Rainer's chair, and knelt on them, facing each other with Rainer in the middle. One unbuttoned Rainer's shirt while the other opened the tab on her trousers and slid down the zipper. Rainer's expression didn't change. She looked as if she wasn't even aware of what was happening.

"For the first elimination," Rainer said, "each of you will turn to your left and face the person beside you. She will be your partner."

My partner was a small, Asian woman who I remembered seeing at rush week but never speaking to. Her eyes were cool and assured, although not unfriendly.

"Each pair will retire to the furniture provided. Before you recline, please remove all your clothing."

Someone laughed. Nervous laughter.

"Please begin."

For a second, neither of us moved. Min, whose name I finally remembered, suddenly swiveled and strode to a broad hunter green sofa ten feet away, directly in front of Rainer. She pulled her sweater off over her head, just as quickly divested herself of her bra, and then pushed her jeans and underwear down and kicked off her shoes. She was naked before I'd managed to follow her. My hands shook as I unbuttoned my shirt, pulled it from my jeans, and, working on autopilot, continued to disrobe. I sensed Kari somewhere close behind me, a soothing presence. Whatever craziness was about to begin, I wasn't alone.

"You and your partner are to pleasure each other

simultaneously, using your mouth, hands, or tongue. The first member of each couple to orgasm will be eliminated. You may start now."

I caught glimpses of the two attendants on either side of Rainer stroking her exposed breasts and abdomen. She was super hot, but I didn't have a chance to watch. I stared at Min, wondering which of us would bolt for the door first.

"I'd like the top, if you don't mind." She smiled, a disconcertingly self-possessed smile. "I'm sure this won't take long."

She was obviously confident. Well, so was I.

"Sure." I stretched out on the sofa, pulled a small throw pillow behind my head so I knew the angle would be good, and let my legs fall open. She deftly straddled me, her knees at my shoulder level, her elbows beside my hips, her arms cradling my legs from underneath. If there was a bell to start, I didn't hear it. Her mouth was on me before I'd barely gotten comfortable between her thighs. My hips jerked and I swear she laughed. I wrapped my arms around her ass and tried not to think about who was watching. Min knew what she was doing. She started out licking on either side of my clit, just enough pressure to make me hard, and ending lower down, stroking the sensitive lining of my inner lips. My clit twitched and pulsed. She was good, sure, but so was I.

I grabbed her ass to keep her from pulling away and closed my mouth around her whole pussy, sucking gently. Her clit was right at the level of my tongue and I sucked it between small, quick flicks on the underside. Her thighs trembled but she made no sound. She didn't have to. She liked it.

Concentrating on her helped me ignore the growing pressure between my legs. If I could keep my mind on what I was doing to her, I might not come all over her face. When she reached down and stroked my opening with two fingers, I wasn't quite so sure. My clit pounded. A hard ball of heat grew and throbbed in my pussy, threatening to explode. I wanted to be stroked, to be filled, to be fucked while she sucked me. I wanted to come in her mouth, all over her. Fuck. I was losing my rhythm, and she moved in for the kill. Her tongue was a magic wand, stroking, teasing, pressing. I was going to come so fucking hard.

I moaned, tensed my ass, and tried to pull away, but she held fast, sucking the shaft between her lips so I couldn't escape.

I had to distract her, or I'd be eliminated very, very quickly. She was disciplined, but I knew she wanted to come, I could tell from the turgid fullness of her clit, the way her pussy lips opened and slicked. Her thighs trembled, and I knew I had her on the edge. Trouble was, she had me there too. My clit was ready to go off in another ten seconds no matter what I did. I slid a finger inside and fucked her while I licked her, but I still couldn't get her to go. I was going to lose the damn competition, and if I did, I might end up leaving Kari there alone. I couldn't do that.

I felt the churning, pulsing blast building inside me, and desperate, I tried the only thing I hadn't tried yet. I ran my thumb between her lips, soaking up her come, and pressed it to her ass, circling and massaging the tight ring of muscle while I sucked her clit. Maybe the surprise was what broke her, but she pulled her mouth off my pussy and cried, "No! No, no, no."

I almost cheered. *Oh yes.*

Her pussy pulsed against my face and she came jerking in my arms, writhing against my mouth while her ass clenched over and over. When she finished, limp and moaning with her face buried against my thigh, I dropped my head back, gasping. My clit was still on fire, but I hadn't come. Yet.

Waiting for my body to slide down from the almost-coming brink, I turned my head, searching for Kari. She wasn't far away. She never was. She straddled the lap of a muscular redhead in a big overstuffed chair six feet away. Her back was to me. All I could see were her toned shoulders, the delicate sweep of her spine, and her round muscular ass, rhythmically flexing as she rocked against the woman beneath her. One of the redhead's arms disappeared between their bodies, and I imagined her stroking

Kari's clit, sliding her fingertips over Kari's slick pussy, bringing her closer and closer to the edge. Kari jerked, her hips starting to shake. Damn it, she was going to come. Watching her get ready to come pushed me right back up to the brink. Fuck, I had to be careful or I'd come by accident.

I heard a moan and realized it was Kari. *Aw, Kari, come on. Don't let her win.* Just when I was certain Kari was about to come all over the redhead's lap, Kari reached back, cupped the redhead's pussy, and in one sweet move, slipped her fingers inside. I grinned when the redhead's legs shot out, stiff and trembling, and her whole body arched off the chair. I heard a yell, knew it was all over. Kari did her nicely, fucking her slowly until she finished. You'd never know it was the first time Kari'd ever done it. As the redhead's legs slowly relaxed, Kari looked over her shoulder in my direction. She smirked, and I could almost hear her say, "Not bad for a beginner, huh?"

I gave her a thumbs-up. Smugly, she turned back and kissed the girl. Hell, she'd just topped like a veteran. Apparently, Kari and I were the top tops in the room, since the other couples were all still going at it. Moans, cries, babbling, and curses filled the air. I concentrated on getting my clit back to baseline. Whatever was coming next, I didn't want to start out at half-mast. First Min and then Kari had me wanting to come as bad as I could ever remember.

After another few minutes, Rainer's voice penetrated the haze of sexual murmurings.

"This round has ended. Those of you who have come will no longer be joining us for the rest of the evening. You will be escorted back to your rooms. We thank you for pledging and for joining the evening's entertainment."

One of the younger sisters came to stand by us. Min sighed and gave me a sweet kiss. "Good luck. You were fantastic."

"Thanks," I said. "And sorry, I guess."

She smiled as she rose and gathered her clothing. "Hey, no problem. There's no such thing as a bad orgasm, right?"

I sat up and pushed my clothes into a pile while she finished dressing. Across from me, Kari did the same. *You all right?* I mouthed.

She grinned. *Super.*

I'd seen her naked before, but somehow, the muted light of the boathouse and knowing she must be as aroused as me made her more beautiful than ever. Her dark nipples, tight and small, stood erect on her perfectly oval breasts. Her lean belly sloped down to muscular thighs and delicate calves. My clit twitched, and I gritted my teeth. Really, really bad timing to be this horny.

As if she was reading my mind, she shook her head in mock disapproval. I could see her eyes laughing. She was enjoying this, for sure.

I jerked when Rainer's voice rang out again.

"We've now reached the final point of elimination. Each of the remaining pledges will please have a seat."

While I'd been ogling Kari, the sorority members had arranged big chairs like Rainer's throne in a semicircle. Eight of them. I glanced at Kari, who lifted a shoulder as if to say *we've come this far*, and we took seats side by side in the half-circle. I didn't know the woman to my left.

She had to be close to six feet tall, with big wide shoulders, a long lean torso, and muscular legs. Must be a jock, a runner or rower or basketball player maybe. Her black hair was clipped short, her exotic features angled and sharp. Her skin was ebony and glistening, her breasts as full and tight looking as mine felt. She glanced at me out of almond-shaped eyes similar to Kari's, but she didn't speak. Everyone was on edge.

Rainer walked to the center of the half-circle.

"You've all proven your sexual expertise, and for that you will be rewarded. Your only requirement to pass this challenge is to exhibit control and stamina while the sisters take their pleasure. You will refrain from orgasm until each of the sisters has finished. To show you that can be done, I'll join you in this exercise."

The two women who'd flanked her before on the footstools stepped into the circle and quickly undressed her as if they had done it dozens of times before. They probably had. Naked, she settled into the chair facing the semicircle so everyone had a view of what was about to happen. Shar placed the red velvet footstool in front of her and knelt on it. Other sorority members formed a line until one was facing each of us. A brunette—a sophomore, I think—wearing nothing but a slinky black bra, matching lacy panties, and a hint of a hungry smile stepped up between my open thighs. Why did she have to hit just about all of my fantasy triggers, like I wasn't hot enough already.

"Begin," Rainer said.

Everyone knelt and my breath whooshed out.

Shar went down on Rainer and, as if at a silent signal, all the others followed suit. I gripped the arm of my chair as a warm mouth closed over me. Out of the corner of my eye, I saw Kari stiffen and I tried really, really hard not to imagine how she must feel right now. I could take it. I'd have to take it. How long could they possibly do this?

My clit tensed and plumped up as the brunette between my thighs teased and sucked me. Okay, if I didn't think about it, didn't look at her, I could do this. I watched Rainer, her expression impassive as the blond head between her legs slowly moved up and down. I could imagine Shar's tongue sliding between Rainer's pussy lips the way the brunette's slipped over mine. Shar reached up and caressed Rainer's tight belly and breasts, moving from one to the other, thumbs brushing her nipples. Rainer watched me watching her and smiled as if highly amused.

Suddenly the mouth on me pulled away and I breathed a sigh of relief. Okay, I made it. And then the sorority sisters got up as one, moved in a choreographed game of musical chairs, and another woman took the place between my thighs. Jeez. This one's rhythm was totally different, faster, harder, fingertips and tongue dipping inside me and then up and swirling around my clit. The increased tempo jacked me up hard and fast.

Beside me, Kari moaned. My thighs tightened. "Don't," I gasped, whether an order for Kari or myself I didn't know. Damn if the woman between my legs didn't laugh. Next to me, the big tough number whimpered. "Fuck, she's gonna make me come."

My vision swam. I was about to come myself. I tried to focus, searching for anything to divert me, and my gaze landed on Rainer again. Her face was set in that same smug expression as if nothing was happening, but I recognized the tension in her body as a redhead this time licked and fucked her. Damn, though, Rainer's control was amazing. I gritted my teeth, met her gaze. If she could hold on, so could I.

Blessedly, whatever timer they could hear must've gone off because they all moved again. How many times were they going to do this? The few seconds when the contact was gone was enough for me to back myself down, but every time my clit twitched, I was closer.

"I don't think I can do this," Kari whispered, her voice ragged and faint. "I want to come so bad."

"Don't," I said, and now Shar was between my legs, parting me, caressing the sides of my clit with her thumbs. I made the mistake of looking down as she licked me. Her eyes met mine, hazy and hot. Oh fuck. "*Fuck!*"

I wrenched my gaze away.

Rainer was chuckling. I grimaced, ground my teeth together. Fuck no. Rainer caressed the back of the head of the woman between her legs, her hips slowly thrusting. Goddamn her, Rainer was fucking her mouth as if she had all the time in the world. I didn't dare try that. If I did, I was going to come in Shar's mouth in a hot second.

The big jock next to me shouted, bucking and writhing in her chair. I couldn't not watch. The sister sucking her off stroked her belly and her breasts until she collapsed, muttering *fuck fuck fuck* over and over again. I realized I'd cupped Shar's neck, pulling her mouth harder against me, the way I did when I wanted to come. I forced myself to let go. I heard two other pledges come, one keening as if in pain, the other hooting wildly. Whenever someone orgasmed, the sorority sisters who brought them off dropped out of the line. Thank God. Maybe I had a chance to win whatever this game was. They all switched places again, and then only Kari and I were left. Along with Rainer.

Rainer, as cool as ever. Her eyes were hooded, her knuckles white on the edges of the chair, her expression remote and superior.

"I'm going to come this time," Kari groaned. "I have to come so bad I don't care anymore."

Paulie knelt in front of Kari. Shar moved into the space between our chairs and a redhead took her place between my legs. When the redhead slipped inside me and started kissing my clit, Shar reached down and played with my nipples.

"Oh God," Kari cried. "It feels so good. She's gonna make me come."

"Me too," I murmured. Enough already.

Kari reached between us and grabbed my arm. I found her hand and held it. Rainer smiled as if she approved.

My clit was on fire, a pulsing ember between my legs. I had maybe ten seconds to go. And then I saw it. A grimace broke across Rainer's face, and she glanced down at the brunette sucking her. Her stomach muscles tightened, etched beneath her skin like carved engravings on a stone statue. She was about to come. She looked over at me, and I grinned, my vision going dark.

"Now," I called, the sweet lightning coiling up my spine.

Rainer shouted, coming at the same instant, and I felt my body go rigid like I'd been electrocuted. I came and came, Kari's hand still gripped in mine, my eyes locked on Rainer's. Harder than I ever had in my life.

Limp and exhausted, I glanced at Kari.

"Nice job," she gasped, laughing.

Rainer rose, as cool again as if nothing had ever happened.

Naked, she passed down the line of pledges, kissing each one, murmuring a welcome. She lingered a minute with Kari and then came to me. Bracing her hands on the arms of my chair, she leaned down, but instead of kissing me, whispered in my ear, "Next time you come tonight, I'm going to be the one making you scream. No one touches you again until me. Do you think you can take it?"

The answer was easy.

Pledge night was over, but the pleasure was just beginning.

IN THE STACKS

Aurora Rey

I love going to the library. The smell of old books, chunky wooden tables, hushed voices. I know it makes me a nerd and I don't even care. The one exception to this, perhaps, is going to the library the night before a paper is due because I haven't even started the research yet. But even then, it's not so bad. Tonight is one of those nights.

When I get off my shift at the bookstore, I stop by my room for a quick shower. Spring is beginning to hint at summer, so I throw on a sundress and a pair of sandals. I grab my bag, making sure my ID and laptop are in it.

The sun is just setting and campus has the feel of hovering between day and night. People are sprawled on the quad, studying or pretending to. A couple of frat boys are throwing a Frisbee while checking out the girls who've just come from getting a spray tan and a blowout for the weekend's parties.

I'm not the only one heading to the library, but it feels a little solitary all the same.

I walk up the steps and past the towering columns covered with ivy. Someone coming out holds the door for me, which is nice; the doors of the main entrance are gigantic and heavy and there is no graceful way to open them.

After passing the circulation desk and the reference station, I head to the stacks. Literature books are on the B-level, which is the sub-basement. I sometimes think about the symbolism of that, but I really like the B-level, so it's hard to complain. No one is standing at the row of computers that link to the library's catalog, so I get to it.

I jot down a handful of call numbers to get me started and make my way to the row I want. I walk down the aisle, scanning the spines for the right combination of letters and numbers. When I get to the shelf where my two most promising sources should be, I notice a couple of gaps between the books.

I look down at my scribbled notes, run my finger along the shelf. They aren't here. Fuck. The entire premise of my paper hinges on an article my professor mentioned about the queer subtext in Nella Larson's *Passing*. And, of course, it's an older piece that isn't in any of the online databases.

The prospect of choosing a new topic makes me nauseous. Sure, I haven't started writing yet, but I've thought about it. Quite a lot, actually. While straightening sweatshirts and restocking folders and highlighters, I'd sketched out my thesis and several of my arguments. Without the source documents, though, I am up shit creek.

I scan the shelves above and below on the off chance someone put the books back out of order. No luck.

"Looking for something?"

I turn in the direction of the voice and there she is, standing at the end of the row. We've never spoken before, but I've noticed her—at the bookstore, in the dining hall, on the quad. A girl couldn't look like her and not be seen.

In jeans and a dark gray T-shirt, she manages to look feminine and masculine at the same time. Short hair and long eyelashes, the delicious curve of breasts and straight hips. She's enough to make my mouth go dry and my insides clench with longing.

She's also in my American lit class. I make a point of sitting behind her so I can stare without being caught. I'm not a total lost cause in the flirtation department or anything, but there's something about her that leaves me tongue-tied and wistful.

"How'd you guess?" I try desperately to make my voice sound normal.

The smile she sends me is slow and easy. I bet she's gotten more than one girl into bed with little more. "Is it the *Lesbian Desire* anthology?"

Is she playing with me? Is she writing on the same subject? My night just got a whole lot better or a whole lot worse. "Do you have it?"

"I do." The glint in her eye is playful, but also a little dangerous. Is she being suggestive or am I just imagining it? Wishing it? "And I'd probably be willing to share."

God. If we weren't in the library, I would fall into bed with this girl on the spot. Even with a paper due tomorrow. "I'd owe you big-time."

I think I catch her looking me up and down, but I can't be sure.

"I'm at the table in the corner." She tilts her head slightly and turns to walk in that direction.

I follow her, and sure enough, the book I need is there, along with a dozen others, a notebook, and a really expensive-looking laptop. I look at her, focused half on the task at hand and half on the way she looks standing there—casual but also kind of like she owns the place.

"That's the one." I point to it.

She shrugs slightly. "Like I said, I'm willing to share. But I'm not done with it, so you'll have to stay here to use it."

I'm sure as hell not going to complain about that. "That's cool. Thanks for letting me join you."

"Of course. Nothing worse than an unsatisfying trip to the library."

After saying that, she winks at me and moves slowly back to her seat. There is something flirtatious in her tone, her body language. Even if I'm not brave enough to flirt back, my body has no problem playing along. I join her at the table and try not to think about the fact that I've gone all hot and bothered.

She starts typing while I pull out my laptop and set up. I steal quick glances at her every so often. I get my first few paragraphs drafted, which is kind of a miracle given how distracted I am. I need to start putting in citations before I move on.

I reach for one of the books, using it as an excuse to look at her again. She glances up at that exact moment and I feel heat race into my cheeks. She smirks and looks back at her screen. Great.

I force myself to focus for about twenty minutes and actually make some decent progress. My eyes do not leave my screen or the book in front of me. When I hear her make a noise, I glance up. She's stretching and rolling her shoulders.

"I don't know about you, but I could use a break."

"Definitely." I stand up to stretch out my back, my rib cage. "I could make a coffee run. Or sodas or whatever."

"Thanks, but I'm good. I guess I had a different kind of break in mind."

I raise a brow, trying to remain calm. She's not suggesting what I think she's suggesting. Is she? "Yeah?"

Great. Be monosyllabic, because that's sexy. I search her face, desperate to find meaning. Instead of speaking, she walks toward me. She comes up close to where I'm standing. I mean, really close. She smells amazing—clean and, much like her clothes, this combination of masculine and feminine that is the stuff my fantasies are made of.

"Yeah." Her voice is barely above a whisper, and the way her lips move makes me a little crazy.

I tear my gaze from her mouth and look in her eyes. What I see in them is both a question and a promise. Fuck. I open my mouth to say something but nothing comes out.

Her gaze flicks down to my mouth and back to my eyes. And then it happens. She closes the small space between us and kisses me.

Her lips are even softer than I imagined they would be. But

after a few seconds, when she realizes I'm kissing her back, her mouth becomes firmer, more demanding. When she pulls away, I'm not sure if minutes or hours have passed. I don't really care.

"I've been wanting to do that," she says.

This cannot be happening. The sexiest girl I think I've ever seen just kissed me. And apparently she's been wanting to. I desperately try to pull my thoughts together so I don't ruin the moment. "I've been wanting you to."

"Is that so?"

She runs her hands up my sides and covers my breasts. The fabric is thin and I'm not wearing a bra. My nipples are hard and tingly. I can barely form words. "And that."

She kisses me again, then turns us slightly. I can feel the edge of the table press against the back of my thighs. "Sit."

I do as she says. If she said to run through the stacks naked while singing nursery rhymes, I probably would do that too, at this point. Her right hand slides up my thigh. Her fingers move up to my hip. Something flashes in her eyes and I see her swallow. She's realized I'm not wearing anything under the dress. It's a pretty passive way to be brazen, but I take it where I can get it. No one's ever caught me before. That I've managed to surprise her gives me a thrill.

"Open your legs."

Again, I obey. I feel her fingers move across my abdomen and then dip lower. I've been turned on since I saw her standing at the end of the row, and it's only gotten worse.

She smiles at me, then steps back. I have a moment of panic that this is all a giant tease. A cruel tease that will leave me edgy and distracted for days.

She grabs a chair and positions it where she was just standing. She sits down and scoots toward me. "Move a little closer to the edge."

I suddenly understand what she's about to do and I have a moment of a completely different kind of panic. We're in the library. It's public and brightly lit and someone could walk by at any moment. I don't even know what code of conduct we'd be violating, but I'm sure it's a pretty big one.

And yet. The panic is no match for how badly I want this, want her. I do what she says.

"Rest your feet on my thighs."

Doing so lifts my knees and pushes my legs farther apart. Instead of feeling exposed, I feel…emboldened. I want her to touch me more than I think I've ever wanted anything in my life.

She slides my dress up and leans forward. I hold my breath. She looks up and locks eyes with me. I nod ever so slightly. I can't believe I'm about to do this. She smiles and returns her attention to my open thighs. She presses her tongue gently against my clit, and I shudder. The air spills out of my lungs unevenly.

Her arms move around me and she works her hands under my ass, not lifting me off the table, but holding me in place. She starts a slow rhythm with her tongue, even strokes from the tip of my clit to the opening of my pussy. Each time her mouth slides down, she goes a tiny bit farther, until she is pushing her tongue into me. She clearly knows what she's doing.

I hear something and flinch. My eyes fly open. I look around, but it's only us. She stops and looks up at me.

"Sorry," I say, breathless with both fear and excitement. "Please don't stop."

I feel her grip on my ass tighten. Her tongue resumes its languid strokes.

I start to move with her, slow undulations that let me relish the way her fingers dig into me as well as the movement of her mouth. Just when I'm really getting into the rhythm, she shifts her tongue and quickens the pace. Her slow strokes become circles around my clit. Without touching the tip, she swirls around and around, working me into a frenzy.

I grasp the edge of the table, trying to maintain some kind of control. When she shifts her focus again, flicking her tongue back and forth right over my most sensitive spot, I stop trying. The slow thrust of my hips becomes a vibration. It's a frenetic race to the edge and I can't stop myself from tumbling over.

When the orgasm crashes over me, I'm not sure how I manage not to scream.

Before I have a chance to come down, to catch my breath, she stands up. I need to put myself together, to say something, but she doesn't give me the chance.

In an instant, her fingers are where her tongue just was. But instead of touching my clit, which honest to God I don't think I could take at this point, she slides them up and down either side of my pussy. Despite having just come, suddenly I want nothing more than to have her inside me.

I force my eyes open and find her looking at me. Her face is intent, but her eyes are questioning. She is in control of this whole thing but she needs to know it is what I want.

"Yes."

She slides one finger into me, then a second. Holy fuck. She feels absolutely incredible. I clench around her, trying to pull her in deeper.

Her movements are slow and smooth. I realize she's not fucking me to make me come, she's fucking me to make me want to. It's working. I'm completely turned on again and it takes all my willpower to keep my hips slow.

I open my eyes so I can look at her. She's staring at me, and the look on her face is one of intense concentration. There's satisfaction too, like nothing pleases her more than having this effect on me.

"More."

She smiles at my request. It's a smug smile, sexy as fuck. On her next thrust, she adds a third finger. I groan.

"Shh."

I remember where we are and bite my lip in an attempt to remain quiet. She starts fucking me in earnest now. She pushes her fingers in so deep I can feel the pressure of her knuckles against my pelvic bone. I rock back and forth against her, desperate to come and desperate not to.

She turns her hand slightly and brushes her thumb up to my clit. Oh, God. Oh, yes. No one has ever touched me like this before. Each thrust is paired with an easy upward stroke. It's exquisite. It's excruciating.

The pressure that has been building starts to erupt. The quivering in my core pulses outward. Every nerve ending in my body sparks alive. Even then, there aren't enough places for the pleasure to go. It ricochets through me again and again.

Eventually, I start to come down. My muscles continue to tremble and my bones feel weak. I realize her free arm is around me. Whether it was to hold me steady or something more tender, I can't be sure.

She eases back, carefully pulling her hand away. "I've been wanting to do that too."

I blink at her, trying to pull together some semblance of a response. "I..."

Nothing else comes out.

"You're beautiful," she says, "and even sexier than I thought."

"Can I..."

She cuts me off with a kiss, then turns away. She tucks her laptop into her bag, picks it up. She comes back to where I'm sitting and kisses me again. "Maybe next time."

I watch as she saunters through the stacks and disappears from view. I realize suddenly that I'm still sitting on the table with my dress bunched up. I tug the hem down and move to a chair, trying to catch my breath. I can still feel her mouth on me, her fingers inside me.

I look around. Another girl from our class has emerged from one of the rows. She gives me a knowing smile. Was she there the whole time? Did she see what just happened? Or is it simply because we're both here, clearly scrambling the night before the paper is due? I don't suppose I'll ever know. She disappears down another row of shelves and I turn my attention back to my work.

It isn't easy. The pleasant ache between my thighs is a persistent reminder of what just happened. And while part of me is sated, her offhand comment has me thinking—hoping—it might happen again. I flip open the book that started everything and find the chapter I need. It's going to be a long night.

THAT'S CONFIDENCE

Robin Watergrove

I've made exactly one friend in college. That's all I had in high school too, and you know what? It's working for me. Her name is Julie. We bonded over our anxieties about shared bathrooms.

She's been invited to a house party and wants me to come along. Someone was griping about how gross the dorms are during the sorority rush, someone else suggested a chill night, no hazing, no competition, no drinking, no drugs, at a friend's house in the suburbs, and it snowballed from there.

"I wasn't invited," I try, weakly.

"Don't make me beg."

"Why are you even going? Do you want to go?"

"Yeah." Julie shrugs. "It's the first party I've been invited to that's not all about drugs and alcohol. Might be cool." She doesn't have to work too hard to talk me into it.

I part my hair a little farther to the side so it sweeps over my forehead like a wave. It falls into my face every time I look down. And I mostly look down. I look at my shoes when I walk, I look at my hands in my lap on the bus ride to the house, I look at the doormat while we're waiting for someone to come to the door.

No one comes. We open the door a few inches and hear voices inside. We enter slowly, looking around like we're timidly robbing the place, and see a group of girls down the hall, in the living room.

I see her profile first. She has long, straight brown hair. I'm immediately self-conscious of my own trying-too-hard hairstyle. The group laughs and she smiles. It's a small gesture, and a big statement. She doesn't use her face to perform for others. It shows what she feels. Period. I'm staring down the hall at this girl when Julie elbows me.

"Take your shoes off." She points to the pile of Converse and boots by the door.

I'm already intimidated. I bend down to untie my shoes, and my chest feels tight. This'll be a fun evening.

Julie heads straight for the living room. I avoid the living room and everyone in it. I lurk in the kitchen and take way too long putting together a plate of chips and weird little pickles. The problem with social anxiety is once you flinch, you can't stop flinching. Like some gifted Pavlovian dog, I teach my body how to respond, first try. I look through the arched doorway at the back of her head, and intimidation shocks through me again.

I'm like the people in those videos about weird fears, who need extensive immersion therapy just to stand in an elevator or look at a picture of a spider. That's me, but with hot girls.

Put me next to a hot girl and I'm all shivers and stutters. Anyone who's quiet and confident. Girls with no makeup and unfussy hair, who wear loose pants and T-shirts. Everyone talks about being hot for "bad girls," and that's what a bad girl looks like.

Bad girls are pretty understated. If she's got big spiky hair or intense makeup or a bunch of rings in her nose, she's like a peacock and porcupine in one. She wants you to be impressed but keep your distance. Bad girls want you to get closer. There was this one girl in high school who sat across from me in art class. She used to wait for me to look up, then she'd hold my eyes for as long as I'd let her. I never talked to her, but I fantasized about fucking her.

I've only slept with guys. Two guys, one who liked to use two condoms and ask me if I was feeling good every twenty seconds, and one who always wanted to fuck face-to-face because he "didn't want to be disrespectful." They never grabbed me or held me down and I never asked for it. But when I dreamt about art class girl, she always had both of my wrists held tight over my head. She'd bury her fingers in my pussy and smirk when I gasped.

It's hard to look your wants in the eye, but when you spend a lot more time wanting than getting, you have to face facts eventually. I want to fuck a girl. Specifically, I want to get fucked by one who really, really wants to fuck me. I want a girl who knows what she's doing and doesn't ask for permission to do it. I want a bad girl.

I told Julie one night. We were talking about goals, and I said I wanted to sleep with a girl before I graduated. She said, "I don't think that'll be a problem. You're hot shit." I hope she's right. I'm an optimist, but I'm also a human statue around beautiful girls, and it's hard to fuck a statue.

I'm standing by the kitchen counter, trying to figure out how many hours I can be around this human kryptonite when a tiny, muffled part of my brain speaks up. *Don't be ridiculous. Why do you make things so hard? Go talk to her.* My stomach knots itself up at the idea.

I eat chips nervously, look down, and brush my hair out of my eyes. *What do you have to lose? Go ahead, embarrass yourself. Baby steps.*

I have so much to lose, says a stronger voice in my head, *I have everything to lose. I can make myself look like a complete idiot in front of everyone here. I was not even invited to this party.*

Fate makes the choice for me. Everyone in the living room starts to wander into the kitchen. Hot Girl comes in and I keep my head down. She has a sexy voice and a soft laugh. I look her over when her back is turned. Cut-up T-shirt over a tank top, cargo shorts, no socks. She's got a smattering of cryptic little tattoos on her arms. My heart is beating in my throat. I need to get out of there.

I go to the bathroom by the front door and wash my hands twice to kill time. Then I scratch the family dog behind the ears and pretend I'm not at a party at all.

Frustration is a perfect partner to intimidation. They snare on each other like razor wire. *Scream all you want*, I tell the tiny voice that wants me to make a move already, *I'm doing my best. And my best tonight is just petting this dog.*

The dog wants to go out, so I follow him into the backyard. I hear them before I see them: a bunch of voices, giggling and talking with words that are basically giggles. I look to the left and see a hot tub full of girls in their bras.

Before I can shrink back inside, someone hits my shoulder. "You coming?"

I turn around. It's Hot Girl. I flinch. Even tiny, frustrated voice is speechless. I say the only word in my head. "What?"

"To the hot tub." She smiles at me and I bite my lip. Not in a cute way, more like someone just clocked me in the jaw. Hot Girl walks past me and I follow her like I'm attached by a string. I leave the dog and the open door and follow her. I don't know how to explain that. I don't know why I follow her.

Hot Girl unzips her shorts and drops them. She's wearing boxers. Tiny, frustrated voice is amused. *Of course she is*, it wheedles me, *are you sure this isn't a wet dream?* Hot Girl sheds her T-shirt to reveal a skintight tank top, no bra. Someone in the hot tub wolf-whistles and everyone giggles.

A blonde in the tub looks over her shoulder at me and says, "Get in!"

Now it's a wet dream, the voice decides. *Or a nightmare*, I counter. I start taking off my clothes as fast as I can without seeming frantic. Thankfully, no one whistles at me when I get in.

I'm shivering like it's freezing cold even though the water is warm. I'm right next to Hot Girl. We're not touching but we're way, way too close. My mild panic blossoms into an all-consuming panic when I realize what they're talking about. A girl with bright red lipstick starts, "Well, my most embarrassing sexual experience was, like…last week." More giggles. They work around the circle; about half the stories are about sex with girls. I'm half listening, half scrambling for a story to share. I have a lot of material, but it's all too earnest, too deeply uncool. Stories of two people who didn't know what they were doing. Nothing like the "I accidentally had a threesome with my computer science TA" story that has everyone rapt right now.

The girl two seats down from me, the one sitting on the other side of Hot Girl, clears her throat. I look past Hot Girl at her. My eyes magnetize themselves back to Hot Girl and I take in her profile again. I'm pretty sure no one's watching and my head is pointing in the right direction and I can't help it. My gaze slides down off her face. Strong shoulders, pale chest. I can see her dark nipples through her shirt. They're just below the water line, halfway between soft and peaked. I want them in my mouth.

You could make a bad girl moan, tiny voice muses. *Put your hands under her shirt. Stroke her stomach, kiss her neck. Go on, bring her to her knees.*

Suddenly, Hot Girl just turns her head and looks back at me. My whole body jolts. I snap my gaze past her and back to the storyteller. Can you do that? Can you just turn around and stare at someone? I feel like she's breaking a fundamental rule. She's still staring.

I wait a moment longer, my face now burning from the embarrassment of being caught, then look back at her. The cringe of embarrassment is closely related to the hot, defensive flare of wounded pride. Something in me prickles and I stare her down.

Everyone in the tub groans. Hot Girl and I both look toward the group.

"No, really!" Storyteller is saying. "You wouldn't believe

how bad it was. She kept screaming and saying 'I'm coming, I'm coming!' when she obviously wasn't." The group breaks up in a handful of quieter conversations. It seems like the embarrassing story circle is done.

Hot Girl's not talking to anyone and neither am I. Too bad the only thing I can think to say is, "What about you?"

She turns to me with raised eyebrows. "What?"

My stomach turns itself inside out. I speak again only because she is expecting me to, not because I want to say, "What's your embarrassing story?"

She laughs once, looks down, and shrugs. "I don't know." Then she smiles at me and I flinch. "I'm not sure. It's all kind of embarrassing. You know what I mean? Sex is clumsy." She laughs again with her eyes down and I laugh too.

It's like someone has snipped a cable inside me. In a flash, the binding anxiety is gone. She seems a little nervous too.

I breathe in, feeling like I've finally come up for air. Then she looks up and her eyes show something I'm not expecting. They're sharp and hot. Eyes that know what they want. They're so direct that I feel like time stutters around me. *She's not nervous. Is she playing with me?* Panic rushes in again.

"What about you?" she says.

I scoff, playing calm while my mind whirls. "I have to tell you one and you don't have to tell me one? That's not fair."

Unfazed, she says, "You go first." Her voice lilts a little when she adds, "Then I'll feel less nervous."

She smiles. She's flirting. I blink. She's flirting with me. A thrill shocks up my insides. *Come on*—tiny voice is growing louder—*say something flirty back.*

I don't flinch when I lie, "Well, the first time I hooked up with a girl, that was pretty embarrassing."

She says, "Oh yeah?" and her lips curl. She looks amused, maybe interested.

"Yeah."

Another group of girls gets in the tub. Hot Girl scoots closer to me to make room for them. Her thigh brushes mine and our knees come to rest together. She says, "Tell me about it."

I stitch together three different mediocre sex stories into one passably bad one like a fucking magician. "Well, she was hot, but she couldn't kiss at all. She just stuck her tongue out and I had to kiss around it. And that was fine for a while, but then it was just way, way too much saliva."

Hot Girl laughs. "I've been there."

I laugh too and mumble, "So I was just like, 'Go down on me already.'"

Now Hot Girl cracks up. She scoots closer to me again. The tub is too full and kind of loud. She tips her head toward me.

When I speak again, my lips brush her hair. "But then she couldn't find my clit. And it's so hard to be like, 'My clit is here. Move over here. No, over here.'"

Hot Girl nods. "I've never understood that. If you can't see it, just pull the hood up. It's the red button." She looks up and grins at me. She's so close that my eyes go wide. She's close enough to kiss.

I nudge her, my heart flips, and I say, "Your turn." I want to touch her again. My paralysis competes with this edge-of-the-cliff urge that says *you could do more, she wants more.*

"Ah." She pretends to think for a little while. My pulse is too high and I feel a little light-headed. "I'm Chloe, by the way." She nods instead of extending a hand—that would be bizarre, a half-naked handshake in a hot tub. I would probably do that.

I nod back. "Nice to meet you. I'm Liz." The introduction feels important, like she wants to know my name, or wants me to know hers, before whatever comes next.

She's still watching me. Easy and slow, like she's opening a door, she lets the glimmer of sex pool in her eyes. I feel fear and curiosity and cringe-worthy, knows-no-bounds lust slip out of my eyes in reply. I stare at her.

"Well," her voice is soft, "you know how things are sort of embarrassing at the time but then, afterward, you keep turning them over in your head, and they don't seem so bad?"

I nod, under her spell. *Look at me like that again.* I'm wet. My pussy is thick and full.

"And you jerk off sometimes, thinking about them?" She adds, "Maybe it really was hot in the moment but you just couldn't see it then, because you were too nervous or whatever?"

Chloe continues, "So there was this girl. I'd just met her and I had a huge crush on her already. We were squished together in the back of a van, going to a show. She was funny, seemed cool."

"I wanted to feel her." She bites her lip. I shiver. "I wanted more than that. And you know when you can tell that a girl wants it too?" I'm so wrapped up in her that I'm barely aware of the other girls packed in close around us. Chloe's voice is low, just for my ears. She says, "So I just…"

She sets her hand on my thigh and I gasp in slow motion. My lungs pull in a breath and it trembles up my spine. My head knocks back and there's nothing I can do to stop it. My pussy contracts, already three steps ahead of me and hopeful.

I try to pull my rib cage closed, tighten my strings, keep my cool. I drop my chin and try to breathe. Chloe keeps talking. "She didn't really respond, so I just kept going." Her fingers start to slip up my thigh. For the first time, I feel like I'm fucking. Not having sex, but fucking, losing myself in something so erotic that it devours me.

Keep going. I'm frozen in place, staring at the water. *Don't stop.*

I whisper, "What did she do?" I try to smile. My pussy is so full I can barely feel anything else.

"She made some joke." Chloe is looking at my lips. "I can't remember. But she was smiling at me, so I didn't stop. She talked and I just…felt her body." Her hand drifts higher, up to my hip and the skin just above my underwear.

I find that the face I was so fearful to look at, so afraid to let see me and all my vulnerabilities, looks just as wrecked. Chloe's eyes are wide and dark. She keeps licking her lower lip. Her chest is rising and falling a little too fast. She presses harder with her fingertips and brings them together, drawing firm lines on my skin.

What does she want? What do I do? How far does she want to go? My voice is so quiet, barely a whisper. "Why was it embarrassing?"

Chloe whispers back. She angles her head like she's going to kiss me. "Because it didn't go anywhere."

I say, "Oh." My mind is blank. I don't understand.

Chloe nods, looking at my lips again. "Yeah. She never did anything. Never touched me back or…showed me she wanted it. So I stopped. I didn't know what else to do."

"What did you want her to do?"

"Show me she wanted it," Chloe says again.

I want to say I don't know how to do that. But we're still on the near side of casual. We're still talking like we're not talking about ourselves, right here, right now. And we are, right? I'm suddenly unsure. Is she just telling me a story and feeling me up because we're all so sexually liberated and easygoing? She's clearly turned on, right? What am I supposed to do? I say, "How?"

Chloe shrugs and her touch goes light. "That's the thing. It can't come from me. If one person dictates the whole thing, it's no fun. I took a chance. Now she has to take a chance. Try something I may or may not like."

I spread my legs. Without hesitation. I clumsily, pushily lift one knee and set it on hers. I stare at her wordlessly, blushing and defiant at once. *Like this? Don't go. Do you like this? Touch me again.*

Chloe's eyebrows knit together, then peak up.

"And if I like it," her voice is a little rougher, "then I could do something else to show her that I want it too." Her hand glides over my thigh. She presses her palm flat against my pussy. I'm too far gone to hide from her. I quiver and my eyes roll back.

I wonder if she can feel how wet I am through the water, how badly I want it. I can't control myself; I roll my hips and huff. *More.*

"Then," I watch Chloe glance around the tub to see if anyone is watching, "I could do a little more. She already knows I want her." Chloe lifts one side of my underwear away from my skin. I'm so turned on that I'm having trouble staying quiet. "So I could show her what I could do for her too." She slides a finger inside me. My mouth drops open.

She's inside me. My mind doesn't believe me. She's inside me. I lean toward her like I'm whispering in her ear, just to hide my face behind her hair. I whimper and she hums from the back of her throat. She's inside me. She's fucking me in a tub full of people.

She starts to move and pleasure overwhelms me. She pulses her finger slowly up and down. I'm so full I'm listless. Useless for anything but getting fucked. It feels amazing. I slouch and let her have her way with me. She massages my knee with her other hand and nuzzles against my head. I'm flooded with that feathery tingling that comes before orgasm.

We need to get the fuck out of this tub. There's a dangerous few seconds where we're both breathing too heavy and practically on top of each other and I'm dying to kiss her, missing all the levelheaded restraints that would normally keep me in check.

I wonder, distantly, if anyone has noticed us, then dismiss it. They would be wolf-whistling. *And who in this tub has actually fucked a girl? I have. I am. Right now.*

Chloe tips her head back and looks down at me. Her cheeks are glowing. She asks, unnecessarily, "You wanna fuck?"

"Yeah."

She pulls her finger out and says, "Wait two minutes, then follow me."

I nod and look down as she climbs out. I breathe in shakily and push it out.

Julie pushes her way over to me—has she been in the tub

this whole time?—and raises her eyebrows. "Getting steamy over here!"

I stare at her. I'm too undone for pretense. I say, "She was fingering me."

Julie's jaw drops. She shakes her head, as if to clear her vision, and whispers, "Are you serious?"

I nod.

Her eyes are wide and animated. "So why is she gone and you're still here?"

"I'm following her in two minutes."

Julie grins at me, open-mouthed, like I've just said we won a trip to Australia. She wiggles in her seat like she's vibrating with excitement, which makes me laugh. My body feels hollow and spent, like I've already had an orgasm.

Nerves knock at the back of my mind. I ask, "Any last-minute tips?"

"No, you'll be fine." Julie's face is serious. "Just remember to breathe and tell her what feels good, ask her what feels good, you know. All that stuff. Just have fun."

I nod and push myself forward onto my feet. Julie grabs my wrist. She whispers, "Remember that you're not doing this to impress her."

I consider that, then nod again. I grab my clothes in one hand and walk back inside. Chloe is in the kitchen, leaning over the sink and wringing out her tank top. *Show you I want it, huh?* I pin her to the counter. My lust-waterlogged body is clumsy. I grab her face and kiss her. I mumble into her lips, "We don't need that shirt," and pull it off. I tongue her nipples and suck on her breasts like it's the most natural thing in the world.

She puts both her hands behind my head. We're dripping on a stranger's kitchen floor, moaning little sounds at each other, shivering in the air-conditioning. Chloe leads me upstairs into a guest bedroom.

She locks the door and wraps me up in her arms again. In the quiet, I feel the first wave of uncertainty since she had her finger inside me. I kiss her back, sucking on her bottom lip, and hope I'm doing this right, doing what she likes. Chloe's a talker. She's a constant stream of murmured words, "oh my God," "holy shit," "good kisser," "come closer," and I'm nearly silent.

Chloe kneels down and tugs me with her. She pushes me back on my ass and crawls forward till our noses are touching. A stronger wave washes through. We're really doing this. My senses sharpen and pull the scene into better focus. Chloe's nosing against me, touching my wet stomach. Her eyes are warm and calm. "You can lick me if you want, but all I want is to go down on you."

I nod. That feels fine. I won't have to do anything I don't know how to do. One of my high school boyfriends went down on me for maybe two minutes, like it was a little performance for me instead of a sex act, so I'm not even really sure what it's supposed to feel like.

She tugs at my underwear and I lift my hips. Chloe moans when she sees my pussy. She touches the lips with her fingertips and says, "Oh my God, you're so fucking wet."

I feel like I've been validated. Not only do I want a girl but she wants me back. She's taking my clothes off and she likes what she sees. She presses on my engorged skin and my head falls back. I can hear the muted sounds of girls outside through the window.

Chloe settles onto her forearms and starts kissing my thighs. I watch her and shiver. My mind still can't believe this is happening. The farther she works up my inner thigh, the more I buck and moan.

Chloe watches my face when she first licks my clit. I freeze, not sure what she's expecting. I keep making noises but I'm struggling to listen to my body, trying to figure out what I feel under the scratchy friction of the carpet, her hands on my hips, the water dripping down the back of my neck and cooling on my arms, her hot breath between my legs.

Does it feel good? I'm not sure. It feels like too much. Like an oversensitive nerve being agitated. I feel exposed and realize my stomach is clenched. *Remember, you're not here to impress her.*

Fuck it, I can't feel anything if I'm too focused on making noise. I take a deep breath and fall silent. I breathe out and my body lets go of its grip. I stop shivering. I breathe in and it seems to fill me up from the bottom. The heady smoke of arousal drifts around under my skin. I lie flat on my back and stretch my arms out to the sides.

Chloe moans a little and nestles deeper. She sets the tip of her finger on my perineum. I look down and see her eyes are closed. My deep breaths are the only sound in the room. They seem to soothe Chloe too. She's moving slower now, licking up from the middle of my labia to the peak of my clit. I breathe in with the stroke, stroke, stroke, and breathe out even slower. Pleasure soaks my loose muscles and starts to lift sounds from my lips.

I didn't expect a bad girl to be so gentle. She lifts the hood from my clit with her tongue and circles it. She pulls back, admires me, then licks again. I'm buzzing. My breathy noises take on a new urgency. Chloe presses harder against me and I moan in reply. She presses harder still, licking faster. She lifts my labia to either side and flicks my clit with the tip of her tongue. Each touch reverberates back inside me and stirs up something deeper. She fucks her finger into me.

That's what I want. *Take charge.* I gasp, "Yeah, like that." *Take me.* Chloe responds, surging against me. Her knuckles press against me as she thrusts deeper. I roll my hips, show her how I want it, show her I can speak her language. I spread my legs wider, and she groans, her brow furrowed. The backs of my legs are purring.

I'm whimpering at her with every breath. She lifts off just long enough to say, "Put your hands in my hair." I stroke it out of her face and tug softly. She nods against me and tips her head into my hand. I feel warm, like I'm giving her something she wants too.

Chloe adds a second finger; I feel like I'm being fucked open. She alternates between long, deep fucks and shallow little curls. The deep ones make sense; it feels like she's tugging on something heavy inside me. But the short little rubs aren't doing anything for me until, suddenly, they are. I feel like she has both hands up inside me, squeezing and drawing everything, veins and nerves and liquid into this one spot. I feel my body winding around that spot, organizing itself around the intensity of it.

I think, hazily, that I'm proud of myself for being this worked up with a girl I just met. When I'm distracted, wondering why I'm not stressed out about how my thighs look, she catches me with just the right pressure at just the right moment. I don't have time to brace myself. It shoots straight to my groin and sparks. I cry out and cry out. She rubs me harder, lighting the spark like a fuse, and I come. My legs lock up and I shudder around her, slurring, "Oh fuck, oh my God, oh my—"

It's much more intense than any orgasm I've ever had with my vibrator. She keeps going and going like it'll never end. My body moves on its own accord, bucking and contracting. She holds my hip and tries to stay in place over my clit.

When she slows, I open my eyes. I look at the carpet fibers in a daze. Chloe is lapping me up, humming and massaging my thighs. Tiny voice pats me on the back. I think, with relative clarity, that I feel complete.

This is who I want to be. Someone who can fuck around with a beautiful girl in a locked room and come, way too loud, in her arms. I feel like I can carry this ease, the memory of this moment, around with me. That I can wear it with nonchalance in the way I speak, the way I smile. That's confidence.

HARD, WET LESSONS

Ali Vali

I'd do her," Bryn Elliott's roommate said as they walked to their apartment at the cusp of LSU's campus. The fall semester had just started, but there was nothing fall-like about the hot Baton Rouge weather.

"Of course you would." Bryn laughed. "You're a little slutty."

"So you're telling me if she offered, you'd turn her down, Mother Teresa?"

The object of their conversation was English professor Maison Davis, new on campus—a recent transfer from Alabama who had the ability to make poetry and short stories riveting. At least to Bryn, but it could also have something to do with the way she looked in jeans.

"No, I'm not an idiot," she said, a little too defensively. "But I'm also a realist. She's hot, but totally out of my league."

"Did you lose your self-esteem at lunch or something?"

"Again no, but I'm a junior and she's teaching, we're not exactly hook-up material." It hit her as they passed through the university gates that her iPad was still under the seat she'd picked toward the front to get a better view of the professor's ass. "Go ahead without me."

"What's wrong?"

"I forgot my iPad and notes. I'll see you later." Bryn wasn't tall but she'd run track in high school, so hopefully she'd make it before someone walked away with the damn thing. "Please be there," she said as she dodged people on the wide pathway, and she wasn't just referring to her iPad.

❖

Maison Davis sat in the large auditorium classroom with a red pen and a surly attitude. If these assignments were any indication, the first week's worth of lectures had amounted to her talking only for the pleasure of hearing her own voice.

"If Robert Frost had developed a gaming system or an iPhone app that revolved around crushing candy, maybe these numskulls would be more interested in the classics."

She wrote another note in big block letters on the upper right-hand corner of the page to a female student who'd actually dotted the *i*'s in her name with little hearts and smiley faces. It was days like this that she thought about changing careers. Perhaps she'd clean fish for a living.

"Please, please, please be there," Maison heard as the cute blonde who always sat in the second row came in and headed to her seat. "I'm so fucked," the blonde muttered a moment later.

"Looking for this?" Maison asked and scared Bryn into falling headfirst into the third row. "Okay, that went well."

Bryn was on the ground holding her head when Maison made it up there, and her tears were something Maison wasn't prepared to handle. Usually, in her admittedly short teaching experience, coeds cried because they'd flunked her course and she was messing up their GPA. Had any of them had the privilege of meeting her mother, they'd know guilt wouldn't work on her; she'd been raised by someone who had a doctorate in it.

"Are you all right, Miss Elliott?" She held her hand out and helped Bryn to her feet.

"You know my name?" Bryn gazed up at her with what appeared to be amazement.

Bryn's open staring had her noticing the blackening spot on her forehead. "Yes, and so will the infirmary when they check out the knot on your head."

"No, really, I'm fine."

"Did you finish medical school already and take my class for fun?" Bryn shook her head, so Maison helped her down the stairs, carrying all her stuff.

It'd be a special treat to go from grading papers to sitting in the infirmary with a bunch of hungover idiots. Never mind that it wasn't so long ago she'd been the hungover idiot trying to prepare for her next hangover on this very campus.

"Does this mean I'm the teacher's pet?" Bryn asked.

"It certainly shoots you up the ladder, Miss Elliott."

❖

"You really don't have to stay," Bryn said as they waited for the nurse practitioner to check her out.

"Hot date you need to get to, Miss Elliott?" Maison glanced up from her papers, almost done since Bryn had kept her eyes closed.

"No, but I'm sure my roommate won't mind relieving you." Bryn smiled, and this time she didn't seem like she was in pain.

"How about you concentrate on clearing your head instead of trying to get rid of me, and this will go a lot smoother." She packed away her work in the old leather messenger bag she'd had since she'd started school, and put it next to Bryn's stuff. "It was my fault you fell, so I don't mind."

The nurse came by and gave them the all clear. Thankfully Bryn's flying act hadn't ended in a concussion. Maison carried their stuff and got Bryn into the passenger side of her truck.

"Hungry?"

Bryn nodded before resting her head back and closing her eyes again. "Whatever you want, I'm not picky."

"Hopefully you outgrow that eventually. There are certain things you should be demanding about."

❖

Bryn walked around Maison's office and studied the few pictures on the wall. The place was full of boxes, as if she'd unloaded the U-Haul and run out of steam. It was a shock to find herself there. They'd stopped so Maison could post the test scores before heading out to wherever they were going to eat.

"Why do you still give written tests?" Bryn asked and thought she'd screwed up her chances of staying when Maison stopped typing and glanced over at her. "Not that there's anything wrong with that."

"There's nothing wrong with questions either, so don't hold back. It's the only way to learn anything." Maison swiveled her chair around and reached to pick up Bryn's iPad. "Do you have a favorite poem, or are you taking my course because you figured it'd be easier than writing essays?"

"I like poetry." She smiled when Maison hiked her eyebrows up. "I also hate writing essays."

"I make you write your answers on paper to remind you that life isn't all about having something like this in front of your face all day, every day. Poets like Brontë, Browning, Dickinson are better enjoyed by holding books than an e-reader. But I guess if that's the only way I can get you to discover their works, then I should shut up." Maison put the device down and tapped her finger on it. "Some of life's pleasures are best enjoyed the old-fashioned way."

"I also took your class because you're much better looking than Dr. Welsh," Bryn said, totally shocking herself by saying something so out of character, but she wasn't about to waste this opportunity.

"That's flattering, but the university frowns on me complimenting my students even if they deserve it." Maison's eyelids were half-closed, as if some inappropriate thoughts were going through her head. "And considering you're the only one who didn't totally bomb my quiz, I'd hate to lose you in my class."

The answer was interesting. It wasn't a "no," or a "you're too young," so she thought of her roommate's proclamation of doing the good Professor Davis. The real reason she'd registered for Maison's class was to indulge her fantasy of putting her hands on Maison's ass and having her beg for more.

"It'd be our little secret."

"Until it wasn't," Maison said, still with that great smile.

"I'm sure you've gotten your share of coed crushes, but I've been waiting for you to get here since last year when they announced your appointment," Bryn said as she opened two of the buttons on her blouse. "There was a story in the school paper about your transfer." She undid two more buttons and smiled at the reaction.

Maison didn't move, but her fingers were white on the desktop, she was pressing her fingers down so hard. "So you're different, is what you're saying?" Bryn almost laughed; Maison's voice sounded slightly higher.

"I'd like to think so." She finished the row of buttons and took a second to congratulate herself for taking time over the summer to update her underwear selection. Maison's eyes betrayed her stance on fraternization. Her gaze wasn't on Bryn's face. "For one, I'm not crazy." Bryn moved to the door and locked it. The sun was starting to set, and she doubted they'd be disturbed.

Maison laughed. "Okay, that's an interesting start."

"I meant I won't go running to the dean if we agree this isn't for us." She dropped her shirt and stood still, wanting Maison to take a good slow look and thanking whatever higher power was giving her all this confidence.

"What else?" Maison asked, clearing her throat, but keeping the desk between them, as if she didn't trust herself.

"You won't have to work very hard to turn me on." She fumbled a bit with the top button of her jeans.

Maison seemed to finally take mercy on her and came around the desk to take a seat in a well-worn leather club chair. "Any woman as beautiful as you, Miss Elliott, deserves a lover's full attention, so why say that?"

"Watching you teach something you're passionate about makes me wet." The declaration had Maison spreading her legs slightly, and Bryn desperately needed her pants off. "I doubt you've noticed me before today, but Tuesdays and Wednesdays are my favorite days this semester."

"I've noticed you."

"I think about you when I touch myself every night."

Maison closed her eyes and took a deep breath, but kept her seat. "So was today planned?"

"Today was me being a scatterbrain because we were talking about how we'd willingly give in if you gave us a chance." She managed the rest of the buttons and kicked off her jeans.

"We?"

"My roommate and me." She moved to the ottoman and very carefully, so as to not touch Maison, placed a foot on the chair arm and leaned back on one hand.

The white lace bra and panties hid very little, so Bryn was sure that Maison had no problem seeing her fingers when she slid them between her legs. "See, I told you that watching you makes me wet."

Maison stared at her slick, wet fingers before looking her in the eye. "You're not calling your roommate, are you?"

"She can fall on her head on her own time. I'm not sharing you with anyone." That Maison nodded was a relief; she really did want her total attention. "Right now, though," Bryn leaned forward and ran her fingers along Maison's lips, "I need you to kiss me."

"Bryn," Maison said, her hands still on the chair, "let's think about this."

"You're brilliant, but thinking is the last thing I want you to do." She grabbed the front of Maison's shirt and tugged hard. "I want you to forget everything and concentrate on this." Bryn moaned when their lips met. "Do you really want me to go?"

"No." Maison kissed her again before leaning back and resting her arms on the chair. "I might need more convincing, though."

Bryn leaned back, anchoring her feet under Maison's legs. She'd never done this for anyone, but she spread her legs and started stroking her clit for Maison's enjoyment. It felt so good, but she wanted to ratchet up her desire so Maison craved to touch her. If that happened, they wouldn't stop until they were both so satisfied it'd leave an impression they couldn't ignore going forward.

She cupped one of her breasts and squeezed enough to make Maison exhale heavily. The material felt rough against her nipple, and she liked the way they were visible enough for Maison to be mesmerized.

"So tell me how you know my name." She moved her hand slowly down her body as Maison squirmed. "There's got to be a hundred and fifty people in your class."

"Not too many of them sit in the front." Maison placed her hands on Bryn's ankles. "And the ones who do don't look like you." Maison spread her legs a little more, and since she had a hold of her, Bryn had no choice but to do the same. "Show me what you want."

Maison's tone had changed and become authoritative. Bryn pushed her panties out of the way, spread her pussy, and kept stroking—only now Maison could see exactly how turned on she was. She slid her fingers over her now stone-hard clit and tried to keep her eyes open to see Maison's reaction.

"Is that all for me?" Maison asked, and the question made her wetter. "Is it?"

"Yes." She moved her hand faster and harder.

"Bryn," Maison said loud enough to get her attention. "Give me your hands." She held her own hand out.

"Please, I need to come."

"You will, but you need to learn a little patience. Think of it as the difference between writing an essay and typing a tweet."

Bryn laughed but did as Maison asked. "It usually takes me a week to write an essay. If you make me wait that long, I'll damage something." Maison's laugh seemed to echo through her body, and she moved closer and went willingly when Maison lifted her to straddle her lap.

"Tell me what you want." Maison reached behind her and unhooked her bra with one hand.

"Done this before, have you?" Bryn asked but didn't want an answer when Maison circled her right nipple with the tip of her tongue. The touch went from her nipple straight to her clit as if they were connected.

"Suck it," she said and slid her fingers into Maison's hair.

"I could," Maison said as she moved to the left nipple, "or you can take those pretty panties off before I have to rip them."

Bryn stood up so fast she came close to falling over, and Maison stood to hold her steady. "Aren't you going to take anything off?" Bryn asked. "You're extremely overdressed."

"If you want it, take it, but if you stop unbuttoning I'll stop too."

"Stop what?" she asked and slumped against Maison when she put her hands on her ass and squeezed. Her begging Maison to fuck her wasn't far off, but she rose to Maison's challenge and started unbuttoning her shirt.

When Bryn reached the last button, Maison had her hand between her legs, and she was having trouble staying upright.

"Please," she said and closed her eyes when Maison picked her up and carried her to the desk. The wooden surface was uncomfortable until Maison laid her back, sat in her office chair, and put her mouth on her. "Please, baby," she said as she put her feet on the edge and spread her legs.

Maison started with a flat tongue but went only to the bottom of her clit. She lifted her head to complain when Maison sucked her clit so hard Bryn's ass came off the desk. When she brought it down, Maison's fingers slid deep into her pussy, and the sensation almost made her come.

"Fuck me," she said and grabbed two fistfuls of Maison's hair, not wanting her to move her head.

Maison was incredible as she went from sucking her to licking her until Bryn could sense the beginning of her orgasm. She squeezed Maison's fingers and grunted when she came so hard she landed on the desk like a wet piece of paper.

"I can see English isn't the only thing you majored in and are passionate about." She enjoyed the feel of Maison's fingers still buried inside her.

"There's more to life than poetry." Maison kissed her clit before lifting her head.

"You're right, but I think you spend a lot of time sitting and reading in that chair where we started, don't you?" Bryn sat up, wrapped her legs around Maison's waist, and kissed her, thrilled to suck on Maison's tongue and taste herself on her lips.

"I do," Maison said slowly, as if she wasn't sure where she was going with the conversation. Bryn gasped when Maison stood and pulled her closer so her wet pussy was pressed to her jeans. It was rough, but it brought her pussy back to life, and she wanted to feel Maison's skin pressed to her.

"Then I think you should have a seat."

Bryn unbuttoned Maison's pants and followed them and her underwear down when they were back at the chair. "Sit for me," she said as she pushed the ottoman out of the way.

Bryn sat back on her heels and stared at her fantasy come to life. Maison looked so good with her shirt open, sitting and waiting for Bryn to lick her dry.

"I'm going to suck you until you come." She put her hands on Maison's knees and ran them down to her inner thighs, liking that Maison spread her legs as far as the chair would allow. She lowered her head and put her tongue very briefly on Maison's clit before leaning back again. "Would you like that, baby?"

"I would, but would you?" Maison said, a bit too smugly for Bryn.

The professor was about to get a lesson in balancing the positions of power. Unlike Maison, who preached about patience, Bryn put her mouth on her clit and sucked hard to press it to her tongue. It must've felt good since Maison reached down and grabbed a handful of her hair. Right now all she wanted in life was to make Maison come hard, fast, and in her mouth.

"Fuck." Maison held Bryn's head in place, unnecessarily, since she had no intention of moving or stopping. She sucked harder, trying to give the same pleasure Maison had given her. "Fuck, right there," Maison said, and Bryn's clit came to life again when Maison's hips moved in time with her mouth. She pressed her thighs together to get some relief but it wasn't enough, so she reached down and started touching herself.

She didn't want to come by her own hand, and Maison must've noticed because she pulled on her hair hard enough to make her head come up.

"Wait, I want—" she said but didn't get a chance to finish when Maison stood and bent her over the front of the desk.

She let out a keening sound when Maison pressed her pussy to her ass and reached forward to put her hand between her legs. "Baby, if anyone is going to make you come, it's going to be me." Maison stroked Bryn's clit.

It was almost too much as she felt Maison pump into her ass and touch her at the same time, but she held out, wanting Maison to come first.

"Shit," Maison said as if all her intellect had deserted her. When her hips sped up, Bryn could tell she was close. The jerky motion of Maison coming made her smile, but she didn't get a chance to gloat. Maison turned her around and laid her out on the desk again.

"Oh God, oh God." She bucked into her mouth and covered Maison's hand with hers when she reached up to pinch her nipple. It took only Maison's mouth and her fingers inside to make her come again, harder than the first time, with her feet on Maison's back.

They didn't move for a long while, and she sighed when Maison pulled out, picked her up, and moved to the chair again, where she settled on Maison's lap. "Are you going to kick me out now?" she asked when Maison put her arms around her.

"You're more intelligent than that. Think of a better question, Miss Elliott." Maison kissed her temple. "The semester just started, but I think there are some hard, wet lessons we can teach each other. Don't you?"

"It could be a homework assignment that would take years to finish."

"You're a fast learner, baby."

"Are you kidding? This is one course I'm going to ace."

GUISE AND DOLLS

Allison Wonderland

I'm not a big fan of coffee, but I could really go for a cup of Jo. Just look at her. She's...Oh, you can't. Well, that's okay. I'll look, and you look forward to my risqué yet respectful descriptions. If she were a dyke, Jo would be the ultimate lipstick lesbian. She certainly has the face for it: more striking than a set and applied with more technique than Meisner. And she definitely has the figure for it: Jo's got enough curves to compete with a crazy straw. She even wriggles when she walks, except she doesn't walk—she struts, hips swiveling like a hula dancer, legs flexing like a ballet dancer. When she struts across campus, the guys say, "Looking good today, Joelle," as if she didn't look good yesterday and might not look good tomorrow. Everywhere she goes, she is besieged by winks and whistles and overtures of fornication.

That's because everywhere she goes, everyone thinks she's straight. And she is. Just look at her. I know—you can't. You'll have to trust me on this one. Everything about her is straight: her teeth, her posture, her hair, her orientation.

Speaking of orientation, that's when I first laid thighs on her. We're both... What? I said eyes. All right, I meant to say eyes. Anyway, we're both students in the Conservatory of Theatre Arts. I thrive on dyke drama, which is why I'm in the Dramatic Writing program. Joelle is a drama queen of a different sort— she's majoring in Performance. During freshman orientation last semester, the Wellness Center put on a bunch of hokey health skits about stress and sex and other collegiate concerns. Joelle was one of the actors in a play called "You Booze, You Lose… Your Virginity." She turned on a pretty good performance. Heck, even my thighs got a little damp. And…I did it again, didn't I? Well, my eyes were damp too, I swear.

"For crying out loud, this is so ridiculous," Joelle remarks, as we make our way toward the dorms. She's not strutting now; she's stomping—across the brick tiles that pave the campus. This place is such an eyesore. All the buildings are brown, like an old-timey radio. It seems like the only campus beautification project the school has undertaken is admitting Joelle. She could beautify… Sorry, I didn't mean to interrupt.

"I'm supposed to tear up at the end of 'Adelaide's Lament,'" Joelle laments. "Adelaide's all groom and doom because the guy she's in love with doesn't want to take the plunge, so she develops this miserable cold, yadda yadda. I have to go from sick sniffles to sob sniffles. The problem is I can't fake it; I have to feel it. Well, I would if I could but I can't, so…I can't. It's such a far cry from what I—" Loose tiles rattle like dishes and I snatch Jo's arm when she wobbles. "If my acting career fails, the only thing I have to fall back on is my ass."

I study the snug hug of Jo's jean shorts—a little too longingly, because I'm starting to feel that customary quiver. I push my spiral notebook up against my chest so that if my body decides to broadcast my craving for Jo to the entire student body, it won't look like I'm smuggling gumdrops under my shirt.

"Sure, I've gotten worked up over somebody before," Joelle is saying, "but it's different with…you know."

"With Brent?" I venture, following Joelle into the residence hall.

"Uh, no. Brent is bent."

"Why? Because he's in the thee-ay-ter?"

"No, because he's gay. You think every guy is after me. I'm"—Joelle unlocks the door to her suite—"After you. I'm not the Big Woman on Campus, or whatever the female equivalent would be. Is there one?"

"Beats me." I stretch out on Jo's bed, the closest I'll ever come to sleeping with her. Her sheets smell like a gingerbread house. I rub my bare legs against the cotton. "And FYI, Joelle, every guy *is* after you."

"Oh, yeah?" Jo sets her script onto her desk beside the Intro to Anthro textbook. "Name one."

"Darrin."

"Darrin?"

"That guy who was in the elevator with us at the Student Center yesterday. Darrin took one look at you and was instantly bewitched."

Jo's eyebrows curve like the pipes on her radiator. "Weren't you?"

I shift on the bed, my elbows thrusting against the mattress, which is ludicrously long and makes me feel puny and pitiful. I'm blushing too, I can tell—the closet is across from the bed and the door is one big mirror. "I prefer Dick," I squeak, a humble homage to the highlighter. "With a capital D and that rhymes with P and that stands for—"

"Pussy," Jo provides, and slides the closet door open. For one merciful moment, the mirror disappears. "Don't hoodwink at me with those pretty eyes of yours," she says, selecting a pair of jeans on a silly satin hanger. "You're more transparent than a pair of pantyhose." She propels the door closed, forcing me to come face-to-face with the numskull in its reflection. "You're also weirdly interested in men," Joelle adds. She takes the jeans off the hanger. "What were you like B.C.?"

"B.C.?"

"Before cunt. Or did you always like lady parts like me?"

"The only lady parts you like are the ones you get to do onstage," I tease, because if Jo ever does give me my LGBT cue, there's no way I'll miss it.

Joelle kneels down, begins fussing with one of the many

straps that trap her feet inside her shoes. The V-neck of her shirt dips into a U.

"I'll do it." I practically throw myself at her feet.

Joelle stands. "It's nice to have friends in low places."

Friends. Why did I pursue a friendship with Jo when I can't pursue a romance with her? I mean, what is it about unrequited love that makes it so appalling and appealing at the same time? I hope the professor covers this topic in my Psychology of Women course. Otherwise, I may have to withdraw. "Um, B.C. To answer your question, I dated guys during that epoch, but I always knew I liked the birds better than the bees, so…Hmm. I think only half that euphemism is effective, but you get the gist."

Jo steps out of her shoes. "So did you ever let a bee sting you?"

"Nope." I flop back onto the bed, the pleats in my skirt spreading out like a paper fan.

"I think I'm allergic to bees," Jo says, unbuttoning her shorts. She grins at me. Looking away is not an option. "You've seen London. You've seen France. Now you get to see my—"

"Camouflage underpants? Who do you think you are—G.I. Jo?" I'm surprised they're so simple, but they're sexier that way: no frills, just thrills.

Joelle trades in her shorts for the pair of pants she got from her closet. She leads them up her legs, slowly concealing their svelte shape with the dark denim.

"Do these jeans make my ego look fat?" Joelle inquires, posing like a paparazzi princess in front of the mirror.

"Colossal." I pat her posterior. "Just like your caboose."

Joelle shakes her fanny in my face. "You can borrow them sometime."

"Oh, so you're going to let me get in your pants?"

"Absolutely."

My smile squirms. "Stop leading me on," I mutter, half-hoping she'll hear me and half-hoping she won't. It's my fault—I shouldn't be flirting with Jo, not when she knows I have feelings for her. And she knows. There's no way she can't know. It's plain as gay. Day. Whatever.

"I'm not leading you on," Jo insists, but her tone is too chirpy, like she doesn't take me seriously.

"You're a leading lady. It's what you do."

"I'm not always a leading lady. Freshman year I auditioned for Peggy Sawyer in *42nd Street*, but they cast me as Dorothy Brock. It all worked out for the best, though, since Dorothy has this fabulous song about wanting someone to be gay with and play with. Not exactly your garden variety coming-out story, is it?"

Jo wants someone to be gay with? Great. Jo wants to play with someone? "Great, I'm in love with a playgirl."

"Luck be a lady. You're in love with me?"

"Like you didn't know." Attagirl—make *her* look stupid.

"I knew you were attracted to me, but amour? I didn't know I could wish you."

She's next to me on the bed, smiling with her straight teeth and sitting with her straight spine and…and…

"Not exactly your garden variety coming-out story?"

"Hey, just because my posture is straight doesn't mean that I am."

"But you look so—"

"Ladylike?"

"Yeah." Stupid Sapphic stereotypes.

"You look ladylike too, except when you sit like that." She studies my signature sprawl. "Look at you. Legs spread. Wide open. Gaping. Legs. Wide open."

"Hey, just because I'm not sitting pretty doesn't mean that I'm—"

"A lesbian?"

"Yeah. Wait, what?"

"Sometimes you're more bewildered than bewitched." Jo jabs my side like she's trying to stick a straw into a juice box. It tickles then tingles. "I hate that about you."

"Is there anything that you love about me?"

She shrugs one shoulder. "Nothing."

"What else?"

She hugs both of mine. "Everything."

I stare at Jo. Could it be that the girl who always has to have the piece of cake with the flower on it wants to have her cake and eat me too?

"Oh, come on," she says, eyes spinning like a compact disc. "You think I've been flirting with you all this time for tits and giggles?"

The whirring in my ears mimics the frozen yogurt machine in the cafeteria. I open my mouth to squeak, but this time no sound comes out.

"Okay, clearly you didn't like that question, so maybe you'll like this one: what does a person have to do to get some lip service around here?"

Nothing, apparently—before I can do or say anything, Joelle is shoving her fingers into my hair, letting them tangle in the loopy blond locks. I guess gentlemen aren't the only ones who prefer blondes.

The kiss is long and long overdue. It is liberal and liberating, decadent yet decorous. It makes me want to do a keg stand (I don't drink), study a broad (but with no space between us), and go streaking across campus (fully clothed).

With lips that taste like tropical punch and a mouth that tastes like blueberry yogurt, Jo's kisses are more amazing than Joseph's Technicolor dreamcoat. *Go, go, go, Jo!* This girl kisses with precision, perfection, panache.

But then, I always figured she would.

Jo College is not your average Jo.

❖

Joelle slams the door of my room. The bulletin board above my desk shudders. The framed poster beside my bed—Marilyn

Monroe lifting weights in blue jeans and the top half of a bikini—jiggles.

"Most people go out with a bang," I remark, retrieving a fallen flyer for Jo's show. "Not you. You come in with one."

"Your roommate isn't here, is she?"

I scan the room: bunk bed, books, basketful of garments that just got back from a trip to the laundry room. But no roommate. "She's in class. Well, she could be in the closet, but let's not go there." Jo gives me the Valley Girl face: snarls in charge. I close my laptop. "What's up?"

"The curtain," she says, dropping into a plastic blue chair that feels more comfortable than it looks.

"You've got four hours till show time."

"I'm not going on."

"Yes, you are."

"Not in my condition." She sniffles. "I think I'm coming down with something."

"You're too hot to catch cold." Jo is the first to growl at me. Her stomach goes next. "You hungry?"

"I'm too nervous to eat."

I slide my desk chair back and make the brief migration to the other side of the room. I kneel in front of Jo, folding my arms over her thighs. "We'll get your favorite: spaghetti SOS."

"That's not a bad idea, actually. I could use all the help I can get."

"Not help, silly. SOS. Sauce on the side."

Jo stops her smile before it peaks at her cheeks. "Don't be endearing. I can't handle it right now."

"How come you're so nervous?"

"My mind is a tabula rasa. The dialogue is going to die on my lips, and don't even get me started on the lyrics." She taps her foot, flaps her hand, groping for the words to the bushel and a peck song.

"Isn't there something about hugging and necking?" I query, and get a weary look in response. Maybe I should show, not tell.

I lift myself onto Jo's lap and wrap my arms around her neck, nuzzling her manicured mane, dark and shiny like black coffee. I don't know if this is helping, but what I don't know can't hurt me. But it can hurt her, so... "I know what you need." Reluctantly, I climb off Jo's thighs and move to stand behind her. "You need a massage," I offer, rubbing her shoulders.

Joelle shrugs against my hands. "I don't think that will be sufficient," she says. "I do, however, think that I'm going to faint."

I frown down at her. "Put your head between your legs."

Jo tilts her head back and regards me as though I'm one sip short of saying so long to sobriety. "So when I pass out I can hit my head on the floor? Do I look like a numskull to you?" She slants her head to one side, her eyes narrowing into buttonholes. "Can't you put *your* head between my legs?"

A fuzzy feeling flutters inside my panties. "You want me to give you a peck on your bushel?" My heart socks my rib cage and my knees knock together like a plastic clacker.

But I'm not too nervous to eat.

I come around the front of the chair and kneel at Jo's feet again. I curl her skirt up across her thighs. No camouflage panties today. No panties period. It's like a stage without an apron, a theatre without an orchestra pit.

It takes a moment for my eyes to adjust, as if someone just turned the spotlight on me.

The curtain is most definitely calling. And this is no time for stage fright. I can do this. I've taken a few improv classes, and the first rule of improv is to always accept what your scene partner gives you. Have you seen what my partner is giving me? I peruse the playing area, all lush lips and liquid lust. Instead of chewing the inside of my mouth, I should be chewing the scenery.

Besides, Jo went up on her lines, so it's only fair that I go down on them.

Those lines are ridged like a desktop globe and slippery when whet.

But let's pace the plot more practically.

I start at the top of the show. Jo's curls, pitch-black like the flats and sharps of a piano, provide the backdrop to a striking set. Not be upstaged, her clit, hard as the head of a tassel tie, begins to vibrate, complementing her vocal cords.

Waiting in the wings is the ensemble, and I see to it that each and every part is featured fairly. Her folds are flavorful—succulent and sugary, like Bartlett pears and conversation hearts.

"You're getting wet," Jo informs me.

My head pops up as if from a trapdoor in a stage floor. "How do you know?"

"Your hair's in the dip."

I glide my hand through my tresses. Smeared strands stick to my fingers. I grip the tips, massage the gel into the blond loops.

Joelle's lips skew into a half-smile, as if she's too worn out to lift up the other side of her mouth. "That's one way to treat split ends," she mumbles.

I duck back down. Whispered whimpers glide past Jo's lips and she grinds her groin against my mouth.

A song pops into my head, and I murmur the lyrics into her sex as if it's a microphone. "I'll know when my love comes al—"

"Adelaide may be getting laid, but she's not singing that number," Jo grouses in a hum-cum-moan.

"I'll know when my love comes?"

"Now you've got my number."

I've also got her licked, and kicking like a chorus girl. I hold her thighs tighter, my nails scraping her skin, like a pencil making light marks in a libretto vocal book. Jo sings my praises as if she were a bell, and the show ends on a high note.

"That was nicely-nicely done," Jo murmurs, looking satisfied.

Perhaps a little too satisfied.

"You weren't nervous at all, were you?" I challenge. "You conned me into cunnilingus." Jo giggles. "You stooped pretty low, you know that?"

"I know," she crows. "Good thing I'm sitting down, 'cause I am rockin' the gloat." She winks at me, her mermaid-green eyes sparkling.

"Take back your wink."

Jo looks me straight in the eye. Well, as straight as she can, anyway. As for me, I can't even see straight, but I can see her eyes darken, the way the house lights go down in the theatre.

So much for intermission. I was hoping to catch my breath, give and get a more in-depth critique of my performance, maybe participate in a post-show talkback with the actor. But Joelle doesn't hold the curtain, already having decided to turn our one-act play into a full-length work.

I'm under her direction now, and then, after she sweeps me off my feet and drags me to the bottom bunk (which, fortunately, is mine and not my roommate's), I'm under her.

Jo rushes through the overture, pulling at my clothes, plying them like she can't get the curtain open fast enough.

The show gets on the road; rides over the speed bump of my hip, zooms past my thigh, passes under my skirt, parks inside my panties.

Jo follows the fold—all of them. "It's like a sauna in there," she remarks, eyes alight with delight.

I squeeze her breasts, the cups plump and cushy against my palms.

"They make wonderful supporting players, don't they?" Jo jives as things continue to heat up.

"Yup," I manage, already approaching the finale. The second act is always shorter than the first.

"Maybe in our next production, you'll cast them in a starring role."

I laugh just as my body starts acting funny, shaking like a fistful of dice.

"Fuck be a lady," Joelle growls, and lifts her hand to her mouth. She blows on her fingers as though they've gone from yearning to burning. "*You* should have auditioned for the show."

I take her hand and take over, because I can take the heat.
"Me? Why me?"

"Because you," Jo replies, and licks the lollipop-like luster from her fingers, "would have made the perfect Hot Box Girl."

FINAL EXAM

Meghan O'Brien

Jess Holt trudged into Newsome Hall, the only all-girls dormitory on the university's sprawling 3,000-acre-plus campus, in a funk to end all funks. She'd just completed the second-to-last final exam of her freshman year at college, but rather than feel relief, the knot of panic that had been steadily gathering in her stomach for the past week now threatened to strangle her from the inside. It was a terrifying, suffocating feeling that made it hard to keep taking normal breaths. She hadn't made it past the common room before an overwhelming feeling of dread forced her to stop, bend at the waist, and grab onto her thighs while she struggled not to pass out. She only dimly heard a voice before a strong arm wrapped around her middle and guided her to a nearby couch to sit down.

"Hey." A hand rubbed her back, chasing away the worst of the attack while slowly returning her to reality. "You all right?"

Jess inhaled, exhaled, then looked up at her caretaker only for her heart to chug impossibly harder. "Mike" McDonnell—whose birth name was rumored to be Michaela—sat next to her on the couch, concern etched across her handsome face. A junior and therefore the oldest student living in their dorm, Mike was the only verifiable lesbian she'd met at college that year, a late transfer who had moved into all-girls housing with obvious trepidation only to become the darling of the mostly straight, largely bi-curious population of first- and second-year underclassmen. Jess had harbored a secret crush on Mike since the very first moment she'd laid eyes on her, excited by her unapologetically butch appearance—the shaved head, low-slung jeans, and various tanks and T-shirts that showed off her muscled arms—and, eventually, impressed by her clear dedication to her education. They'd struck up a casual friendship over the course of multiple, sporadic evenings studying in the common room together while their roommates were getting laid or had otherwise rendered their rooms inhospitable, but they weren't exactly *close*. At least not as close as Jess had often fantasized.

Flushed, Jess nodded. "Sorry."

"Don't be." Mike stopped rubbing her back, though Jess wished she wouldn't. She knew Mike tried to play it safe, with freshman girls especially, though she also knew she'd slipped at least once that year and engaged in a heated make-out session with a bold, curious former homecoming queen who happened to be Jess's roommate. According to Zoe, Mike had *also* fooled around with at least two other girls in their dorm, though only at parties, and only to second base. Mike had never behaved flirtatiously toward her at all, much to her despair. Even now, Mike's expression was pure platonic friendship. "You okay?"

Jess looked away, embarrassed by her desire to fall into Mike's arms. No one knew she liked girls. Not anyone in her hometown, and sadly, even after an entire school year, nobody on campus either. Her one overriding social goal for freshman year had been to confirm what she'd suspected about herself since the onset of puberty (maybe even before), yet she'd failed to make more than a small handful of friends, none of whom she'd come out to. It was difficult to imagine saying the words aloud when she'd spent her entire life until that point living in a small, conservative town where silence around this topic felt imperative to her very survival. Next week she'd return to that same town, still unkissed, to spend the summer in her parents' house without having attained any confirmation that she *really* did know who she was. What a *waste*.

"No," Jess mumbled. "I mean, yeah, I guess. Thanks."

"Tough exam?" Mike tilted her head. "Harsh comedown from an all-nighter?"

"My exam went great." Jess smiled tightly, wishing she could relax enough to give off a friendlier vibe. If the main source of her depression was the idea of going home without having even been *kissed* during her first year of college, the best possible way to treat what ailed her was to thoroughly charm the only lesbian she knew. But Mike was so *sexy*, especially with the tattoos she'd accumulated that year—one on each arm, both intricate enough that Jess had no idea what they actually represented since she'd only chanced subtle, fleeting glimpses when she was certain Mike couldn't see. The idea of kissing *Mike*—wet dream Mike, who'd been the inspiration behind months of self-induced orgasms—was too surreal, too *fantastical* to entertain. Shy girls like her didn't hook up with sexy, intelligent butch goddesses like Mike. At least not at this school. Jess's face burned as her mind raced over these thoughts and more, making her worry that Mike might know exactly what she liked, after all. "Just...end-of-the-year blues."

Mike returned her smile, kindly. "One more exam for me. Feels like yesterday I was freaking out about having to move into an all-girls dorm, and now it's over. I'm actually kind of sad about that."

Jess thought about the fan club Mike had accumulated since she'd arrived. "Why wouldn't you be sad? All the girls love you."

Mike snorted, sheepish. "When the university told me I'd be living here, I worried that all these straight girls fresh out of high school would see my haircut and the way I dressed and totally shun me. I didn't count on the rampant bi-curiosity, though I suppose I should've."

"Lucky." Jess battled true envy at the thought of how wonderful it must feel to be yourself and not only be accepted, but *embraced* by the people around you. Even if it was only because they wanted you to feel them up. "The girls' dorm is like the lesbian jackpot, right?" The L-word felt strange to say aloud, but she loved being able to with someone who wouldn't judge.

"I suppose." Rubbing her head, Mike scooted back another inch until she'd established a respectable distance between them. "But I've tried to be good. Even if straight girls tend to get insanely forward when they're tipsy, I'm pretty sure indulging their curiosity *too* much would be the road to hell, or something."

"At the least, it could stir up drama."

Mike grimaced. "I *hate* drama."

"Me too." Now that they were talking, Jess's body relaxed as she recalled that Mike was not only sexy, but also, simply, a lovely person to be around. Evenings in the common room with Mike were something she'd truly miss over the summer. Memories of their time together would surely dominate Jess's masturbatory life for years, and yet the connection they'd formed in real life wasn't sexual at all. Perhaps that was what made it so compelling, so ripe with possibility. "Will you live in the dorm next year?"

"Nah. Talk about feeling like an old lady!" Mike chuckled. "I rented an apartment a block away. I move in next week."

"Oh." Jess tried to not let her disappointment show. "Well, I'll miss seeing you in the common room whenever I'm sexiled."

"Maybe next year *you'll* be the one sexiling."

Jess lowered her face, bashful about the suggestion. "Probably not."

"Well, hopefully you'll get a roommate who doesn't do that to you quite so often." Mike stretched back against the arm of the couch, drawing Jess's attention to her leanly muscled, tattooed arms, then to the stripe of bare skin revealed when the hem of her shirt rode up. "Not everyone is as big a player as Zoe."

Jess couldn't help but picture Mike kissing Zoe with her hand up the front of her shirt, as Zoe had told the tale. Burning with envy, desperate for *something*, the comment slipped out before Jess could think. "According to her, you would know."

She was surprised when Mike blushed. *Blushed.* "Yeah."

Mike coughed. "That was…a lapse in judgment brought about by one too many beers." She sought out Jess's gaze in a way that suggested she desired forgiveness. "It happened a month after I moved in. I didn't know her—or you—very well at that point."

"You don't have to explain yourself to me."

"I know, but…" Mike shrugged. "I like you, and…I don't want you to think Zoe's my type or anything."

Jess didn't understand why Mike cared. She *wished* she did, because the answer felt important for reasons she didn't dare linger on for fear that doing so would only cause her to embarrass herself. "I get it. Drunk college parties often lead to bad decisions. If kissing Zoe is the worst decision you made all year, then you probably did all right."

Mike hesitated. "And you? Any bad freshman-year decisions?"

Jess's eyes filled with tears that she tried and failed to suppress. She watched Mike's blurry face fall before tightening in anger.

"Jess," Mike said steadily. "Did someone hurt you?"

Guilt-ridden over making Mike believe she'd triggered a painful memory, Jess shook her head vigorously. "No." She forced a laugh and wiped her tears away. "No, I'm sorry, not at all." Hurt her? Nobody had even *touched* her. "No bad decisions. No good ones, either."

"But your exam went great," Mike said, clearly trying to help. "At the end of the day, that's what college is all about."

"Maybe." Jess bit her lip and met Mike's gaze, which held so much compassion it made her want to confess everything. Crush aside, Mike was a *friend* who might have also struggled to come out at some point in her life. Perhaps she could offer advice, or at the very least, reassurance. Imbued with sudden courage, Jess conducted a quick scan of their surroundings. Once she confirmed they were alone, she looked back at Mike, heart pounding. Before she could second-guess, she whispered, "I'm…I like…I'm like you."

Mike leaned in, brows furrowed in a way that made it obvious Jess's quiet declaration had failed to register. "You *like* me?"

Horrified by the misunderstanding, Jess blurted, "I said I'm *like* you. I'm a…" She lowered her voice. "Lesbian."

"*Oh.*" A slow grin took over Mike's face. "Am I the first person you've told?"

Jess nodded as yet more heat suffused her face, making her worry about the likelihood of a self-induced burn. "I grew up in a tiny, conservative town of three thousand people. I can't imagine telling anyone there, not unless I wanted it to get back to my folks. They'd drag me to their preacher, who'd tell me what an abomination I am." She took a breath, not wanting to dwell on those thoughts. "You're the only lesbian I've ever met."

"Shit." Mike inched closer and put a tentative hand on her arm. "Sorry. My parents disowned me when I was seventeen, so I get it. I haven't seen them in years."

"I fully expect to be disowned at some point in the future." Jess tried for nonchalance, but fell short. "Honestly, right now it feels like it might be a relief. I could just get on with my life and stop worrying about what they'll think."

"I'm not sure you'll *ever* completely stop worrying, but not having to hide—and not being judged by the people who raised you—*is* a relief. That's where I got the idea for this tattoo, after my parents kicked me out." Mike lifted the sleeve of her black V-neck T-shirt to show Jess one of the designs she'd wanted so desperately to see. The word FREEDOM was inked into the pale skin in bold, clear print. The last letter dissolved into a flock of small birds that whirled around in flight. "So I'd always remember the silver lining, regardless of the consequences."

The whimsical portrayal of a poignant concept elicited an automatic smile. "It's beautiful."

"Thanks." Mike gestured awkwardly at her other arm. "The other's along the same lines, but it's hard to see properly with my shirt on."

Jess swallowed and looked down, sure that hadn't been a come-on, wishing it had. Stuttering, she said, "I don't know when I'll be ready to tell them. I sorta feel like maybe I should at least *kiss* a girl first." Terrified that Mike would take the confession as an invitation, equally terrified she wouldn't, Jess couldn't tear her eyes away from her knees. They bobbled nervously as she fought the urge to flee. "You know, to be sure about everything before I break their hearts."

"Why, do you feel confused?" Mike spoke so gently that Jess couldn't bring herself to leave. "Do you even *like* guys?"

"No." Jess giggled. "Not really."

"You don't have to kiss someone to know." Mike again touched her arm, this time with an encouraging squeeze. "I realized when I was six years old. My parents probably did, too."

Jess nodded, because yes, she didn't have to be physically intimate with a woman to know she desperately wanted to. Still, college was to have been her first opportunity to truly *know* in a way her gut simply couldn't, and she'd wasted the entire year buried in schoolwork, too shy to pursue the one experience, more than any other, she yearned to have. "I get that, I just…" She exhaled, unable to admit how badly she wanted sex. Good girls *didn't*, or so she'd always been told, and yet she *did*. So much that the thought of waiting until next fall to try again made her want to weep. "I'd hoped to make at least one bad decision before returning home to a summer of hellfire and damnation."

"To earn the judgment?"

Mike's obvious amusement emboldened Jess to lock eyes. "I guess. And to have the memory to help me survive it."

Mike looked around the room, then before Jess could react, threaded her fingers in Jess's long hair to pull her in for a soft, lingering kiss. It was nothing more than a light press of their lips, a brief mingling of their rapidly expelled breaths, but it caused Mike's hand to tighten on her head before she slowly drew away. Mike whispered, "Did that help?"

Jess stared as Mike licked her lips, aroused by the knowledge that she was tasting the fresh coat of lip balm Jess had applied after her exam. "A little. Yeah."

Mike fisted her hands on her knees, exhaling in a rush. "Damn, girl. You're not making this easy."

"I'm not?" Jess wasn't sure how to take that. She sure *felt* easy, at least as far as she understood the term. "Sorry."

"No." Mike stared at her with an intensity that made Jess's entire body tingle. "You've got nothing to apologize for."

Uncertain how to take Mike's change in mood, Jess looked away, embarrassed. "Thanks for the kiss."

"Did it clarify anything?"

Jess couldn't suppress the smile elicited by the memory of Mike's supple lips against hers. "Yeah."

"And?"

Helplessly, Jess threw up her hands and blurted, "I want to have sex with women."

A loud whistle from across the room shattered the illusion of their solitude. "Way to go, Jess!" Miranda, who'd sat behind her that semester in Spanish, pumped a fist in the air while her friend Carli giggled. "Finally, a sign of life!"

"Hey," Mike responded, friendly yet stern. "Back off, okay?"

"No harm intended." Carli wrapped an arm around Miranda. "She started celebrating her last exam hours ago. Don't mind her."

Mike waited until Carli led Miranda away, then craned her neck to force Jess into eye contact. "Don't listen to her. You're worth ten of any other girl in this dorm. Believe me."

Jess nodded silently. She wasn't sure what was left to say. Flayed open and vulnerable in a way she'd never allowed herself to be before, with anyone, she considered going back to her room, crawling into bed, and hiding under the covers until her exam the following afternoon. Yet part of her longed to see what Mike would say next. Where might this already unbelievable interaction go? Did she dare hope that maybe—*maybe*—she was about to get the chance she'd waited for all year? "I appreciate that."

Mike carefully tucked a lock of hair behind Jess's ear. "Do you…" She exhaled. "Do you *want* to see my other tattoo?"

Jess was pretty sure she knew what Mike was really asking. She bit her lower lip. Nodded. "Yes."

Mike's throat jumped, leading Jess to the earth-shattering conclusion that she wasn't the only one eager to explore their chemistry. "All right, but…*shit*," Mike muttered. "Naturally, my roommate is fucking some guy in her bed right now." She glowered, awash with regret. "Do you have somewhere we could go?"

Jess had never been more grateful to have a party animal for a roommate. "Zoe hasn't been home in three days. She's shacked up with her boyfriend at the frat house this week, trying to fulfill her alcohol-fueled idiocy quota before the semester ends."

Mike brightened. "So you want to…"

"We can go there." Jess stood, then steadied herself against the couch as a tidal wave of light-headedness hit her. "Whoa."

Mike wrapped an arm around Jess's waist to help her straighten. "I've got you." The look of concern reappeared. "You *sure* you're all right?" As they stepped away from the couch, Mike hugged her gently. "I don't want to take advantage if you're not, you know?"

Alarm swept through Jess at the thought of scaring Mike away with her timidity. "I haven't been drinking. I'm in my right mind. I'm just…" She exhaled, trying to calm herself. "Nervous."

"So you've never done *anything*, with *anyone*?"

Jess wished Mike didn't sound so incredulous. "Never." She waited a beat. "Well, I kissed this super-hot butch chick once, a minute ago…"

Mike chuckled. "Sounds exciting."

"It was."

As they approached Jess's door, Mike said, "I need you to

know I don't expect anything, okay? If we just talk, cool. If you want to look at my tattoo, then call it a night, no problem."

Jess appreciated the sentiment, but the closer she got to sharing another kiss with Mike, the higher her confidence soared. "Thanks, but…" She paused in front of her room, but rather than get her keys, she turned to place her hand over the tattoo she hadn't yet seen, sliding beneath the shirt sleeve as she did to savor the heat of Mike's skin. "I wouldn't mind a *real* kiss. At least."

"A *real* kiss, huh?" As Jess fumbled to fit the proper key into the door's lock, Mike swept her long hair aside to plant a kiss near her collarbone. She whispered, "I can think of a *few* types of 'real kisses' you've never tried. Which do you want first?"

Jess shivered so violently she knew Mike had to notice. Indeed, hot breath washed over her throat as Mike groaned in response. Hands trembling, Jess managed to unlock the door, allowing them to stagger into the room with Mike's lips still attached to her neck. Once inside, they broke apart so that Jess could flip on the overhead light. Immediately, Mike's hands returned to Jess's waist, spinning her in place to cage her against the door. Overwhelmed, Jess put her hands on Mike's shoulders and gripped tightly, desperate for the security imparted by not only Mike's physical, but also her mental strength. "You *really* want to do this?"

Mike backed off, searching Jess's eyes. "You can't tell?"

"But you don't like drama." Jess kicked herself for bringing up reasons they *shouldn't* fuck. What was she doing? "And the road to hell…"

"You're different."

"Why?" Jess wasn't trying to talk Mike out of this. She just didn't want to feel like she'd pressured her into anything.

"Well, even though I kept telling myself you're too young for me, I've been crushing on you for months. Don't think that's bullshit, either, 'cause you're smart, you're motivated, you're pretty as anything, and you've got *fantastic* tits." Mike appeared bashful enough about this revelation to make Jess believe it might be true. "Also, we have shit in common. *Difficult* shit. I know what it's like to feel alone in the place where you grew up. And…I remember how being with a woman that first time validated all of my struggles, how it actually affirmed my identity, in some crazy way." She grinned, clearly reminiscing. "I also remember how fucking *incredible* it was to finally get laid. My first time was with an experienced, slightly older woman. She taught me a lot and made me feel nothing but *good.*" Stepping back, Mike lifted Jess's hand to kiss the knuckles. "Is it wrong to feel excited about having the chance to give *you* a first time like that, too?"

Breathe, Jess coached silently. *If you pass out now, you'll never forgive yourself.* "Not wrong."

"Good." Mike moved forward, pushing their hips together, then their breasts, as she pinned Jess against the door. "First *real* kiss, then? Using our tongues?"

Beyond coherence, Jess could only nod. She parted her lips when Mike pressed into them, then moaned when a tongue swept through her mouth, blazing a trail of exploration that left Jess's panties instantly drenched. Mimicking Mike's movements, she learned to kiss by example, until Mike's hips began to grind against hers in what she assumed was unspoken approval. Close to orgasm merely from dry humping against the door, Jess keened in disappointment when Mike broke away minutes later. "No, don't stop."

"I have to, or else I'll pass out." Mike shook her head as though trying to regain her senses. "Or get too excited."

"Too excited for what?" Jess felt strangely detached while watching her finger trace a path down over Mike's breast to circle the erect nipple that poked through her thin cotton shirt. "I thought we'd already established that you're getting lucky tonight."

"Yeah, but…" Mike exhaled shakily, shifting her weight from foot to foot as she endured Jess's teasing touch. "At *your* pace. Which I guarantee is a few speeds slower than mine right now."

Jess could practically *feel* Mike's sexual energy boiling up, threatening to overflow. Rather than be frightened, the tension only made her wetter. Signaling her readiness to continue, Jess said, "Show me your tattoo?"

Mike's eyes flashed. "Good idea." She took a step away and turned her back to Jess.

When she stripped off her shirt to reveal an intricately drawn wing that extended from her spine to her shoulder, then down along her arm—positioned to appear as though the appendage was tucked safely against her back—Jess gasped in admiration. "Gorgeous." She traced her fingertips over the detailed feathers covering the shoulder blade. A chill ran through Mike's body, drawing her attention to the goose flesh she'd left in her wake. "Another symbol of freedom?"

"Yeah." Mike turned to face her, tossing the shirt away. Her breasts were beautifully shaped and proportioned, larger than Jess had expected, and topped with dark pink nipples that appeared so painfully aroused that, without thinking, Jess lifted a hand with the intention of warming the turgid flesh of one with her palm. She stopped abruptly, worried she was being too forward. Mike grabbed her wrist and guided her to cradle the firm mound, chuckling at Jess's loud whimper upon making contact. When Mike released her, Jess rubbed her thumb over the nipple, causing it to tighten further and tearing a whimper from deep in Mike's throat. Mike rumbled, "They're *extremely* sensitive."

"Oh." Jess positioned the nipple between her fingertips, wanting so badly to pinch. "Do you like having them touched?"

"Very much." Mike wobbled when Jess gave into her desire, tugging lightly on the nipple, rolling it between her fingernails. "But do you think we could sit down for this part?"

"Good idea." Jess led Mike to her narrow twin bed, shoving the lone teddy bear she'd brought from home to the floor. "My mom packed that, *not* me."

"Cute, either way." Mike smirked, planting her hands behind her hips on the mattress as Jess sat beside her. "Will you take off your shirt so I can look at you while you touch me?"

Shyly, Jess tipped her head and tugged her T-shirt off. Unlike Mike, she wore a bra, and struggled for a moment with the clasp before Mike released her from its confines with a single flick of her thumb. Jess shrugged out of the modest undergarment, casting it to the floor before instinctively folding her arms over her naked breasts. "Thanks for the assist."

Mike dropped her gaze to Jess's chest. "May I see you?"

"Yeah." Battling a wave of self-consciousness born from the simple reality that nobody but her parents, her physician, and herself had ever seen her nude, Jess peeled her arms away from her breasts while staring at the comforter to avoid seeing possible disappointment in Mike's eyes. "Sorry."

"No more apologies," Mike murmured. Then, "Jess, you're *perfect.*"

Hearing only honesty, Jess looked up. "Yeah?"

Mike appeared to struggle to tear her attention away from Jess's small, rosy-tipped breasts. "They make me want to jump straight into another type of *real* kiss." She poked her tongue out, briefly, before meeting Jess's gaze. "May I suck on one?"

Jess's inner muscles clenched, sending a wave of pleasure rolling through her body. "*Please.*"

Mike scooted closer and curled a steadying hand around Jess's hip. She bent to first kiss, then lick, the tip of her right breast. On instinct, Jess held on to the back of Mike's head, simultaneously puffing out her chest to encourage Mike to take more into her mouth. As incredible as tongue kissing had been, this was astronomically better, an act she'd imagined thousands of times without ever actually appreciating just how *divine* it would feel. She moaned when Mike varied the suction of her lips, alternating from soft to hard, and the movement of her tongue, fast to slow. With her free hand, Jess reached beneath Mike's chest and cupped a heavy tit in her hand, massaging, then manipulating the hard tip with her thumb and index finger. Mike moaned loudly against her, easily matching Jess's intensity with her lips, teeth, and tongue.

After a few minutes of pure bliss, Jess whispered, "May I kiss *you* now?"

Mike pulled away without argument. She lay back against Jess's pillow with her arms above her head, hands resting lightly against the headboard. "I'm yours to do with as you please."

Somehow this was better than any fantasy she'd ever dared to entertain. Swept away by how unreal everything seemed, Jess noted that she was barely trembling anymore as she stretched out alongside Mike's solid body. She leaned to kiss the tip of one hard nipple, then licked it, testing the flavor of Mike's skin. Mild, but her mouth watered for more, compelling her to capture as much of the firm flesh between her lips as she could. Mike moaned and squirmed beneath her, wordlessly encouraging Jess to keep doing what she was doing. Jess kissed from one breast to the other, sucking, teasing, *worshiping*. After many minutes of this, shortly after Jess crawled over to straddle Mike's hips while she explored, Mike suddenly stiffened and quaked beneath her, crying out in a way that Jess recognized from her own self-exploration. Sitting back on Mike's hips, Jess stared down at her face, dubious that anyone could *actually* get off like that. "Did you…?"

Mike groaned, still twitching. She grabbed Jess's hips and rolled their bodies so she was on top. "Yeah. I did."

"You can *do* that?"

Mike rewarded her with hearty laughter and a deeply passionate kiss. "Yes," she murmured, pulling away. "You really, truly gave me an orgasm just by playing with my tits. That enough to get you through the summer?"

"It's a fine start."

Mike rocked her hips against Jess's, then slipped a denim-clad thigh between her legs to press against her damp crotch. "Don't worry, sweetheart, we're not done yet." She captured Jess's wrists and pulled them over her head so she was completely pinned beneath Mike's strong body. "I still need to make *you* come, don't I?"

Jess couldn't think. "Oh…"

Mike relaxed her hold on Jess's wrists, then rolled off to the side. "There are a few different ways I could go." She circled one of Jess's agonizingly erect nipples with her finger, then moved to the other one, causing Jess's inner muscles to clench in a way that made her suspect she wouldn't be able to hold out very long. "I could *try* to do what you just did, or…" She dropped her hand to the waist of Jess's jeans, playing with the button, tracing the zipper. "Or you could take these off and let me show you my favorite way to *really* kiss."

Jess pinched herself, literally, in disbelief. "What do you…?"

"Ever fantasize about letting a girl lick your pussy?"

Jess nodded. She'd masturbated to visions of *Mike* going down on her; she'd simply never imagined it would happen for real. "Sure."

Mike smoothly unbuttoned and unzipped Jess's jeans, then sat to slide them over her hips and down her legs. "Did you rub your clit while you thought about it?"

Jess pushed aside her embarrassment. There was no place for it here. "Yeah."

"Until you came all over your pretty fingers?" Mike tossed her jeans onto the floor as Jess nodded again. She inhaled sharply when Mike rested her hand over the soaked crotch of her panties. Mike beamed as she flexed her fingers. "You're so *wet.*"

"Sorr—" Jess began, but Mike cut her off, shaking her head.

"I *love* a nice wet pussy in my mouth." Mike rubbed her fingers up and down Jess's labia, pushing against the fabric until it was thoroughly saturated with her juices. "I want you to watch how I eat you, all right?" She winked. "Consider it a lesson, from me to you."

Jess nodded silently as Mike stripped away her panties to reveal her dark, glistening patch of pubic hair. She struggled not to close her eyes as Mike stared down at her vagina, using her thumbs to spread the slippery labia while she settled onto her belly between Jess's open thighs. She wanted to see what happened next every bit as badly as Mike wanted her to watch. Despite everything she'd been raised to believe, nothing had ever felt more righteous than the first, careful touch of Mike's tongue against her sensitive inner lips, nor had anything brought her closer to heaven. Fisting her hands in the comforter, Jess braced herself against the headboard and stared intently as the sexiest woman she'd ever met gave her the most intimate kiss imaginable.

"*Fuck*, you taste good." Mike hoisted Jess's thighs over her shoulders, licking her again and again before giving her clit a careful kiss. "My best advice is to go slow. Concentrate on her labia and opening first." Mike paused to demonstrate, using her tongue to circle the hole Jess had never dared to breach on her own. "Be gentle with her clit until she begs you to suck on it, either with her words or by pushing your face into her cunt."

Jess blushed at Mike's crude language, but more so at the rush of wetness it unleashed. Her thighs quivered so exaggeratedly it made her feel foolish. She struggled to keep still. "It feels… so…"

Mike entangled her fingers with Jess's, holding her hand, and took a break from licking to stare up into her eyes. "Like it?"

"Yes!" Using her free hand, Jess nudged Mike back down. She didn't miss the way her mildly forceful move made Mike grin. "Keep going…*please*."

Mike laughed, then dragged the flat of her tongue up Jess's labia, ending with a swipe against her swollen clit. Jess gasped at the sight, and at the absolutely breathtaking pleasure Mike's actions caused. She doubted she could withstand much more, not when Mike's hot mouth felt *this* divine. Not wanting to finish before allowing Mike to cross home plate, Jess begged, "Go inside me."

Mike pulled away, face shiny with juices. "You sure?" She lowered her free hand. Jess jumped as a careful fingertip probed at her opening. "Have you ever been penetrated before?" When

Jess shook her head, Mike exhaled unsteadily. Hot breath washed over Jess's hotter flesh, triggering chills throughout her entire body. "I don't want to hurt you, so we'll take it slow. Just...try to relax."

Jess couldn't imagine how. Her entire body thrummed with sexual tension, with the overpowering need for release. "Okay."

Mike lowered her mouth to Jess's clit, lapping at the sensitive ridge of flesh as she applied slightly more pressure to her slick opening. Massaging the tight ring of muscle with her finger, Mike stroked in time with the rhythm of her tongue while dipping ever so slightly inside. Jess sensed the resistance of her body to the invasion and had to battle her instinctive urge to pull away. Willfully, she rocked into Mike's tongue and hand, focusing on the bliss of the former to mitigate the mild discomfort caused by the latter. Refusing to chicken out *this* close to her ultimate goal, she moaned, "Please, Mike, just *do* it."

As soon as the words left her mouth, Mike pushed inside her vagina while sucking her clit with so much finesse that Jess began to come around the finger inside her even as it slid home. The brief flash of pain instantly transformed into the most ecstatic pleasure Jess had ever experienced, a million times better than anything produced by her imagination—truly the ultimate affirmation that this was *exactly* what she wanted for the rest of her life. Jess squeezed Mike's hand so hard she worried about breaking fingers, then finally went limp when, after what seemed like hours, the internal convulsions began to subside. Weakened by her climax, Jess allowed her rubbery thighs to fall open on the mattress, but didn't pull away from the tongue that continued to explore her every nook and cranny. Mike's finger still rested inside her, and when she withdrew halfway only to sink deeper inside, Jess was stunned to feel her body once again stir to life.

"Got any more studying to do tonight?" Mike gave her clit a noisy kiss, then eased back so Jess could watch the long finger disappear into her greedy hole. "'Cause if not, there's plenty more I can teach you." She brought her thumb up to brush over Jess's clit, causing her to cry out. "Starting with hand jobs and multiple orgasms."

Jess had studied enough. Apart from her last exam tomorrow, she was happy to devote the remainder of her freshman year to remedial sex education. "I'm in."

"Good." Mike shot her a devilish grin, using her elbow to pin Jess's thigh to the bed while she slowly, deliberately, fingered her vagina until she elicited a shuddering moan. "Now, pay attention. There'll be a test later."

"Yes, ma'am." Jess gasped when Mike's tongue joined the thumb on her clit, introducing her to an entirely new concept in pleasure.

One that would *definitely* get her through the summer.

FIRE OR FLAME

Nell Stark

Kerry didn't recognize the man sitting at the porter's desk of Duke Humfrey's Library, and she reached for her ID while bidding him a good evening. Just over one week remained before the beginning of Oxford's Michelmas term, and this was probably a popular time for staff to take a last-minute vacation before the faculty and students returned en masse to the university.

Once he waved her through, Kerry headed toward Selden End, her favorite place to work. As always, she spared an admiring glance for the vaulted ceiling, covered with ornate panels depicting Oxford's crest. No matter how many times she made this journey, it never failed to inspire in her a sense of awe. This part of the library was over five hundred years old, and its tall bookshelves had been constructed in the seventeenth century. Kings had studied here, and prime ministers, and illustrious scholars who had gone on to change the history of Western thought. Oscar Wilde had walked where she did now, and C.S. Lewis, and J.R.R. Tolkien. In her more fanciful moments, she imagined them as ghostly presences, watching over her intellectual progress.

Bemusedly, Kerry wondered what those men would think of her, if they were alive today. Three years ago, she had been fresh off her first international flight, wide-eyed and eager for all the opportunities a Rhodes Scholarship could offer. Now she was the Duchess of Kent—a title that King Andrew had bestowed upon her when she married his daughter, Her Royal Highness Alexandra Victoria Jane, second in line to the throne.

Oscar Wilde, at least, would approve.

Their marriage was nearly half a year old, but Kerry hadn't even remotely grown accustomed to being addressed as "Your Grace"—especially since she had never been graceful at anything except football. And now, with the academic year about to commence, she would have to learn to answer to yet another unfamiliar title: "professor." Upon the completion of her scholarship, Oxford had offered her a position in the History of Art department, where she was charged with expanding its Architecture curriculum. She preferred to work on her lesson plans here, in one of the university's most architecturally rich spaces, where all she had to do was lift her head for inspiration. Besides, the prospect of working at her nearby flat held no allure when Sasha was obliged to be in London for the evening on business.

The library was usually quiet after five o'clock, but tonight, it was positively deserted. As she continued on past the empty chairs and pristine tables, past the silent bays filled with books older than this room in which they were housed, she didn't see another soul. The prospect of having the most venerable room in the Bodleian all to herself was at once exhilarating and more than a little eerie. Kerry turned to the left once she reached Selden End, hoping her usual corner spot would be as unoccupied as the rest of the floor had been…

…and was suddenly frozen to the floor by the sight of her wife, the Princess Royal of the Commonwealth of Nations, perched atop the table completely nude. One elegant leg was crossed over the other, and her skin, tawny from the week they had recently spent in the Seychelles, glowed in the lamplight.

For a moment, Kerry feared she was dreaming—that she was back on the airplane from JFK to Heathrow, and that the past three years had all been a flight of fancy produced by the subliminal desires of her unconscious mind. The sluice of terror down her spine should have been enough to wake her if she were indeed asleep, but she pinched the skin below her left knuckles, just in case.

She was awake. Sasha was real. Their marriage was real, and her wife was really here, in what amounted to the most epic seduction in all of history. Paris, Lancelot, and Romeo were amateurs by comparison. Princess Alexandra had just upstaged them all.

A peal of silvery laughter filled the room, and Sasha shifted position, leaning back to brace herself on her palms. The movement revealed the perfection of her breasts in all their pale, rose-tipped glory. "Did you honestly just pinch yourself?"

Kerry tried to speak, failed, swallowed, and tried again. "For a second, I thought everything—you, us, this—might be a dream."

Sasha's expression went from amused to fierce in an instant. "Come *here*."

Her imperious tone befitted a princess. Kerry dropped her bag and obeyed, her breath catching as Sasha opened her legs to invite her between them. Sasha wrapped her arms around Kerry's neck but held her back when Kerry tried to close the space between them.

"This is real." Sasha's eyes were bright. "You are *mine*."

And then Sasha pulled her down, joining their lips in a kiss at once triumphant and tender. When Kerry moaned at the sweetness of it, Sasha slipped her tongue inside. Kerry reached for her, one hand at her hip and the other ghosting up her spine. Sasha's skin pebbled beneath her touch as the kiss went on and on and on.

When Sasha finally pulled back, they were both gasping. "Incredible," she whispered, dragging one thumb across Kerry's now-swollen lips.

Kerry's brain was short-circuiting. She wanted nothing more than to push Sasha down to the tabletop and bury two fingers inside her, but the shrill voice of logic held her back.

"How much time do we have?"

"As much as we want."

Sasha wrapped her legs around the backs of Kerry's thighs and tugged, pulling her pelvis flush with the edge of the table. The delicious pressure sent desire arrowing through her, and she shivered in its thrall.

"How did you—" Kerry couldn't think, nor could she stop herself from grinding shamelessly against the source of the friction. Sasha's breasts filled her vision, begging for her touch. She wanted so badly to give in to her need. "What—"

"Today is our third anniversary."

The words startled Kerry enough that she raised her eyes to Sasha's. How could it be their third anniversary when they had only been married for a matter of months?

Sasha traced Kerry's cheekbones with her thumbs. "Three years ago, in a childish fit of rebelliousness, I skipped an engagement with the Rhodes Trust to go dancing at a new club. But fate intervened and brought you to me despite my stupidity."

Comprehension dawned. Kerry would never forget that first, incendiary kiss they had shared in a back room at Summa, but she hadn't realized that Sasha regarded it as a watershed moment— nor had she considered its fragility.

"I didn't want to go out that night," she said slowly, reliving it in her memory. "Harris had to persuade me to be social." She tightened her grip on Sasha's waist, anchoring herself against a wave of dread. "I've never thought about how close we came to never meeting. That's terrifying."

"It is." Sasha leaned in to kiss one corner of her mouth and then the other. "But look at us now—how far we've come." Her full lips curved in a mischievous smile. "Not to mention how many times."

The knot of tension in Kerry's chest dissolved with her laughter. "And you're here to add to that running total?"

Sasha's eyes darkened. "I'm here to finish what we started

three years ago." She ran her fingers through Kerry's hair before tugging lightly. "I love you. I always will. But that night wasn't about love—it was about lust. We were interrupted then, but no one will interrupt us now." She moistened her lips in clear anticipation. "So relax. I've taken care of everything. And now I'm going to take care of you."

With a shuddering sigh, Kerry abandoned her lingering anxieties. She raised her hands to cup Sasha's breasts, glorying in the incomparable softness of her skin and the swift tightening of her nipples. When Sasha threw her head back and moaned, Kerry rolled both nipples between her fingers. Sasha's hips bucked.

"Lie down." Kerry freed one hand to push gently against Sasha's chest. "Let me have you."

Sasha's eyes snapped open. "No." She sat up and grasped Kerry's wrist. "I said I would take care of you, and I meant it. Now unbutton your shirt."

"But—"

"Don't even think of arguing." Sasha's hands went to work on her belt buckle, but her eyes remained locked with Kerry's. "You are going to get naked, and then you are going to take my place on this table. And then *I* am going to fulfill one of my fantasies."

"Y-you are?" Kerry could hardly muster enough breath to stammer. Usually, their lovemaking was a sensual battle of equals, but right now, Sasha was demanding everything she had to give. Never had Kerry wanted to surrender so wholeheartedly.

Sasha glared up at her in the act of drawing down the zipper. "Take. Off. Your. Shirt."

Kerry fumbled with the buttons and cursed when her right sleeve caught on her watch. By the time the shirt fell to the floor, Sasha had pushed Kerry's pants below her knees. Kerry steadied herself against the table as Sasha nipped at the elastic band of her underwear, and when Sasha suddenly pressed her lips against the thin fabric at the apex of her thighs, Kerry groaned in pleasure.

"I can feel how swollen you are." Sasha rubbed two fingers against the damp swatch where her mouth had been. "And how wet."

"For you," Kerry choked out.

"That's right." Sasha hooked two fingers in the fabric and pulled until Kerry was standing in a pool of her own clothing. "Now, sit."

Kerry boosted herself onto the table and watched in dizzy fascination as Sasha made quick work of her shoes. Once Kerry was naked from the waist down, Sasha ran her hands up Kerry's legs, lingering on her thighs to massage the muscles there, sliding her thumbs dangerously close to the heart of Kerry's ache.

"Oh, please." Kerry didn't want to be reduced to begging already, but she simply couldn't help herself.

Instead of obliging her, Sasha stood. Her expression was smug, but Kerry could sense the tenderness beneath it. "You can be as impatient as you like, but this isn't going to be quick." Sasha reached out to toy with the straps of Kerry's bra. "Hands over your head, now."

Sasha took her sweet time pushing the fabric up and over Kerry's breasts and nibbling at each inch of skin she exposed. Fireworks burst beneath Kerry's skin at each scrape of Sasha's teeth. When she bit down gently on one nipple, a cry escaped Kerry's lips before she could clamp them together.

Sasha pulled away, looking extremely self-satisfied. "You don't have to be quiet," she said as she pushed Kerry's legs up and apart until her heels touched the tabletop. "The guard at the front is under strict instructions to wear earplugs."

Before Kerry could even attempt to form a response, Sasha dropped to one knee. Spellbound, Kerry watched as Sasha spread her open with gentle fingers, and she shivered as the cool air washed over her exposed sex. Her reaction brought an exultant smile to Sasha's lips.

"Keep your eyes open for as long as you can," she murmured, each puff of breath a teasing caress.

And then she leaned forward to touch the very tip of her tongue to Kerry's clitoris in a kiss as light as it was tantalizing. Kerry's eyes slammed shut as her body surged, instinctively trying to get closer. But Sasha's grip was unyielding. Again and again, she brought her mouth to Kerry in a series of delicate touches expertly designed to make her go insane. Kerry flung one arm over her eyes and clutched desperately at the table's edge with her other hand. Pleasure coiled in her abdomen, ready to spring, and she groaned with the effort to rein it in.

"Sash—I...I c-can't..."

When Sasha closed her lips around her and sucked, electricity jolted down Kerry's spine and she cried out again. She clenched deep inside, teetering on the precipice of ecstasy...but the next stroke of Sasha's tongue never came. Quite suddenly, she was gone.

Kerry reached for her and found only empty space. Her eyes snapped open, but the world was out of focus. Her heart clattered against her ribs in a sudden surge of panic—

"You're so beautiful." Sasha's voice was accompanied by the warm pressure of her palm between Kerry's breasts. "So desirable. So *mine*."

Kerry's vision cleared on a powerful wave of relief, just in time to watch Sasha kneel on the table between her legs, breasts swaying in the grip of gravity. But when Kerry tried to sit up, the princess's firm hand held her down.

"You're exactly where I want you." Sasha punctuated her words by bringing the index and middle fingers of her free hand to Kerry's mouth. "Suck."

Kerry obeyed gladly, hollowing her lips around Sasha's fingers as she let her tongue dance across the tips. All she could think about was just how incredible Sasha would feel inside her, and she did everything possible to convey the magnitude of her need. When Sasha's hips rocked restlessly against her, Kerry knew she had succeeded.

"Stop." Despite her obvious arousal, the syllable didn't

tremble. Sasha held up her hand between them, wet fingers glistening in the muted light of the Bodleian's lamps. "I'm going to fuck you now."

Kerry wanted to watch, but her muscles turned to jelly at the first touch. Sasha pushed inside slowly, filling her one fraction of an inch at a time, insistently working her way deeper and deeper. Kerry could only gasp for breath as a powerful jolt of pleasure rippled through her.

"I love how you feel inside." As she spoke, Sasha began to withdraw, almost as slowly as she had entered. "So hot. So tight. So responsive."

"Don't go," Kerry said hoarsely, struggling to raise her head enough to meet Sasha's gaze. She tried to close her legs to hold Sasha in place, but Sasha stopped her with a sharp slap to her stomach.

"Don't you dare." She brought her nails into play, drawing fiery lines down Kerry's abdomen. The sweet pain only amplified her pleasure, and her head fell back against the table. "Keep your legs spread, *Your Grace*. I want you open and vulnerable."

Kerry's strangled laugh became a gasp as Sasha filled her again, swiftly this time. Heat blossomed beneath her skin and she became molten around Sasha's fingers, her fluttering muscles offering their own silent plea.

"Oh, you just got so wet." Sasha's voice was taut in triumph, and she began to move in earnest now, fucking her with deep, rhythmic strokes that ignited a sharp ache in Kerry's belly.

When Sasha began to curl her fingers at the apex of every stroke, Kerry dug her nails into the wooden tabletop in an effort to anchor herself to reality and stave off the rising tide of her climax.

"You. Are. Mine." Sasha punctuated each word with a sharp thrust. "You are *always* mine. Wherever you are, every moment of every day. You. Are. Mine."

The pressure was unbearable, and Kerry's thighs began to tremble. "Yours," she managed to choke out.

Sasha brushed her thumb against Kerry's clit and hummed in approval when Kerry's head thrashed. The last shreds of control were inexorably slipping away, like a star on the razor's edge of supernova.

"Say it again." Sasha's voice was low and hypnotic, weaving a spell between them. Every movement of her hand tightened the knot of Kerry's desire.

"Yours."

"Again," Sasha demanded. "Promise me."

As Kerry gasped for the breath to speak, Sasha thrust hard, hooking her fingers deep inside the embrace of Kerry's body as she rubbed firm circles against her clit. Light and heat fused in a glorious conflagration, and Kerry half screamed, half sobbed that final "Yours" as her body convulsed in the grip of ecstasy so intense it bordered on agony.

Sasha held her down and fucked her through the eye of the firestorm, pushing Kerry from one orgasm to the next until she had wrung every last ounce of sensation from her trembling body. When Kerry's muscles finally slackened, Sasha gently withdrew and bent to cover her face with kisses.

"I love your passion," she whispered as she smoothed the damp hair from Kerry's brow. "I love your intensity. I love you, Kerry."

Kerry had nearly slipped into unconsciousness, but she still registered Sasha's solicitous touches and heard the quiver of need in her voice. Need. Sasha needed her. But when she tried to raise one arm to embrace her, Kerry found she could barely move a finger. And when she tried to speak, her throat was raw from the abrasive force of her own screams.

She swallowed hard and tried again. "Sasha."

"Hmm?" When Sasha's lips met hers, Kerry tasted herself. Epiphany struck, galvanizing her into action. It took every bit of strength she had to raise both hands and cup Sasha's face, but she finally managed to create just enough distance between them for her to speak.

Sasha was frowning at having been interrupted. "What—"

"Sit on my face."

Darkness swallowed Sasha's emerald irises like an eclipse, and her tongue darted out to wet her lips. She might be speechless, but the fine tremor of her fingers against Kerry's stomach was all the answer Kerry needed.

"Now. Please." Kerry moved one hand to Sasha's hip, urging her up. "I need you."

As Sasha settled above her, Kerry wrapped both arms around her thighs. The rapid rise and fall of her breasts was mesmerizing, but Kerry forced herself to look past them and meet Sasha's gaze.

"Go slowly." Sasha's voice trembled.

Her obvious desire was intoxicating, and Kerry's exhaustion burned away on a surge of adrenaline. "As my lady wishes," she said, before pulling Sasha down.

She was deliciously wet, and Kerry took great delight in licking up all the evidence of Sasha's arousal before focusing in on the swollen bundle of nerves that was the focal point of her desire. Kerry tongued it lightly for several minutes, constantly varying her rhythm to deny Sasha the build-up she required for release. The longer Kerry teased her, the more urgent Sasha's movements became, until she was clutching at Kerry's hair and grinding against her mouth.

Kerry couldn't get enough, but neither could she stand to wait any longer to feel Sasha come apart above her. After tightening her grip on Sasha's legs, she sucked lightly on Sasha's clitoris even as she continued the flickering motion of her tongue.

"Fuck!" Sasha's interjection was accompanied by a tug on Kerry's hair so sharp it brought tears to her eyes. Kerry didn't mind one bit. Sasha was finally starting to lose control. Her muffled curses quickly gave way to an inarticulate keening, inspiring Kerry to increase the pressure of her lips. Sasha writhed frantically against her before releasing a thin wail and falling forward, her back arching like a bow over Kerry's head as her body shook in the throes of climax.

Kerry stroked her thighs as she coaxed out each aftershock. When Sasha went limp, Kerry eased her down to the tabletop and held her close, cradling Sasha's head in the dip between her shoulder and collarbone. As the minutes passed, Kerry could feel their heartbeats and breaths synchronize. Above her, the gold lettering on the Oxford crests twinkled like constellations. *Dominus illuminatio mea.* She would never glimpse it again without thinking of this moment.

"What are you thinking?" Sasha murmured sleepily.

"That you are my light."

Sasha blinked adorably in confusion. "Your light?"

Kerry gestured toward the ceiling. "My comfort. My inspiration. The spark of my desire." Suddenly, she laughed.

"What?" Sasha pulled away to regard her suspiciously. "What's so funny about that?"

"I'm just remembering the oath I had to take when I first received my library card."

Sasha's frown deepened. "Remind me. I'm sure I had one, back in my undergraduate days, but I didn't set foot here very often."

Kerry tried to remember the exact language. "It's a translation of Latin, I think. Something about promising not to *bring into the library or kindle therein any fire or flame.*" She caressed one corner of Sasha's mouth with her thumb. "The way you made love to me…I thought I might spontaneously combust."

Sasha propped up her head on one elbow. "That spark has always been at the heart of us—from that very first night, three years ago."

"Yes. I love that. I need that."

"I do, too." Sasha inched closer and slid one leg between Kerry's to rejoin their bodies. "Our life is going to change now that you have your position here."

Kerry felt a pang of uncertainty. "Do you wish I hadn't—"

"Shh. Don't jump to conclusions." She grasped Kerry's chin to hold her gaze. "You're going to be a brilliant teacher. Oxford is lucky to have you." Her eyes narrowed. "But you're mine before you're theirs. That's what tonight is about. Even when you're here late, working—even when I'm in another time zone or on another continent, working—I need you to remember that."

"Sasha." Kerry bridged the space between them to press their foreheads together. "I meant what I said in the heat of the moment. Yours. I promise I'm always yours."

STUDY BUDDIES

Carsen Taite

I'd never, ever gotten a B. I stared at the page, willing the letter to morph into the acceptable, but knowing the nausea of reality wasn't going away anytime soon.

Straight-A Annie. I took pride in the name even though I knew my undergrad roommates had only called me that to get under my skin. Determined to keep my streak in law school, I'd spent the first week of classes scouting out the 1L's with perfect pedigrees. Harvard, Yale, Princeton. Serious, dedicated, smart. Everyone knew that being in the best study group was the only way to ensure *success*, and I'd picked four like-minded souls to run with me to first place.

But the number of Bs on my grade report was all the evidence I needed to prove that I'd chosen poorly. The members of my study group were loaded with smarts, but completely unfocused—more interested in booze than books. Unlike me, they didn't need to graduate top of their class since their families were captains of industry, retail, and investment.

Now the second semester was about to start and I'd spend it digging out from under, determined to go it alone rather than risk my future with a bunch of legacies who were guaranteed a bright future because it was their birthright. I slid into my seat and scanned my notes, trying to settle my stomach as the crotchety Torts professor took the podium and selected his first victim.

"Ms. Ardmore, please give us the facts of *Palsgraf v. Long Island Railroad.*"

Damn. I hate professors who go in alphabetical order, but I'd read the seminal case twenty times the night before, so I took a deep breath and rattled out the key facts. He didn't even bother acknowledging how well I did before he started firing off questions about proximate cause and duty. By the time he moved on to his next victim, the whole experience was a blur. The Bs in my pocket had undermined my self-confidence, and I couldn't assess whether I'd held my own or sounded as foolish as my inner voice assured me I had.

When class was finally over I strode quickly out of the room, not wanting to run into any of the members of my previous study group. It was best if we made a clean break of it. As I reached the door I saw, out of the corner of my eye, someone pointing at me, and I turned to see Lila Swanson and her study buddy, Diane Wilson. Their heads were close together and they were whispering and smiling and not even trying to hide the fact I was the subject of their discussion.

That was new. These two were the talk of the school, and I didn't think they gave anyone else the time of day. Lila was a Pepperdine girl and Diane was a Berkeley grad, but neither had the grades I did, and their most distinguishing fact was their jaw-dropping beauty. Lila was a tall, tan, breathtaking blonde, and I had an easier time imaging her on a surfboard than in a courtroom. Equally stunning, Diane was the perfect contrast with fair skin and full waves of shiny jet-black hair. I'd nicknamed them Salt and Pepper, but they didn't fit into my criteria for success, and I had no desire to know them. I nearly tripped over the steps rushing out of the room, anxious to get away from their scrutiny.

An hour later, I was sitting in the library, reading up for tomorrow's classes, when I sensed someone behind me. I glanced over my shoulder and saw two someones. Salt and Pepper. Before I could say anything, they took a seat on either side of me. Even seated, they towered over me. Lila scooted her chair closer. My breath hitched and my heart started pounding. I wrote off my reaction to a bout of claustrophobia, and I started to push back from the table when Lila leaned toward me, her breasts gliding along my arm, and my escape was derailed by the sudden realization that the room was freezing cold and Lila wasn't wearing a bra.

Damn. I tore my gaze away from her stiff nipples and turned toward Diane, who was licking her lips like she'd just eaten a very delicious meal. I was in the middle of a sexpot sandwich. I had no idea what they wanted, but I decided to head them off. "I'm studying."

"Alone?" Lila asked, her voice low, sultry, and not at all studious.

"Yes."

"What happened to the rest of your elite group?" Diane murmured.

I shrugged rather than answer. I had lots of pages to read and no interest in rehashing why I was going it alone. Creating a course outline that covered a semester's worth of work was a daunting enough task without being distracted by silly questions, no matter how gorgeous the interrogators.

"I hear they all bombed their exams," Lila said, speaking to Diane over my head before turning to me. She placed a hand on my arm. "What about you? How did you do?"

I shot a look at her hand, but I'm fairly certain I accidentally spent a few seconds staring at her breasts instead. Too damn distracting. What the hell was this? Some kind of "gang up on the used-to-be-head-of-the-class girl" day? "Look, I'm trying to study here. Maybe you could find someone else to gossip with." I showed them I was serious by moving my arm. A little.

They exchanged knowing smiles and stood up, like they'd rehearsed their departure. Before they left, Lila dropped her voice to library low and whispered, "You're super smart, but smart isn't everything. If you're going to be successful, you need to surround yourself with the right people, and you might need to look into some different study methods. When you're ready to admit doing it on your own isn't getting the results you want, give us a call."

Before I could respond, she tossed an envelope on the table, and she and Diane flounced away. I waited until they were out of sight before inching the envelope closer. When I turned it over, I saw my name written in flowery cursive on the outside and spent a few minutes pondering what might be inside. For a brief moment, I let myself bask in the awe of receiving a personalized missive from two hot women, but then my rational brain kicked in and I dropped the envelope to the table and pushed it away. Whatever it was, it—like them—was a distraction, and one that I could ill afford.

But maybe the unknown was the distracting part. Unable to stand the suspense, I ripped it open and shook the contents out onto the table. Three things. The first was a notecard with a few lines in the same flowing cursive as the writing on the outside: *If you want grades like these, come and check out our study group. We think you'll like our special method. Every Tuesday and Thursday at seven p.m.* I recognized the address as one close to campus.

Special method. Right. I started to toss the homemade invite aside, but first I picked up the other two slips of paper that had fallen from the envelope. I held one in each hand and looked between them in disbelief. Lila and Diane's first semester grade reports. Straight A-pluses. Each of them had a perfect 4.0. Maybe there was something to their special method after all.

❖

I stared at the walls in my apartment. Bare, white walls. The walls of a student who was steadfastly focused on her studies. Until last week that had been me. Since the visit from Salt and Pepper in the library, I'd been completely and utterly distracted.

The words on the pages of my textbooks swam in lazy circles, encouraging me to ponder things I shouldn't. Lila's perfectly round breasts and Diane's luscious lips topped the list. I shifted in my chair, but the friction of my clothes was almost enough to send me over the edge. I'd abandoned last semester's study group and the safe zone of the library to home in on my work, but distraction still dogged me and I was doomed to failure.

A cold shower, a cold drink. I craved something to calm my raging hormones, something to quell the ache pounding between my thighs and blocking my ability to absorb anything having to do with Torts or Property or Con Law. I walked the six feet to my tiny kitchen and grabbed a bottle of cold water. While I stood at the counter, alternately drinking the water and rubbing the icy bottle on the back of my neck, I spotted it. Its pretty pink edge poked out of the pocket of my day planner. The envelope Lila and Diane had left behind at the library. The envelope I should have tossed in the trash on my way out of the building, but instead had tucked inside the planner where I kept all my important notes. I'm not proud of the fact I'd opened the envelope no fewer than a dozen times over the past seven days, but up until this moment I could brag that I hadn't acted on my impulses.

One more time. I shucked the note card out of the envelope and traced my fingers over the page, strangely drawn to the pretty paper, the flowery script. I held it close to my nose and inhaled the light citrus scent. Was it Lila's or Diane's? I shook my head as if that would clear the disjointed and very non-studious thoughts floating around inside, but I knew it was useless. There was only one way I was going to get back on track. I tore at the barrette I relied on to keep my hair from being a nuisance and shook out the unruly waves. Before I could change my mind, I shoved my books in my bag, grabbed my jacket, and scanned the address on the invitation one last time. I needn't have bothered. I'd committed it to memory days ago.

❖

"She's here."

Lila stood in the doorway of the apartment facing me, but she spoke the words over her shoulder. I stood on tiptoe, but was still too short to see who else was inside. Was it Diane? Was it only Diane? Secretly, I hoped no one else had received the pretty pink invite.

I heard voices. Several of them. Damn. A small part of me wanted to back down the hallway and scurry back to the safety of solitude, unwilling to admit I wanted, let alone needed, any help. I'd started the school year with so much promise that it seemed insane that I was standing, books in hand, at the door of the pretty girls, hoping they would be the solution to my straight-B blues.

I took a step back, but Lila's long, soft fingers slipped around my wrist and tugged me toward her. With one foot in the doorway and one ready to flee, I wavered, but her whispered voice dripped silky promises against my ear. "Let us show you what we have to offer. You won't be sorry."

Years of discipline hadn't prepared me to resist the charm of a beautiful woman, which was probably why I'd made a vow to avoid them until I'd accomplished my professional goals. Juris Doctor, judicial clerkship, associate at a high-power firm, partner. The natural progression had been my guiding light, but if I didn't get my grades up I'd be working out DWI pleas at the public defender's office. I took a deep breath. Thirty minutes. That was plenty of time to figure out if this little side trip was worth my time. I looked up at Lila and nodded.

Diane was perched on the couch with Oki Nakamura, which did not compute. Oki was the top student in our class, on track for the best clerkships, the most coveted job offers, and the last person I would have expected to see sitting here with the West Coast contingent. I'd always assumed Oki studied alone, thinking no one else could offer anything in exchange for access to her massive brainpower, but here she was, her unbuttoned blouse juxtaposed with the books by her side. While I tried to form a question that didn't sound impertinent, Lila motioned to the living room. "Go join the girls while I get you something to drink."

She disappeared around the corner and Diane waved me over, patting the couch cushion on her other side. "Annie, join us. I promise, we don't bite." She accented the words with a wide and gorgeous smile, and as I gazed at her perfect winter-white teeth, I had a flickering thought. Too bad.

"Hi, Annie." Oki smiled too, but her expression was more cautious than inviting. "I have to say I'm surprised to see you. I know Lila and Diane can be convincing, but you seem a little high-strung for our group."

Diane slid a hand down Oki's bare thigh. "Now, Oki, be nice. I think Annie will round out our group nicely. Her answers to Professor Millwood's questions are always spot-on, and even you have trouble with the finer points of property law."

Oki blushed a shade and started to scoot away from Diane, but before she made it an inch, Diane pulled her back and kept her close by delivering a movie-star kiss that melted Oki into a puddle of goo.

Oki Nakamura morphed from better-than-everyone-else scholar to cuddly sex kitten, but I could not look away. Truth was, for a brief moment I imagined it was me Diane was kissing. I closed my eyes and fell into the fantasy of soft lips, hungry with desire, claiming me and shooting pulsing surges straight to my core. When my eyes fluttered open, Diane and Oki were staring at me with teasing smiles. I was flushed and wet and so completely out of my element that I wished I could melt into the floorboards and disappear. Realizing I could accomplish a much less dramatic exit, I turned to walk away and stepped smack into Lila's arms.

"Wait, don't go," she said "We haven't even cracked a book."

Her sultry voice made "crack a book" sound like a euphemism for something that would only interfere with studying, but I desperately wanted to do whatever that was. Really badly and right now. "But..." I waved at Diane and Oki, who were no longer staring at me, instead finger-feeding each other snacks from a tray on the coffee table.

"But what?" Lila didn't wait for my answer before grabbing my hand and leading me to the sofa across from Diane and Oki. "Here's how it works. We've developed a system for learning the material based on risk," she stopped and traced a finger along my neck, "and reward."

Before I could ask one of the many questions that came to mind, her lips were on mine, soft and gentle and then hungry and fierce. I stiffened for a second, but instinct is a strong force, and next thing I knew I opened my mouth and invited her in. As our tongues touched, I groaned and shifted on the couch. My clothes were too tight, the room was too warm, I was on the verge of exploding when she pulled back and licked her lips like a sated feline.

"That's the reward," she murmured. "You'll earn plenty of them if you dare to employ our methods. See," she slid her hand along my thigh, "all you have to do is study with us."

Her long, soft fingers were stroking the crease of my thigh and I could barely breathe, let alone process her words, but my brain kept insisting that I try. "So, we like quiz each other and if we get the answers right, then…"

"Something like that," she said.

I pointed to Diane and Oki who, locked in a torrid kiss, had abandoned any pretense at being polite. "Doesn't look to me like there was any quizzing going on there."

"Here, let me show you how it works."

Instantly, Lila's lips were back on mine, but this time, her hands tugged at my sweater and she pushed it up over my head. After a moment, she broke the kiss and leaned back and studied my expression, which I'm positive was a cross between "fuck me now" and "what is the relationship between the pounding between my legs and the future I've dreamed about." Heat rose off my skin, and the involuntary arch of my chest toward her signaled the "fuck me" thought was winning, but as I moved closer, she scooted away and settled back against the couch, an aggravating few feet away.

"Wait." I struggled to keep the desperation out of my voice.

"Don't worry," she said. "We're not done. So, Ms. Ardmore, tell me the difference between replevin and repossession."

"Wait, what?" My brain struggled to shift from highly aroused to highly confused, and I barely registered the out-of-context words.

She slid closer and traced a single finger along the edge of my bra. Her light touches left a blistering trail and I groaned, but my relief was short-lived. "Tell me," she said again, her voice sharp and commanding.

I pulled out of my haze long enough to glance over at the other couch. Oki was sans blouse and bra now, reclining against a pile of pillows. I heard her whisper something about duty of care followed by Diane tonguing her way from Oki's navel to her taut nipples.

Hot, wet heat shot between my legs, and I swear my arousal heightened my mental acuity. I sensed a pattern. This time, when Lila asked me to tell her the answer, I did, delivering memorized definitions from my Property Law text, punctuated with short breaths. "Repossession. Self-help. Take it back yourself. Replevin. Go to court. Ask a judge to give it back." Spent, I held my breath and waited impatiently for what came next.

She unbuttoned my jeans and within seconds her insistent fingers slipped into my cotton briefs and slid through my soaking center, over and over. I gripped the couch cushions tight and pressed hard against her hand, torn between the pleasure of her touch and the dread of knowing another question was on its way.

It wasn't long, but this time she didn't stop stroking while she asked. Her voice in my ear was a buzz threatening to derail my sure path to orgasm. Something about mortmain, testator, future interests. My brain knew these words—I was sure, but I was more sure the increasing pressure against my clit was obliterating my ability to put together words beyond "I'm going to come."

Her strokes braked to a featherlight pace, enough to tease, but not nearly enough to give me the release I absolutely had to have. My eyes fluttered open and Lila was right there, her blond waves falling forward against my shoulder, her mouth pouty with want. "You will come, but first you have to answer the question."

She licked her way down my neck to my chest, pausing to unfasten my bra and pinch and tease my aching breasts. *The question. Some words. They're all linked somehow. A common theme.* My mind ticked through its library of knowledge while my body arched and shook and moaned. She was back between my legs now, this time with her hands and mouth, and her hot breath blew circles of ecstasy over and around my swollen clit. She paused there, like she was waiting for the magic phrase to unlock my orgasm, and just as she started to pull away, the answer came to me in big, bold, capital letters and I shouted, "RULE AGAINST PERPETUITIES!"

Before the last syllable left my lips, Lila's mouth enveloped my clit and her velvet tongue delivered firm strokes. I bucked beneath her and vaguely remembered hearing light applause from the other couch as the orgasm roared through me.

When I finally opened my eyes, Lila lay next to me and Diane and Oki were lounging naked on the other couch, tangled in each other's arms. Lila's smile was unquestionably smug. "See how much easier it is to recall what you've learned when you're relaxed?"

She was right. This study group would take me places I'd never imagined.

PLAYING WITH ROMEO

Robyn Nyx

I can do this. I play for ninety minutes in front of hundreds of people every week—this is just a five-minute performance for one guy.

Ryley clasped her hands together and cracked her knuckles. She stepped onto the polished-to-perfection boarded stage and looked out into the theatre. The director sat three rows in, legs crossed, with his fluorescent clipboard at the ready. He looked like the previous twenty or so auditions had made him want to pluck out his eyes and stuff them in his ears. Shakespeare. The language of poets. It wasn't like his words were made to roll off the tongue of the average American, but it was something Ryley had felt a passion for since junior high. Sad though it was, she could still quote the opening act of Othello on command.

"Ryley Donovan?"

"Yes, sir, that's me."

"Alara—our Juliet—just stepped out for a moment. Would you tell me why you're auditioning for the part of Romeo, please?" His voice grew louder with each word so that by the time he got to *please*, he was shouting.

"It's my favorite tragedy, closely followed by *Othello*. Romeo and Juliet's love transcends societal conventions— that idea appeals to me, given what I am." At *I am*, Ryley had motioned to herself, as if she needed no further explanation. "I don't like social boundaries."

The director smiled, and Ryley thought her words might have meant something to him. He was in his late fifties, and with a camp Southern accent that couldn't have been easy to grow up with.

"So you'll turn the Elizabethan tradition of boys playing female characters on its head, then. I like it. You make a handsome boy."

Now Ryley smiled. There was a certain power in being a beautiful girl *and* a handsome boy. So many options. So many straight girls wanting to dip their toes...and tongues...in. *Enter stage right, a most stunning Juliet.*

"Okay, let's do this—this is the last Romeo for today? Please make it so, Dida."

Perfectly straight blond hair reached her ass and swayed from side to side like a hypnotist's watch, mesmerizing those who stared too long. Eyes the color of Five Flower Lake in China. The sharp strut of a young woman comfortable in her own skin. *If only the audition included a kiss.* As she stopped a few steps away, Ryley saw her gaze pass over her with ennui.

"I promise I'll be better than all the rest," Ryley muttered, not loud enough for Alara to catch. Her eyebrow raised inquisitively, maybe a little confused. *She thinks I'm a guy with an effeminate voice.* She stepped in a little closer. *Looking for stubble, sweet lady?*

"Alara, meet Ryley. Juliet, meet Romeo. When you're ready..." Dida's impatient voice interrupted the strange silence.

Alara lifted her script to fill the intimate space between them and nodded at Ryley that she was ready to begin.

"What man art thou that, thus bescreen'd in night, so stumblest on my counsel?"

I'm no man, Alara, but I'll happily counsel your stumble into my bed. "By a name, I know not how to tell thee who I am: My name, dear saint, is hateful to myself, because it is an enemy to thee. Had I it written, I would tear the word."

"My ears have yet not drunk a hundred words of that

tongue's utterance, yet I know the sound; art thou not Romeo, and a Montague?"

And you'll know my tongue, if you're so inclined. "Neither, fair saint, if either thee dislike."

"How cam'st thou hither, tell me, and wherefore? The orchard walls are high and hard to climb; and the place death, considering who thou art, if any of my kinsmen find thee here."

I'll climb mountains if that's what it'll take for you to let me fuck you. "With love's light wings did I o'erperch these walls; for stony limits cannot hold love out: and what love can do, that dares love attempt; therefore thy kinsmen are no let to me."

"If they do see thee, they will murder thee."

I bet you've got a jock boyfriend. Will he want to kick my ass or watch us together? Yuck.

They continued to exchange lines, their eyes never leaving each other. She could see Alara trying to figure her out as she looked up and down Ryley's body, searching for the telltale sign of a bra beneath her T-shirt, searching for a bulge in her just-too-baggy-to-tell jeans. But Ryley wasn't giving away any outright confirmation. *You're just gonna have to ask, and, please God, be interested when you find out. I have got to have my mouth on those breasts.*

Ryley delivered the last line of the audition slowly, her voice wet with wanton lust. "I am no pilot; yet, wert thou as far as that vast shore wash'd with the furthest sea, I would adventure for such merchandise." *And you are some beautiful merchandise.*

"Very nice, Ryley, very nice. Alara, I think we've found our tragic hero, wouldn't you agree?" Dida was up from his seat and advancing toward them, wringing his hands with excitement.

Alara pursed her lips before breaking into a tight smile. "You mean you've found yours, Dida?" Her tone was playful, gently accusing him of unethical thoughts.

"Oh, my dear girl, Ryley's not my type—we'll be doing some gender-bending with this season's Shakespeare. Seems like she's your perfect Romeo, though."

He winked at Alara, and her face flushed. *Question answered.* "When do we start rehearsals?" Ryley was eager to get started, both on the play and on bedding Alara. This college life was fast becoming all it promised to be. Only two weeks in, and she already knew what skirt she'd be chasing.

"Tomorrow. Be here at five, and we'll go through to ten p.m. Make sure you've eaten—I can't stand to hear stomach growling interrupting dialogue. Be prepared to work very hard every night for the next month."

"Yes, sir." Ryley smiled and saluted Dida, who tipped his head in appreciation at the gesture before strolling away to gather his clipboard. "Do you want to get some coffee?" Ryley had decided to waste no time in getting to work on Alara. "We could run some lines? Or just talk about how you see us playing out..." She let the last sentence hang, waiting to gauge Alara's response.

She tutted and shook her head. "Us playing out?"

"Yeah, Romeo and Juliet. Us."

"Okay. I'll play along. Are you already in love with me, then, Romeo?"

"Hard not to be. I'm only human, and you're a damn fine woman. If you don't mind me saying so."

Alara smiled widely, as if she didn't really believe Ryley was coming on to her. "You're funny. Let's get coffee."

❖

"So, what's your story?" Alara wrapped both of her tiny hands around the oversized bucket of a latte, and Ryley immediately thought about those fingers tracing patterns on her body. She shivered with the reaction that coursed straight to her already throbbing pussy.

"My story? Do I have to have one?" Ryley hated small talk, and she didn't like talking personal stuff. There were far better things to discuss. And do.

"Everybody does. What's yours?"

"Can we just skip the formality of meeting and get to know more interesting things about each other instead?" She wasn't a big fan of talking about herself, and hearing Alara's voice would be far more entertaining.

"Like what?"

"Like, how you like your sex."

"You're very cocky for a freshman. You talk like you're nearly thirty and have fucked your way across half the States already. Give me your background, and then I'll decide if I want to talk about sex with you." Alara's phone bleeped an incoming message again, and she read it with a smile. She'd already sent and received seven texts between the theatre and the coffeehouse; it got Ryley to thinking there *was* a girlfriend already installed. That was no surprise, she was a goddess. Question now was, were they exclusive? *Is there even such a concept in college?*

"Fine, I'm from a tiny little place called Amsterdam—New York, not Holland. My dad works in a warehouse and my mom's a waitress. I've got three older brothers, and they all work in blue-collar jobs. I'm the great white hope of the family and I'm on a full-ride soccer scholarship. That's me. What about you?"

Alara pulled out a nail file and started work on her left hand. "I'm one-eighth Cherokee and I hail from Oklahoma. I'm lucky enough to be here because UNC had to fill a quota. I'm a junior majoring in Theatre Study, and I'm part of the Kappa Kappa Gamma sorority, so I get to live in a pretty, historic house with twenty-nine other girls. I don't know my dad, and my mom's had just about every job she could ever have had. She pulled us both up by the bootstraps, and it's my responsibility to take that one step further by graduating from college."

Trying to ignore the possible boredom that had driven Alara to pull out her manicure gear, Ryley pressed on. "So now we know the boring stuff. Tell me what kind of girls you like."

"Wow, you're straight in there, aren't you?"

Alara giggled a cute laugh that made Ryley want to pull her into her arms and kiss her…*everywhere*. "Yep. So?"

"I'm a classic femme, Ryley, I love stone butches."

Ryley's hopes sank…just a little. Maybe Alara could still be turned to the dark side. She motioned to herself, just as she had at the audition. "So *this* is not for you?"

"Well, you're hot. There's no denying that. You've got that andro, pretty-boi thing going on. It's not *un*attractive."

Not unattractive. Nice. Ryley scoffed and pushed her chai tea away, preparing to leave. "It's dark, let me pretend to be all butch and I'll walk you home."

Alara looked a little taken aback, but pushed her chair away from the table and got up to leave. "Okay, but when we get back to my place, there's something I have to show you in my room."

Ryley pulled on her letterman jacket and opened the café door. "See, I can be a gentleman, just like your butches." She couldn't hide the slight scorn in her voice. Alara was right, she did have a boi thing going on herself, and Ryley had nothing against stone butches. She had nothing against any woman who fucked other women…except when it meant they stopped *her* fucking a woman she liked.

❖

They'd sneaked up the stairs to Alara's room, narrowly avoiding the house mom and the chef, both of whom were on the lookout for stray college boys trespassing in their girls' territory. Little did they know, girls could be just as dangerous.

Although Alara had seemed to put the brakes on a possible sexual encounter at the coffeehouse, as they'd walked back to the sorority house, she'd linked her arm through Ryley's and huddled in for warmth against her chest. Ryley thought she might have been chosen as the gay best friend, unthreatening and safe to be around, another theatre lesbian to hang out with. She'd decided to drop her off and think about a new strategy for the coming month. The days when lesbians just stuck to a particular kind of lesbian…surely those days were in the past. *Why limit yourself, Alara? You've no idea what you're missing out on.*

Alara made her intentions crystal clear when she pulled Ryley into her room and pushed her up against the closed door. She looked unsure, but tipped her head up to kiss her. Ryley didn't need a second invitation and bent her head to meet her lips.

"I've never really touched a woman before…" Alara whispered her confession into Ryley's ear as she slipped her arms underneath Ryley's jacket and raked her nails across her back.

Ryley sighed deeply. "I think you're gonna do just fine judging by what your touch just did to me." Ryley took Alara's face in her hands and kissed her hard. "Do you share this room?"

"No. It's private. You just have to put up with the noise from adjoining rooms and people walking down the hallway, is all." Alara punctuated her words with eager kisses before breaking off, switching on her bedside lamp, and lying down, waiting. "And there can't be any screaming…"

"You might be the most beautiful woman I've ever seen."

"You can save the lines, Ryley, you had me at *with love's light wings.* Get over here and show me your cockiness is warranted."

Ryley hastily tore off her jacket and tossed it aside. She pushed Alara's legs apart and knelt between them, leaning down to kiss her while her hands began to explore the perfect breasts she'd so admired earlier.

That was when the door opened.

And closed.

And it became clear that Alara did have a butch girlfriend after all. One about six feet tall and standing by the door with her big, beefy arms crossed.

Ryley jumped off the bed and waited for it to come.

"Don't get up on my account, Romeo." Her voice was surprisingly gentle given that she'd just walked in on her girlfriend making out with someone else.

Alara slid out of the bed and was enveloped in a tight

embrace, accompanied by a heated kiss. "You were supposed to be here when we got back, Jesse."

"The student council ran on, you know what Ira's like." Ryley picked up her jacket and started to move toward the bedroom door. "So I'll be leaving, then?"

Jesse stepped into her path, shook her head, and laughed. She reached for Ryley's face and ran her fingers across her cheek. "No, beautiful boi, you're not going anywhere. My lady wants to learn how to fuck a woman, and she chose you, given that you came on so strongly. I'm here to teach her." Her fingers trailed a path down Ryley's neck and onto her chest. She squeezed her small breast, hard. "You're nearly all muscle, Romeo. You'll be perfect for her." Jesse took Ryley's jacket from her hand and threw it on a nearby chair. "Take off your T-shirt."

Ryley took a moment to breathe the situation in. She'd wanted to end up in bed with Alara, and that was where this was heading. She didn't care much for butches per se, but she'd had her fair share and Jesse was butch sexy—tall, dark eyes, wicked smile. When it got down to it, there was something attractive in every woman. She looked at Alara, and her eyes were swimming with desire. *"She wants this, and she chose you."* It's not often *you get a hall pass to fuck a beautiful femme, granted by her butch.*

She took a step back from both of them, took the hem of her T-shirt, and pulled it over her head. Slowly. She enjoyed the breathy gasp that Alara elicited and the growl that came from Jesse.

"Nice six-pack. Your biceps look like they could go for hours, but you won't be needing that kind of stamina tonight." Jesse sank onto the bed and sat against the headboard with her legs spread. Ryley could see she was packing and felt her clit jump at the thought of seeing Alara's mouth making it disappear. Jesse patted the space between her legs. "Take off your boots and join me."

Ryley did as instructed. With her back to Jesse and her head on Jesse's chest, Ryley slipped her arms under Jesse's knees and held on to her calves. She could feel the hard dildo pressing into the middle of her back and nestled against it.

Jesse thrust her hips just a little. "Patience, Romeo, we'll get to that. Alara..." She gestured for her to join them, and she got on her knees between Ryley's legs. Jesse took Alara's hand and pressed it to Ryley's chest. "Feel it, baby. See how she reacts when you touch her...Use your nails."

Ryley groaned as Alara raked her nails from her nipple to the belt of her jeans. Alara's hair fell over her shoulders and caressed Ryley's stomach as she moved downward. She sighed deeply; there was something crazy sexy about a woman with long hair.

"She likes that, did you see her hips rise, baby?"

"Yes." Alara's voice was husky and her breaths shallow. "Your body's amazing."

Ryley smiled. "Thanks, I work hard at the gym."

"And on the field, Romeo. I've seen you play; you play hard and rough. Is that the way you like to be fucked?"

Ryley let out a gasp that answered Jesse's question when she pinched her nipple hard.

"I want to be inside her," Alara whispered.

"Did you file your nails like I told you?"

Ryley couldn't help but smile—*that's what the texting was about.* All of this must've been planned from the moment Alara found out she was a girl.

"Of course I did." Alara flicked Ryley's belt buckle open and slowly undid her jeans.

Ryley fixed her eyes on Alara's small, delicate hands. They were perfect, just like the rest of her. The way she was undressing her was making her waterfall wet. And Jesse was helping with that too: she'd balled one hand in Ryley's hair and the other was across her face, finger-fucking her mouth.

Alara pulled Ryley's jeans off and sat back on her heels, admiring the view. She ran her fingers over Ryley's lips. "You're so slick."

"She's wet for you, baby, you did that. Slip a finger in."
Alara did so, then let out an appreciative groan as Ryley's pussy contracted around her finger. "That feels so fucking good." Ryley pushed down onto Alara's hand, desperate for more. "Fuck me, babe."

Jesse yanked Ryley's head back. "Pipe down, Romeo, I'm the one giving the instructions. You just lie here and let my lady appreciate how your wet boi-pussy feels."

Ryley swallowed hard. *Fuck, this butch knows how to use me.* "Sorry."

"Put another one in, baby, and drive it deep. Our boi-toy likes it hard, remember?" Jesse removed her hand from Ryley's mouth and clamped it around her breast. She squeezed hard and Ryley hissed. It was quickly followed by a loud groan as Alara pushed in another finger, then a third. Her right hand reached up to Ryley's other breast and she crushed her nipple between her fingers.

"Now can I fuck her?" There was impatience in Alara's voice.

"Sure, baby, use her fierce."

Alara pulled her fingers almost the whole way out before thrusting them back in brutally. Ryley cried out and Jesse clamped her hand over her mouth.

"Shh! We don't want to wake the house mom—if she bursts in on this, my lady'll be kicked out of this fine house and maybe even the college. Bite down on my hand if you need to scream."

Ryley nodded and made use of her offer as Alara worked herself into a nice, even, firm rhythm. Fucking her hard and fast, pulling out and making Ryley raise her hips to chase her fingers, then powering back in, forcing the pleasure right through her.

"That's right, baby, fuck her hard. She's loving it...feel how wet she is for you. You, baby." Jesse was moving her hips to match Alara's rhythm, and her cock was solid against Ryley's back.

"Fuck me, this feels so fucking good. I feel so fucking

powerful." Alara pushed her words out almost as hard as she was fucking Ryley.

"You're a fucking goddess, baby."

Ryley nodded and bit harder on Jesse's hand. To say she'd never fucked a woman before—this girl was a natural. Ryley felt her orgasm building, felt the fire ball in her pussy before exploding into the room with a scream muffled by Jesse's hand. When Ryley opened her eyes, she focused on Alara, who looked like she'd just discovered fire. She slowly withdrew her fingers and lifted them to her mouth. She took a second to appreciate the copious amount of come on her hand and watched it trickle down her wrist before she tentatively tasted Ryley's juices with the tip of her tongue.

She sighed and nodded approvingly. "You taste good."

"Nectar of the gods, baby, lick it all up." As Alara followed Jesse's instructions, Jesse pushed Ryley upright by the shoulders and spun her around to face her. "Time to take care of me, boi-toy." She undid her own belt and jeans and pulled out a seven-inch black silicone dildo that made Ryley falter. Sucking cock wasn't really part of the deal.

"I can't…"

Jesse put her hand around the back of Ryley's neck and pulled her down toward it. "Sure you can."

Ryley hadn't really been on the other end of a dildo before, and the smell surprised her. *Not rubber, but chemical-y, kind of. Not so bad.* She opened her mouth to take the head of Jesse's cock, but gagged instantly when she was pushed down on it. She pulled away, unsure how to continue.

Alara placed her hand on Ryley's shoulders. "Let me show you." She knelt down beside her and wrapped her hands around the base of Jesse's shaft. She traced her tongue from its tip to her hands, back up and then down the other side. Watching her made Ryley wish she'd brought her dildo to college. Instead, it was in a locked drawer at home, all lonesome and unloved.

Jesse wrapped Alara's hair in one hand and kept a firm

grip of Ryley's neck with the other. Ryley dipped down to join Alara. They worked Jesse's dildo together, and the way she was moaning was like it was actually part of her, making it all the more erotic. Jesse's pussy responded in kind. As they reached the tip of the thick silicone, they kissed before working back down to the harness.

"See, Romeo, my lady'll make you a good little cocksucker. She's the best there is."

Alara took almost all of Jesse into her mouth. She gagged a little, but kept going. Jesse pushed her hips up and pressed Alara's head to meet her. As Jesse relaxed and let Alara control the pace, it suddenly hit Ryley that Alara was the one in complete control. It was *her* with the power, not Jesse. What she was doing with her mouth and hands was giving the satisfaction, the pleasure, and she could choose not to. Ryley settled back to watch Alara's grace and Jesse's need, a powerful combination. They continued the dance until Jesse quietly grunted her orgasm and released both of them.

Alara looked at Ryley and caressed her face gently. "Thank you. For letting me."

Ryley smirked. "Thank *you*."

Alara nodded to the door, indicating it was time for Ryley to leave, and rested her head on Jesse's stomach.

Ryley slipped from the bed, pulled on her clothes hurriedly, and opened the door.

"Romeo?"

"Yeah?"

"See you after rehearsals tomorrow. My lady wants to learn how to suck a woman off."

Ryley grinned and closed the door behind her. *I'm gonna enjoy this college life.*

EXTRA CREDIT

Fiona Riley

Tristan gave her long, lean body a once-over and smirked. "Lady killer."

She fixed her faux-hawk for good measure before she glanced down at the reflection of her bulge in the full-length mirror. She turned to the side and cocked her head, wondering if it was too obvious. She smoothed her hands along the front panels of her button-down shirt, skimming over her small, perky breasts and settling over the crotch of her pants. The light pressure she applied to the bulge instantly stimulated her clit, and she smiled. It had taken a little extra time to figure out how to attach the harness to the dildo and make it more discreet, but she was pleased it still gave her the stimulation she desired. Colleen, her new friend with benefits, would be at that West Campus party tonight, and Colleen had expressed her interest in experiencing a strap-on during that quick and dirty fuck session from the library last week. Tristan, ever the gentlewoman, promptly used her extra cash from her work-study gig to acquire the necessary toys and equipment. Tonight was the first night she'd attempted to don it under clothes, and the idea was both terrifying and thrilling.

She turned from the mirror and checked her email one last time before she left to meet up with her friends to pregame before the party. She frowned at the new message in her inbox. It was from her TA, informing her that she had left off the final two sentences of her midterm essay in her digital submission and a completed version was required before nine p.m. Tristan looked up at the clock in a panic. "Fuck! That's fifteen minutes from now."

She hastily fired off a response email telling the TA she would be right over and reprinted the last page while cursing Word for a formatting issue that could cost her a passing grade this semester. As she flew out of her dorm to race across campus to the TA's office, she collided with Colleen.

"Off to someplace in a hurry, Tris?" Colleen's hand found Tristan's bicep and traced the rolled cuff of her shirt along her forearm.

Tristan composed herself and smiled. "Just dropping off something before I get ready to hit up that party later. You still planning on being there?"

Colleen stepped closer and slid her hand down Tristan's forearm to playfully trace the waistband of Tristan's pants. "That all depends." She paused at the button over Tristan's crotch. "Any further consideration to our study sesh from the library last week?"

All concern over her grade slipped from her mind when Colleen gently pulled up on the button and in turn shifted the dildo against her clit.

"Uh, yeah, quite a bit actually."

Colleen looked amused. "Is that so?" She stepped even closer this time, pressing her ample chest against Tristan's, letting her hips brush against Tristan's front, her eyes widening a bit as her mouth fell open. "Oh. I see. Yeah, I'll be there."

Tristan watched the subtle blush form on Colleen's cheeks and gave herself a mental high five. "Good. I'll see you later, then." Feeling bold, she leaned forward and pressed a lingering kiss to Colleen's lips. "Bye."

The high she felt from their exchange helped her sprint across campus, each stride stimulating her a little more, the look on Colleen's face present in her mind as she struggled to juggle the folder with her final paper in it and hold the door open for that pretty co-ed entering as well. She couldn't help herself—life was short and college was full of hot women.

The elevator dinged as she motioned for the pretty brunette to exit first, sparing a glance at her watch and rushing toward the right as the hot mystery girl went left. The door to her TA's office was slightly ajar and she ungracefully knocked/fell into the door, causing it to swing open. Her TA, Prishka Moovari, was stepping out of another woman's embrace and smiling. The sudden intrusion drew her attention.

"Tristan, I didn't think you'd make it." She glanced back at the woman she was just hugging. "Thanks again for everything. I have to settle some finals stuff."

The other woman nodded and passed by Tristan without giving her any acknowledgment.

"She seems friendly," Tristan joked, to ease her own discomfort over interrupting what appeared to be a personal moment.

"You seem late." Prishka pointed to the clock overhead, which read five past nine.

"Fuck," she muttered reflexively. "Uh, sorry. I got here as fast as I could."

Prishka seemed unimpressed. Tristan took a step forward with the folder held out in front of her when a loud noise from the hallway behind her caused Tristan to pause.

"Can you close the door? I'd like to wrap up this grading before I leave tonight," Prishka asked.

Tristan complied and added hopefully, "Does that mean you will accept me being a touch late?"

Prishka's previously impassive face struggled to conceal a smile as she moved around the desk to sit in her chair. "A touch, huh? I suppose. I mean, you did hustle over here," she motioned toward the light beading of sweat on Tristan's brow, "or is it just hot outside?"

Tristan got the distinct feeling Prishka was flirting with her, but when Prishka reached out and took the folder, busying herself at the keyboard in front of her, Tristan second-guessed herself. Prishka was a few years older than Tristan and had recently started work on her PhD. She was stunning and was notorious for wearing ass-hugging skirts around campus. Tristan had spent most of the semester fantasizing about the gorgeous TA, much to the deficit of her grade. That was the only reason she'd bothered racing over here in the first place. Today was the last day of the semester before break, and she needed all the points she could get. Not that she minded spending a few minutes of her Friday night with Prishka, but she had a date with a hot girl and some moaning later on.

The only seat across from Prishka's desk was occupied by a box full of books and plaques. Tristan stood dumbly in front of the desk and surveyed the room for the first time since she arrived; the walls were bland and uninspired. Nothing in the office held any personalization. In fact, upon closer inspection, the box seemed to hold all of her possessions. Prishka's fingers flew over the keyboard and her brow was furrowed in focus as Tristan's gaze fell to the three opened buttons on Prishka's silk shirt.

"Are you going somewhere?" Tristan shifted in front of the desk. All of that flirting and running and interrupting her hot TA hugging another woman was making her clit throb.

Prishka paused her typing and looked up in time to see Tristan's attention focused south of her face. "I'm moving offices and will be in another building next semester. That woman leaving was my old office mate." She leaned back, crossing her legs, and surveyed Tristan curiously as Tristan's eyes followed the hand that adjusted the hem of her skirt.

"Oh, cool." Tristan knew Prishka had seen her eyes drift; she wondered if it would affect her grade.

Prishka uncrossed her legs and sat forward, moving the mouse and typing something before she looked up. "Okay, all set. I have to admit, you wrote a really great paper, Tristan."

"You sound surprised." Tristan wondered if the knowledge that she was packing was making her more bold than usual. She definitely felt hyperaroused, but even this line of banter felt out of character for her.

"You've seemed a little distracted in class this semester. I guess I'm just impressed that you actually retained the material."

"Harsh," Tristan replied playfully, but her smile faded when Prishka's gaze traveled down her body and halted at her crotch, currently at Prishka's eye level. Tristan reflexively dropped her hand to cover the bulge, immediately losing any cool points she thought she might have accrued.

Prishka raised an eyebrow, but a smile graced her full lips. "Packing some extra credit there, Tristan?"

Tristan lightly squeezed the bulge as she reconsidered her earlier dismissal of Prishka flirting with her. "I guess that depends on whether or not I need extra credit."

Prishka seemed to consider this. Tristan began to panic that she had misread their banter. She shifted again, this time anxiously, as Prishka stood and pressed her palms flat to the desk, her expression unreadable.

After what seemed like an eternity, Prishka straightened and walked to the front of her desk, perching at the edge, her head cocked to the side as she exhaled. "I suppose one always needs a little extra credit, don't you agree?"

Tristan smirked and stepped forward, releasing her bulge and tracing her fingers along the edge of the desk, stopping just short of Prishka's hand. She lowered her head and spoke to Prishka's lips, her confidence swelling with Prishka's acknowledgment and reciprocation of her flirtation. "How much extra credit do I need?"

Prishka's lips parted and she let her fingers touch Tristan's on the desk beside her. "All the extra credit."

"Good thing I came prepared." Tristan leaned forward and cupped Prishka's jaw with one hand as she pulled Prishka's hand against her bulge. "Better a *touch* late than never."

Prishka smiled and leaned forward, connecting her lips with Tristan's as she stood and pressed her palm against Tristan's crotch. She moaned as Tristan slipped her tongue into Prishka's mouth and wrapped an arm around her, lifting her up onto the desk with ease.

The kissing was aggressive and heated as Prishka's hands continued to press and rub against Tristan's front. Tristan sucked on Prishka's bottom lip and palmed at her chest, unbuttoning the silk blouse easily and cupping her breasts. She made short work of discarding Prishka's shirt and bra, pinning the smaller woman to the desk while her mouth went to work on pert nipples.

Prishka panted as Tristan teased her nipples in time with her movements against Tristan's bulge. She unbuttoned Tristan's pants and reached in, releasing the dildo from its confines, and gripped the shaft for the first time, seeming to assess the size and texture with a playful tug.

Tristan groaned at the pressure against her clit as Prishka put on the condom Tristan handed her and promptly began to jerk her off. She leaned back and unbuttoned her shirt while Prishka slid off the desk and stood, helping Tristan readjust the dildo in the harness to settle more squarely over her sex. Prishka's free hand lingered over Tristan's ice hockey–toned stomach and slipped beneath Tristan's sports bra to twist her nipple while she stroked up and down on the shaft.

"Fuck." Tristan squirmed at the attention to her chest and clit. She stood to her full height and braced Prishka's hips, turning her to bend over the desk. Prishka hissed as the cold desktop touched her naked breasts, and she reached back to continue to tug on Tristan's dick while Tristan massaged Prishka's chest, leaning down onto her. Tristan's free hand pulled on the straps of the harness to secure it to her hips, a difficult task to complete as Prishka continued to tug insistently at her package. Tristan dragged blunt nails up Prishka's thigh until she reached the hem of her tight skirt, slipping underneath it to press lightly against the soaked front of her thong. She leaned forward and kissed between Prishka's shoulder blades as she teased the minuscule piece of wet fabric and asked lowly, "Are you ready for me?" Prishka moaned and pressed her ass into Tristan's dick, finally relinquishing her grip in favor of clawing at the edges of the desk. Tristan pulled the thong down and pushed the skirt up over Prishka's hips while she savored the soft, velvety feeling of Prishka's lips on her fingers, swirling and teasing, collecting wetness as she palmed Prishka's ass and spread her cheeks. Prishka's hips rolled against hers, another low moan as Tristan dipped through Prishka's swollen lips and traced her entrance with firm pressure.

"Yeah, Tristan, fuck me..." Prishka's head fell forward against the desk, one hand reaching back to press Tristan's hand more firmly on her ass. "I'm ready for you, I'm—"

Two firm fingers entered Prishka, and mutterings were replaced by a deep groan when Tristan pressed a thumb to her asshole before she moved back down to thrust in and out. She grasped Prishka's wrist and moved it to her chest with a grunt. "Pull on those until they hurt."

When Prishka nodded and began working the flesh of her own chest hard and fast, Tristan withdrew her fingers and wiped them along the dildo. She angled the head and dragged it through Prishka's wetness, careful to pay close attention to the whimpers and shudders when the now-slick head bumped against Prishka's swollen clit and up to her puckering ring.

Prishka's hand on the edge of the desk clutched tightly when Tristan pressed the slick head of the dildo against her entrance. "Y-yes, mmm..."

Tristan resisted the urge to plunge into Prishka and get back the rhythm that Prishka's hand had been providing just moments ago; she chose instead to slip the head in and wait for Prishka's sex to adjust to the new girth, thoroughly enjoying the painfully pleasurable expression on Prishka's face, her eyes squeezed shut as her breathing became more ragged. Prishka whimpered and pressed her ass back quickly into Tristan, rolling her hips to invite Tristan deeper.

Taking Prishka's cue and feeling her body relax and buzz at the same time, Tristan eased into Prishka, thrusting in and out until Prishka took all of her on the fourth thrust with a pleased moan and a plump lip squeezed between perfect teeth. Tristan leaned forward and angled upward with her thrusts as Prishka's hand clawed at her tits and let out the sexiest noise Tristan had ever heard. Tristan's clit was on fire as the dildo slammed against her again and again the harder and deeper she drove into Prishka.

"Ugh, God, fuuu-harder!" Prishka made no attempt to keep quiet, and Tristan was grateful to have closed the door when she arrived. Prishka spread her legs farther apart and got up on her elbows to allow Tristan's thrusts to bottom out.

Her upper back and shoulders flexed as Tristan's rhythm and force got faster and more intense. Prishka was pushing back with every thrust, and her beautiful musculature shone with beads of sweat between her shoulder blades. Tristan leaned forward to lick along Prishka's spine as she reached around to cup Prishka's generous, swaying chest. Prishka's breaths were short and ragged as Tristan started to lose her composure. She slapped Prishka's ass with her free hand and grunted, "That's right, come for me."

"D-Don't stop." Prishka rested her head on her forearm, her fingers frantically rubbing her clit in time with Tristan's thrusts.

The louder Prishka got, the more difficult it was for Tristan to keep a rhythm, her own orgasm swelling to the point of breaking. Prishka cried out as she began to tremble, and Tristan pressed her thumb firmly against the tight ring of Prishka's asshole, with a sharp thrust forward pushing Prishka over the edge. Prishka sagged forward with a throaty moan, and the pulsing and pulling of Prishka's core propelled Tristan into her own orgasm with one last desperate thrust.

"Fuuuuck," Tristan groaned. Her legs quivered from exertion

and she leaned her full weight against Prishka, slumping onto the desk, her head foggy.

Prishka shifted beneath her, slipping out the dildo and rolling over. She shuddered as Tristan's dick rubbed against her clit in the position change, shifting forward until it pressed into her belly. She looped her arms around Tristan's sweaty neck when Tristan straightened up and caught her breath. Tristan kissed her slowly while the tremors continued to inundate her system, sparks and flutters prevalent with every pass of her tongue along Prishka's, her body humming with fatigue and pleasure.

"That was pleasantly unexpected." Tristan pressed one final kiss to Prishka's lips before she guided Prishka's legs back to the ground and looked around for Prishka's discarded clothes with a soft chuckle.

"Mmm, I'll say." Prishka dressed quickly, wiping her mouth as she repositioned her skirt.

Tristan discarded the condom and gingerly tucked her dick back into her pants, straining at the almost overwhelming pressure it instigated over her buzzing clit. Prishka found Tristan's zipper and tugged on the fabric, causing Tristan to wince.

"That's for being late. Next time, make sure you get your assignment in on time." She took her soiled thong from Tristan's hand and tucked it into Tristan's front pocket, intentionally brushing her fingers along Tristan's bulge to make her shudder.

Tristan reached out and grabbed Prishka's wrist as she turned to walk away, pulling her in for a hard and deep kiss. "If this is what happens every time I turn something in late, I can promise you that I will never make a deadline again."

Prishka laughed and stepped out of Tristan's embrace with a shrug. "I'm teaching a new class next semester, open enrollment ends tomorrow."

"Will there be opportunities for extra credit?" Tristan glanced at her phone to see three missed calls from Colleen. She smiled. Tonight was off to a great start.

"Perhaps." Prishka sat in her chair and reorganized the papers on her desk. As Tristan turned to leave, she called out, "Oh, Tristan?"

"Yeah?" Tristan paused with her hand on the doorknob.

"I didn't really need you to bring in that last page. I just wanted to see if you would. You got an A for the class, by the way. Have a good break." She smiled and went back to typing as if nothing had transpired between them.

Tristan shook her head with a laugh as she started texting Colleen on her way out: *Best. Class. Ever.*

BODY SHOTS

Janelle Reston

I selected a women's college for one reason: I was desperate to get laid.

After all, my high school counselor had practically guaranteed it would happen. Well, okay—those weren't his *exact* words. When he asked me to name the colleges I was thinking about and Smith, Mount Holyoke, and Sweet Briar came up on the list, he said, "Don't you know those are girls' schools?"

I nodded. Some of my friends thought it was weird, but it wasn't like I needed boys around. I wasn't interested in fucking them.

He cleared his throat. "Only lesbians go to girls' schools, Madison," he said, then hedged. "Except maybe Sweet Briar. Lots of Southern belles there. I don't think Southern belles can be lesbians."

That decided it. I crossed the coed schools from my list and focused on women's colleges north of the Mason-Dixon Line.

College was going to be great. I'd hook up with my roommate. We'd invite the whole hall over for nightly orgies. Sure, I'd go to classes and do my homework, but the rest of it would be one big blur of lesbian sex.

My counselor, it turned out, was misinformed. Within three hours of arriving on campus, I found out more than half my hallmates had off-campus boyfriends. My roommate plastered her side of the room with pictures of Zac Efron, Chris Evans, and

Harry Styles. Obviously, a girl can be queer and still like men, but that was not the case with her.

Fortunately, there was also Frankie.

It was the second week of school and I was in one of the private shower enclosures, singing to myself—a habit I hadn't managed to break yet even though I was now sharing a bathroom with thirty near strangers. Halfway into the song, I realized my voice wasn't alone. Someone had joined in with a rich, silky harmony that echoed pleasantly against the tiles.

"Who's that?" I said, peering out from behind the curtain. A tiny woman in glitter eye shadow and a swirl-patterned minidress was standing at the sinks, a toothbrush hanging from her mouth. Her hair was in a messy knot on top of her head.

"Sorry," she said, still brushing. Her mouth was foaming with paste, but somehow she managed to look cute anyway. "I didn't mean to interrupt you."

"You didn't. I just wanted to know—well, you have a nice voice." She was too adorable to be real. I wondered if she was some kind of siren, seducing unsuspecting first-years with impromptu duets. I wouldn't have minded. Unless— "You're not trying to recruit me to an a cappella group, are you?"

She spat into the sink. "Absolutely not. I just sing when I feel like it. Rugby's my thing."

That was a jolt. "No offense, but you don't look like a rugby player." Even though her arms were as buff as Michelle Obama's, it was hard to imagine her petite bones were much thicker than a bird's.

She laughed. "People like me can squeeze through those big piles of players."

We started hanging out a little, sitting at the same table in the dining hall or doing impromptu duets in the dorm living room. I asked her if she was into girls.

She laughed and set down her French fries. "Are you asking me that because I'm a rugby player?"

"No," I said. "I'm asking because...I'm asking." That wasn't the truth. I was asking because I had a huge-ass crush on her, but I didn't have the gonads to say so.

"Fair enough. I've been intimate with women," she said, then gave me a sly look, "and I'd like to be intimate with a woman again."

That sly look haunted me. Had she been flirting with me? Was she implying that it was *me* she wanted to be intimate with? I thought about it a lot the next few days. I also thought about her fingers, her voice, her pert little ass. I thought about what her body might feel like over or under mine, how her lips would feel on my throat, how her tongue would feel between my legs. I wore out the batteries in my vibrator.

That weekend, she invited me to a post-game rugby party.

"Aren't those just for the players?" I said.

"Nah," she said. "We can bring as many guests as we want."

As many guests as we want probably meant this was not a date, but I dressed my casual best anyway, choosing a sexy-cute fitted shirt and shorts. Underneath I wore my favorite bra and thong panties—a black silky set with tiny brass accents on the hips and cleavage. I didn't set my hopes on revealing them to Frankie, but they made me feel more confident in my skin.

Frankie knocked on my door at nine p.m. She was wearing a faded, sleeveless black minidress that would have made her look like Audrey Hepburn if it hadn't been made of vinyl. It clung to her every curve: shapely hips and ass, muscular thighs, and breasts that looked just the right size to fit completely in my hands. There was a long zipper that went up the front, with a pull-tab shaped like an arrow. It pointed straight up to her cleavage. I tried not to stare.

I assumed there'd be a whole group of us walking over, but it was just us. Maybe this *was* a date. We walked close to each other as we crossed the campus, our hands sometimes brushing as we moved along. I became aware of my thong shifting against my labia and asshole with each step. By the time we got to our destination, my panties were thoroughly wet.

The party was in the common room of one of the older dorms. It had a wooden floor and a ceiling that must have been twenty feet high, with tall leaded-glass windows that looked like they belonged in a church. When she walked in, a loud cheer of "Frankie!" went up and echoed against the stone ceiling.

I followed Frankie like a smitten puppy to a cluster of couches and sat down next to her, trying to follow the lively conversation about scrums, blood bins, grubber kicks, and face balls. Frankie served as my translator, leaning in to whisper explanations of what was being said without interrupting the flow of conversation. Her voice sounded lush and intimate, like she was reading love poems to me rather than explaining sports terms. At one point she came so close I thought I felt her lips brush against my ear. My nipples went hard from arousal. I almost moaned.

Once I was familiar with the jargon, Frankie turned away from me to join back in with the main conversation. But she stayed sitting just as close, setting her hand on my thigh as if she was trying to keep our connection. It wasn't in an indecent spot, exactly—maybe about a third of the way up from my knee, just below the hem of my shorts. But every once in a while she'd absentmindedly brush her fingertips back and forth along my skin—tiny movements, really, not more than a few millimeters. Still, each one felt monumental to me. I couldn't help wondering what it would be like if she touched my clit that way. Or better yet, what it would be like for *me* to touch *her* clit that way. Would she moan? Would she grind into my hand and cry out my name? Or was she a quiet lover whose arousal was told in quiet, gasping breaths?

I imagined myself between her legs, tongue lapping at her labia, her fingers in my hair. Her hands would coax me gently, guiding me to the places where my attention gave her the most pleasure, showing me how to bring her to higher and higher levels of ecstasy. What would she want me to do to her? Nibble at her clit? Curl my tongue into her cunt and lick at her sensitive walls?

Move down farther to bathe her delicate pucker in my saliva and her desire? I wanted to do all of it, and more.

Frankie's voice brought me back to the moment: both of us fully clothed, on a couch in a common room, surrounded by people. "Body shots!" she shouted. "That's a great idea!"

I had no idea what she was talking about. I assumed it had to do with rugby. All I knew was that I was sitting in a room full of other women, so drenched in arousal that my thong couldn't hold it all. It had flooded the fabric, spreading to the insides of my thighs and down my ass crack.

Frankie turned to me. "You game, Madison?"

"Sure, when I get back," I said, no idea what I was agreeing to. "I just need to run to the bathroom."

I did so, cleaning myself up as best I could. If I'd had any sense, I would have jerked off while I was in there to defuse the building tension in my body. But I didn't want to. I was enjoying this state of high arousal and the way it made my skin buzz.

When I got back, the party had transformed to a much more raucous affair. Frankie was lying supine on a table, a glass of tequila on her pelvis and a lime wedge perched pulp side out between her teeth. An upperclasswoman stood over her, sprinkling salt from a shaker between Frankie's breasts. An electric energy sparked between them. The rest of the partygoers were watching and shouting encouragement.

Call me naïve, but I had no idea what was going on. I didn't party in high school, and this was one of my first parties at college. So I'd never seen anyone do body shots. I froze in my tracks, taking in the scene. It looked so private it was almost unbearable to watch, but I couldn't have turned away even if I'd wanted to. Frankie was a magnet to my eyes. She looked giddy and ready to be devoured.

"Do it, Shawnda!" someone hollered to the upperclasswoman. And with that, Shawnda bent low over Frankie, tonguing her salted cleavage. Frankie squirmed and gasped. She let out a delighted giggle. Her face and collarbone went pink with what I assumed to be arousal.

My clit throbbed.

Shawnda then worked down Frankie's zipper to slurp the tequila out of the shot glass perched just above Frankie's snatch. When Shawnda had about half the tequila out of the glass, she pushed her tongue in to lap up the rest. Frankie's nipples went hard, visible like pebbles through the vinyl of her dress.

My trip to the restroom had been pointless. I gushed again. I shifted my legs and the thong moved over my labia in a frictionless glide. It felt amazing, so I kept shifting my legs—back and forth, back and forth—as Shawnda licked every last drop of tequila from the symbolic orifice.

If I thought the tequila drinking was hot, I had another think coming. Shawnda crawled up Frankie's body and tongued at the lime wedge held in Frankie's lips, sweet tight circles and then tiny nips. I figured the next thing to happen would be Frankie spitting out the lime wedge for a real kiss that would turn into hard-core lesbian porn right before our eyes.

Or maybe that's what I was hoping for.

But it ended. Shawnda yanked out the lime wedge with her teeth and stood up with raised fists like she'd just made a touchdown—or whatever it is they call it in rugby. Frankie jumped up to receive the applause of a cheering throng, and the two women gave each other high fives and smacked each other on the ass like football buddies.

"I'm so turned on right now!" Frankie shouted. "And I know whose hot body I want to lick!"

"Frankie's choice! Frankie's choice!" the throng began to shout in unison.

Her eyes scanned the crowd. As soon as she met my eyes, she pointed at me and licked her lips. "You're the one."

My breath caught in my throat. Frankie made a little come-hither motion with her index finger, though she might as well have been reeling me in on a fishing line, as incapable as I was of resisting her wishes. I walked toward her and lay down on the table, my breasts heaving in anticipation.

She bent over and whispered in the same intimate tone she'd used earlier, "You done body shots before?"

I shook my head.

"You don't have to if you don't want to."

"I want to." There was a pang of desperation in my voice. Good. I needed her to know what she was doing to me.

She smiled. "There are two ways to do the tequila. I can put it in a shot glass and set it on your pelvis or stomach and then drink out of it. Or you can pull up your shirt and I can drink it out of your belly button."

If words alone were capable of making me come, those words certainly would have done it. I closed my eyes and took a deep breath. I grabbed the hem of my shirt and pulled it up to reveal my belly and the low-cut waist of my shorts.

"Beautiful," she said. "Now the salt can go anywhere. Do you have a preference?"

I couldn't think of anywhere that I didn't want her tongue. I shook my head.

"I'm going to have my way with you now, Madison." And then she added, her voice a bit lower, "I've wanted to have my way with you for a while now."

She popped the lime wedge into my mouth and I lay there, willing myself not to moan as she started her work. The tops of my breasts barely peeked out of my shirt, but she licked every bit she could manage, sprinkled me with salt, and then licked me again. I'd been to second base before, but this was something altogether different, and hotter, with so many eyes on me and the cool tickle of salt contrasting with the warm tickle of her tongue.

I swallowed a whimper.

She licked up higher, up along my collarbone and neck, sprinkling trails of salt as she went. "Want to lick your thighs next," she murmured into my ear.

I groaned around the lime, nodding eagerly.

Frankie walked over to the far end of the table, positioning herself between my feet. She started at my ankle, with little nips and kisses up my calf that became more open-mouthed and wet as she approached my knee. The spectators went wild as she licked just above it on the inside of my thigh. They hooted and hollered and shouted her name. But none of their exuberance could match how I felt, seeing and feeling this gorgeous woman in such an intimate pose with me. She was close enough to my cunt that she could probably smell my arousal. I gushed a bit more at the thought.

And then she was at my belly, pushing up the hem of my shirt, her hands ghosting over my skin. Someone handed her the bottle. She tipped it gently. A slow, thin stream trickled over my belly and into my navel. I had masturbated in the shower before, aroused by the rush of water against my skin. This was something like that, only more refined and delicate—the difference between using a vibrator to buzz the whole of your snatch or focusing its attention on the hardening nub of your clitoris.

The tequila filled my navel and spread across my belly. I sucked in my stomach to keep it from dripping down my sides. She looked up at my face and licked her lips. "Now's where I get to pretend I'm eating you out," she said, and dove tongue-first into the pool.

I bit hard into the lime. Juice squirted onto my cheeks. I closed my eyes and tensed my muscles, knowing that if I relaxed for just a moment I would lose all control.

Frankie continued laving me, her tongue everywhere on my belly, then dragging along my sides to chase droplets of tequila that had escaped. Cheers bounced off the stone walls and ceiling. Their vibrations felt like an impending orgasm. I squeezed my thighs together instinctively as Frankie licked the last drop of tequila from my skin.

But Frankie wasn't done with me yet. She crawled the rest of the way up my body and lowered herself on top of me, slotting her thigh between my legs as she sucked the juice from the lime.

It took all my willpower not to hump against her, as hungry as I was to feel her heat between my legs.

Though my clit didn't get to touch her, my mouth did: she pulled the lime wedge from between my teeth, spat it to the floor, and began to kiss me in earnest—lips against lips, tongue against teeth, soft desperate moans mixing in the connected caves of our mouths.

At some point I became conscious of my name being chanted. Frankie became conscious of it too. She pulled away, just enough so I could see her face as she spoke to me. "The way body shots usually go, it would usually be your turn to drink next."

I shook my head. "I don't want a drink. I want to go somewhere and fuck you."

"Good," she said, and kissed me again. "I want that too."

She stood up and took me with her, wrapping an arm around my waist as she announced over the boisterous crowd, "Madison is forfeiting her turn!" There was no shortage of catcalls as she pulled me by the hand out of the room.

We didn't make it back to our dorm. We ran down the hall to the nearest bathroom and made a beeline for the showers. I guess that's romantic in a way, making love for the first time in a place so similar to the one where we met.

We kicked off our shoes and tore at each other's clothes as soon as we got into the shower stall. She undid my shorts and slipped her fingers under my thong before I even had her dress half-unzipped. "Goddamn, you're wet." She bit my ear.

"I'm so close to coming already, I swear." I yanked down on the front of her bra, freeing a pert, round breast. Her nipple was hard as a rock. I sucked on it and she let out an airy moan.

She rubbed a finger lightly around my clit—not touching it, just teasing. "If I make you come now, do you think you can come again tonight?"

"I could come all night," I panted. "I'm so hot for you."

She kissed me fiercely then, all tongue and teeth, plunging into my mouth as she plunged her fingers into my hungry cunt.

I grunted and spread, grinding into her hand as I grabbed at her zipper. "Need to touch you. Need to feel how wet you are."

And what a gorgeous sight when her dress fell open and she let it slide to the floor. I ran my hands over her bare stomach and her delectable ass, pushed down her red panties to expose her soft bush. The hairs near her slit were drenched with her arousal, and when I ran my finger over the wetness, she shuddered. I used my toes to pull her panties down the rest of the way to her ankles, and *oh* was that a delight, feeling the way her fingers shifted in my cunt, stroking across my G-spot as my leg rose and fell.

She stepped out of her panties and I raised my leg again, holding it up at the perfect angle by pressing my foot against the stall wall.

"Is this the spot?" she murmured, her breath hot in my ear as she stroked my G-spot again.

I couldn't answer. I just cried out, the sound echoing against the tiles.

She looked proud of herself, but her pride turned to desperation as I parted her bush and ran my fingers over her swollen labia. She shivered and spread her legs, moving closer. "Need you everywhere," she said. She led my hand around to her voluptuous backside, down the narrow furrow of her crack. When I touched her asshole, her body jolted. "Yeah, right there," she said. "You have me so close." She straddled my thigh, spreading her lips against my skin and drenching me in her arousal. She was so wet and silky against my leg, and I swore I felt her clit swell more with each roll of her hips. She rocked back and forth, working my finger into her hot, tight hole.

"I want to taste you," I moaned into her mouth. "I want to lick your cunt and your ass the way you licked my belly."

She lost it then, grinding into me and gushing onto my thigh, warm and slick with the faintest smell of honey. She fucked against me and kept coming, jerking her fingers deep into me with each shuddering wave that rolled through her body. I bit her shoulder to keep from shouting again as I came. Against my closed eyelids I saw shocks of bright white light.

We collapsed against the wall, our chests heaving. Slowly, I became aware of our surroundings: the clinical tile walls, the shush-shush of running water in the shower stall next to us. She wrapped her arms around me and held me close. She kissed up and down my neck.

"Sleep over with me tonight?" she said. "My roommate's gone for the weekend."

"As long as you're not hell-bent on actually sleeping."

She laughed. "Not at all."

It was the beginning of a beautiful relationship.

SWIM GIRL

Rion Woolf

When people ask how it all started, I tell them about that aqua-blue Olympic-sized pool where the cusps of moving waves glinted in the overhead light like diamonds. I tell them the water was my whole world, the only place I felt safe and where I found a strong sense of inner peace.

Until the professor began training in the lane next to me.

I started my day at five a.m. in the university pool. I saw her a few times in the weeks before classes started. She strolled out of the locker room and into the pool area like a woman who owned the sport of swimming. Her broad, well-muscled shoulders and slim waist tapered down into the sexy V of her crotch that made my breath hitch. Then there was the bare expanse of her powerful thighs. Lord, just the sight of this woman thrilled my flesh in the way tender folds of skin shiver when they get too close to an open flame.

The two of us shared this Olympic-sized body of water—her in the fast lane, me in the steady lane. Sometimes I'd stop at the end of the pool and watch her long, lean body propel through the water. She made it look so easy, as if the water was helping her along rather than holding her back. She was older than me, possibly early thirties, and had a body chiseled by the hand of a goddess. She had a way of shaking out the water from her short, dark hair that knocked the breath right out of me. Add in a defined chin and strong cheekbones—God! This woman made me physically want in a way I ached for Ruby Rose on *Orange is the New Black*: physical, steamy, flesh-grinding, put-your-mouth-all-over-me sex.

We met in the women's locker room a few days before the fall semester started. She smiled and looked out at me with dark, smoldering eyes through a tangle of wet bangs. "I've been wondering who my competition is," she said, tossing her towel on the bench between us. "I'm usually the only one here this early in the morning besides the maintenance woman. I'm Ellen."

Her warm, strong handshake left me wanting more of her touch.

"Are you in training, Kinsey?"

"A triathlon in November."

Ellen rolled the dial and opened her locker. "I haven't seen you around campus."

I couldn't look her in the eye as I spoke. The words tumbled out of my mouth like a rambling train, but I couldn't slow them down: I'd transferred to the university, a senior, for the world-class facilities (did I *really* say that?) and to be closer to family.

She nodded in a way that gracefully ignored my nervousness. "Your major?"

"Psychology."

"Interesting." She flipped open her locker and I caught the edge of a tattoo on the swell of her bicep, rainbow-colored. "I teach history on campus. I can give you a few pointers on the Civil War and your stroke if you like." She gave me a perfect smile that must have taken a few years in braces to achieve. "I'm on the Masters team. I've been swimming competitively since I could walk." Ellen pulled a mesh bag out of her locker with a large, colorful, circular emblem of a stick-figured swimmer that read *Swim Girl*.

I accepted her offer while my eyes trailed over every centimeter of Ellen's racing suit, so tight that had it not been colored black, it would have been hard to recognize where her skin began and ended. *Stop staring*, I cautioned myself, but I couldn't drag my eyes away from the half-naked woman before me with taut muscles still golden brown from the summer sun.

"I'll see you around?" she asked.

I nodded and watched Ellen walk to the showers, my heartbeat nearly rocketing out of my chest. She tossed the towel over the wall hook. Then with her back to me, she slipped the straps of her suit slowly down one shoulder and then the other. I stopped breathing when she rolled the racing swimsuit down over her breasts, over her belly, then over the round of her perfect ass. Once she stepped out of her suit, she stood there a moment, completely and gloriously nude. Her sculpted back shone in the overhead lights and my body called for hers—I felt this undeniable pull. Everything inside me wanted to go to Ellen. Just when I thought I couldn't stand another second, she stepped into the shower and pulled the curtain closed behind her.

I'd been with a few men—college boys, if you could call them men—and was not impressed. My body, though, longed for the touch of another woman. I'd kissed a lot of girls on drinking binges and tried drunk scissoring with Casey Smith in her dorm room on my twenty-first birthday, both of us laughing so much it hardly worked. There was a moment, though, when we got it right, when our legs weren't in each other's way and our pussies locked together, those mouths of ours open and hungry for the other. I felt like I could explode and melt and fall apart all at the same time. What I would have given to feel all those explosions again with Ellen. Every fiber of my being begged to follow her into the shower that morning, my cunt wet and pulsating and not caring one bit whether we were in a public facility or that Ellen was a professor and I was a student. Body to body, that was all that I wanted.

❖

A week after classes started, I beat Ellen into the pool for my workout. After a warm-up, I settled into a long and steady three-mile swim. I loved how the water held me, the way it perfectly encased every inch of my body.

I hadn't been able to forget Ellen. I'd looked into her on campus and found out she indeed specialized in the Civil War—the Battle of Gettysburg, to be exact. I suddenly had a newfound interest in Gettysburg and in all things Civil War. I never knew history could be so sexy.

Somewhere after I'd hit the one-mile marker, I turned my head to take a breath and saw Ellen standing on the side of the pool. She stood with her hands fisted at her hips like a swim coach, watching my stroke.

Ellen met me at the shallow end of the pool and jumped in. "You're fighting the water," she said. "Flailing. You need to streamline your stroke."

The pungent bite of chlorine surrounded us. She turned so I could see the side of her body, and there was the tattoo I'd caught a glimmer of in the locker room. The size of a half dollar, the tattoo filled the space right below where her shoulder met her upper arm and featured the same colorful emblem I'd seen on her bag with a stick-figured swimmer: *Swim Girl*. With her arm straight and her thumb against the outside of her upper thigh, Ellen ran her thumb up to her armpit before reaching out for the stroke. I stood beside her with the water up to my waist when she reached for my hand to show me the stroke. Her touch cloaked in water jolted through me like pure electricity.

"Keep your arm as close to your body as possible," Ellen said, adjusting my stroke, holding on to my elbow a little longer than she needed to. "Every movement in the water must be intentional."

My intention at that moment? Not to stare at her breasts.

I utterly failed.

I thanked her later in the locker room while she gathered her items for the shower. "I'm not the best swimmer," I admitted.

"You're better than you think." Ellen smiled. "What you need is confidence."

"I've heard that before."

She reached for my hand the way she had in the pool, this time winding her fingers through mine, nudging me toward her. I held on to Ellen, this almost-nude goddess before me, and surprised myself when I leaned into her until the tip of my nose and lips brushed against the long slope of her warm, smooth neck. Pure heat blazed between my legs. Both of us froze, barely breathing, wanting so much more.

Bang! The locker room door swung open. "Maintenance!"

Ellen and I jumped away from each other, and I turned back to my locker. A woman with a mop and bucket waved hello to us and went into the section of the locker room with the toilet stalls. Ellen headed to the showers. I stood at the locker, holding on to the cold metal edge to try and catch my breath. She was a professor, for God's sake! What was I thinking? I'd never been so forward with anyone before, so wanting, so confident.

The curtain to Ellen's shower wasn't completely closed, and in that gapped space, I saw her. I nearly dropped my towel and shampoo. I stood motionless, transfixed. The shower water rolled down the solid slope of Ellen's torso in rivulets, the suds slipping down between the swell of her breasts, over her hips, and down over the backs of her knees. She turned under that river of water with her eyes closed, letting me see every part of her. Her hand reached up for her left breast and she grabbed it hard, beading the nipple between her fingers. She let out a soft, deep groan muffled by the sounds of running water.

I didn't realize what I was doing while standing there watching her, until I looked down. My hand worked my own nipples into taut pebbles beneath my suit. Red and hardened under my fingers, my breast swelled with an uncontrollable arch of my back. I wanted Ellen to teach me so much more than my stroke.

Then…country music. Twang coming from an old radio. As

if the maintenance woman in the locker room wasn't enough of a pussy blocker, she also played and sang country music as she cleaned. I would have found it all hysterical if everything in me hadn't been aching for Ellen.

I stepped into the shower stall next to Ellen and let the cool water blast hard against my skin, pouring down over my head and into my face. I watched her feet move beneath the stall's wall—perfectly trimmed toenails, tall arches of beautiful feet. Water beat against my back. I pressed my open palm against the shower wall the way people do when they visit death row inmates behind the glass barricade. I wanted to push the wall down and fall into Ellen's arms.

It couldn't be possible—could it? A woman like Ellen could never be into someone like me. She was a professor! What did I have to offer her? I was twenty-two, with no job prospects after graduation and very few friends. Questions like these swirled in my mind, but my body was crying for something more. With soapy hands I reached between my legs and rubbed the tender folds of skin. Ellen's fruity shampoo filled the air and I watched the white lather spread between her pretty toes. The water pounded against my swollen breasts as I kneaded my clit between my fingers until my pussy creamed. Pressure. Wanting. Heat. Burning. I came, grabbing the shower wall to hold myself up, biting my arm to quiet my cries.

When I left the shower, Ellen was already gone. But the maintenance woman wasn't. She sang about long-lost women and too many beers and eyed me suspiciously while I dressed in record speed. I couldn't shake the feeling that the maintenance worker *knew*. It scared me to think that she would be calling her other cleaning pals that evening to tell them about what happened in the women's locker room.

Professor and student.

Scandalous.

❖

When the running phase of my training began, I stopped going to the pool. I told myself it was to give my body a break, but I wasn't fooling myself. Ellen scared me; or, more specifically, the way she made me feel scared me. How could this woman make me wet with only a smile?

I'd managed to avoid Ellen on my morning runs through campus. My strongest sport had always been running, but since I met Ellen I couldn't focus. When I should have been thinking about the way my foot struck the pavement and the roll of my heel, I was contemplating how her toes must taste and imagining the grind of her hot, wet pussy against mine. The fact that she was a professor scared and excited me all at the same time. I'd heard the stories of students who'd slept with their professors, most of those tales ending with the professor getting fired and the student transferred. I didn't want to end Ellen's career. Besides, I wasn't even sure what I wanted from Ellen beyond sex. Most days, nothing—sex with no attachments. Then my guilt kicked in. What kind of girl did that make me?

One morning I took a different running course through campus and came upon Ellen crossing the trail. Her aviator sunglasses reflected the morning light back to me. She stopped for me, her Swim Girl bag tossed over her shoulder. Fall had arrived. Ellen wore jeans that hung low on her waist, hugging her hips in just the right places, and a white button-down that I wanted to pull off her with my teeth.

"How is your training going?"

"Good," I said, trying to slow my breath to speak. "You?"

"We have a big meet next weekend."

After I wished her luck, I told her I'd be rotating sport training again soon. Then I added, "I miss the pool and watching you swim."

"You watch me swim?"

My face burned. I hadn't meant to say that.

Ellen laughed and I noticed a dimple on her right cheek I'd never seen before. I wanted to reach out and touch it.

"That's good," she said. "I like that you watch me."

When she turned to walk away, I stood beside the trail and watched Ellen go until I could no longer see the bounce of her bag or the shift of her hips through the crowd on campus.

❖

The Masters swim meet had men and women over the age of thirty from all over the country competing in the campus pool. I slipped into one of the top bleachers and scanned the order of events. My Swim Girl was competing in four.

After the awards were presented and Ellen had four medals around her neck, most of the teams had showered and were leaving the facility. She gathered her towel and looked up. When her eyes met mine, she smiled. Finally, she lifted her hand and made a signal to me: *come here.* I pushed through the locker room door after Ellen, my flip-flops squeaking against the wet tiled floor.

"Not just a swim girl," I said, "but a champion swim girl."

She turned and smiled, that little dimple winking at me. "I'm glad you're here."

"Me? Miss your meet? No way."

She rummaged through her bag for shampoo and soap. "My Kinsey. Always watching."

A woman left the last occupied shower stall. Ellen watched her go to a locker and then held my eyes with hers. She mouthed, *come with me.*

I followed Ellen into a shower stall, and she pulled the curtain closed behind me. Outside, the woman opened her locker. Ellen nudged me against the wall and leaned her weight against me. "I need your help," she whispered. "Will you help me?"

I nodded, breathless. "Anything."

Her hands slipped under my T-shirt and I lifted my arms for her to pull it off. She hung it over the wall, and her fingers undid the button and zipper of my jeans, letting them fall. Her lips grabbed my ear, suckling the lobe. I stepped out of my jeans. "Anything?" she asked.

I groaned as her tongue circled the outer rim of my ear.

She unhooked my bra. My tits hardened at once. She held my left breast in her hand and kissed me, our lips wet and biting for more.

"Help me out of this racing suit," she said.

Someone else came into the locker room. Women chatted about the awards. A hair dryer buzzed on.

Ellen turned on the shower. The water sprayed against us, cold at first, then warming up. She let the water run down over her shoulders, the hanger of her collarbone, and the strength of her torso. I'd never seen anything more beautiful or perfect in all my life. I stood still, watching her, taking in every inch of her in that skintight racer suit. Ellen looked out at me, her hazel eyes meeting mine, and for the first time, I saw a bit of hesitation. Just a flash, but it only made me want her more. She looked at me through her dark eyelashes as I stepped forward and wound my fingertips beneath the strap of her suit.

The water rained down on us, and with her back to me, I rolled Ellen's suit down over her chest, my hands gripping her breasts hard, then down her taut belly. She leaned back, into me, and groaned.

Down.

Down.

Down over the swell of her hips and the pulse of her strong thighs. Down to her beautiful feet where I pulled the suit away from one foot and then the other. She looked at me on my knees, her lips open, her chest pumping with breath.

"This can be nothing more for me," Ellen whispered into the spray of the shower.

"Nothing more." I almost laughed with relief—a woman after my own heart.

I reached up for her hips and ran my hands down her legs, pooling in the backs of her knees. The realization I'd never done this before settled across her eyes, and she reached for me, the palms of her hands cradling my cheeks. She pulled me to her spread legs and her fingers wound through my wet hair, guiding my tongue. I rolled that swollen, shining pink clit over and over my tongue and moved faster to her soft groans. I wrapped my hands around her, my fingers gripping and kneading the fleshy planes of her ass, my mouth opening further and further for more of what she had to give. My own cunt swelled and pulsed with Ellen's grunts and moans and the water spilling all about us. Her hips rocked forward when she came, the walls of her pussy pulsing and throbbing around my tongue in a way that made me come, too.

Ellen pulled me up to her by my hair. Soft moans escaped her mouth as she licked her come from my face. I held on to her, hugged her tight, afraid if I let go my legs might collapse beneath me.

"You're stronger than you think," Ellen whispered. Her mouth closed over mine again and her hands—her *hands*! My God, where did she learn to do this? The water helped them to slide over my body, her fingertips feeling every ounce of me, setting my skin on fire beneath her touch. My pelvis rocked forward, desperate for her, and she obliged, plunging one finger in me, then two, circling my clit and sucking it much like she had my ear. She brought me close to the edge, closer still, then backed off. Over and over again until I felt like I might go mad.

I quickly learned she liked to hear me beg. "Please," I whispered.

"Please what?" Her fingers dove deeper inside me while her thumb teased my clit. "Tell me what you want."

"Your mouth on me. Please!"

When I finally came inside her mouth, the tears ran from my eyes and I groaned so deep and so long I couldn't believe there was such a noise inside me. I collapsed against her, the water spilling over us, and the wetness of me running down the drain between our feet.

❖

We met for a swim and more showers long after I placed in the triathlon and she won many more swim heats. We experimented with other areas of the locker room while the maintenance woman blared her country music and belted out the lyrics. Ellen taught me how our bodies could connect in ways I never dreamed and how my body had the power to drive her to ecstasy the same way she did me. I went through my senior year in a lust-filled Ellen haze.

Outside of the pool and locker room, Ellen and I never spoke, never called or texted, never emailed. I passed her a few times on campus; she smiled and nodded, that wicked little dimple making an appearance for me. I showed up at all of her swim meets, sliding into the top bleacher. I watched Ellen and her beautiful stroke, fingering the new colorful tattoo I got on my upper right arm with a stick-figured swimmer—*Swim Girl.* After the awards ceremonies and the medals clanged around her breastbone, I met her in the women's locker room showers.

And then I graduated.

I never saw Dr. Ellen Johnston again.

Many people tell me I've lived out their fantasy. It seems like everyone has dreamed about sleeping with a professor at one point or another. When people ask me what I remember most, I tell them about Ellen's strong, broad shoulders that pulled her through lap after lap and her long, long legs that went on for miles. I tell them about the Civil War and the way the water shone like sapphires in the light and washed every part of me clean. And then I tell them about the chlorine, that chemical smell that bit my nostrils and never really left me that whole year. Even now, the smell of chlorine makes my eyes tear and women in racing suits make me wet with want.

A GIFT FROM McGOVERN

Lea Daley

In the staff restroom at Kensington Center, Drew Malachi washed her hands for the prescribed thirty seconds, scarcely aware of her reflection in the mirror. That fine-boned frame, shorter with each passing year. The startling silver of her hair. Fair skin sagging beneath luminous eyes and networked with more than laugh lines these days. But when she reached for a towel, the executive director zeroed in on her hands, now so aged. Exactly as she remembered her grandmother's. And how had that happened? Sometimes it seemed only a few short years since she was young. Only months since she'd met Zoe Compton.

Dear, dear Zoe. Her best friend. Her partner for four decades. Her perfect balance in an imperfect world. Delivered to her by random fate. Because their entire history rested on a snap decision Malachi made at the University of Wisconsin during election season in 1972...

When she agreed to attend a political rally, she was in avoidance mode. Where Drew should have been was hunkered down in the library cramming for an algebra midterm. To no one's surprise, she'd come close to flunking the exam the next morning. She wasn't just mathematically challenged—the part of her brain meant to engage with numbers seemed to be missing altogether. In retrospect, though, she wouldn't regret that

D-minus, because the jostling throng outside Randall Stadium had shoved her hard against another student. A tall woman with incisive hazel eyes, thick brown hair, and a mesmerizing smile. Someone who wouldn't have crossed her path anywhere else on their sprawling campus. Thousands of political signs waved overhead and the roar was deafening. But though she believed in George McGovern and—like virtually everyone in Madison—confidently expected he'd trounce Nixon at the polls, something set her apart from other demonstrators. Drew was simply incapable of performing on command. Wondering whether she'd get a response, she looked up at her accidental companion and hollered, "I can never make myself chant!"

The woman leaned down. "Neither can I! I'm just part of the body count!" Even in a half yell, her voice was mellow, with an intriguing undertone that shivered through Drew. "I figure I've done my duty if I show up to wave a placard!"

Which made Drew glance at the hands holding that sign. Largish. Square and strong. Trustworthy. *You airy-fairy idiot!* she chastised herself. *How can hands be trustworthy?* And then she noticed what the woman was trying so hard to hide under her oversized sweater, her rumpled Army jacket: an hourglass figure that half the guys on campus had undoubtedly dreamed about. Malachi raised her eyes again, saw the stranger was studying her, too.

She knew what people always noticed first: Her delicate build. Gray eyes fringed with dark lashes. Clear, pale skin devoid of makeup. Long, straight hair—just then partly concealed by a fluffy pouf of a hat, protection from the chill. Much later Zoe would insist that she'd done her level best to pull back from Drew that night. Because she'd instantly concluded that this gorgeous creature was out of her league—besides, the woman didn't look like a dyke.

Still they'd stood side by side through all the speeches, chatting in the occasional lull, feeling a thrill of tension twining between them, weaving some inexplicable connection. When the rally broke up, Drew found herself fighting the tide, working hard to stay close, succeeding.

"I'm freezing," she announced as the crowd swept them along. "Want to join me for hot chocolate?"

Even though nothing was worse than falling for a straight woman, by then Zoe would have joined Drew for a week in hell—which she'd admit shortly thereafter. Throwing caution to the wind, she nodded. "I'd love to. I'm Zoe Compton, by the way."

"Drew Malachi."

The chocolate wasn't the only thing hot that night. There was a fiery encounter with Nixon supporters after the rally. Cries of "Tricky Dick!" rose around them, quickly segueing into howls of "Dick's a prick!" Guys from every point on the political spectrum were all jazzed up from hours of impassioned exhortation, eager for a little scrimmaging. With breathtaking speed, a testosterone-fueled scrum formed. Drew and Zoe only managed to escape that mob by dashing around the ragged outskirts. Holding hands.

Next there was the excessive heat in the Student Union—or so it had seemed to Drew, who removed article after article of clothing while both women sipped cocoa from scalding mugs. That enormous Cossack hat went first. Followed by her gloves, her crocheted muffler. Then her heavy wool coat and a cardigan sweater. Zoe watched as those clothes piled up in their booth, visualized adding the remainder to the heap. And within a matter of hours she'd confess that she was startled when Malachi returned her steamy glances. With interest.

Zoe was completing a master's degree in computer science, exhilarated by her new and promising field. Drew was a senior, an early childhood student, brimming with zany stories from her work-study job at the lab school. They couldn't have been less intrigued by one another's majors—or more turned on by their chance proximity. Long before either was ready to separate, it was time for the Student Union to close. After Drew donned all the clothing she'd shed, the pair stepped into an icy autumn night, each desperate to prolong the encounter, neither sure how to swing that.

"I have an apartment off campus," Compton had volunteered at last, with a wary expression suggesting the offer might sound too overt, too crude.

"Lucky you," Drew replied, knowing her roommate was already asleep, already snoring lustily.

"It's just a few blocks away. If we went there, we could keep talking…"

"Not to mention…" Malachi said, looking directly into Zoe's smoldering hazel eyes.

"I'm thinking the same thing."

Zoe had only slept with earthbound mortals in the Math Department. And Drew had only fantasized about being with a woman. Feared that. Longed for it. Just inside Compton's door, she said, "I haven't done this before. Have you?"

"A few times," Zoe answered, unwinding Drew's muffler, removing the hat. "Never with anyone like you."

"Then you can show me how it's done." Not feeling frightened at all.

"It begins like this," Compton murmured, bending to kiss Drew, then breaking away, visibly shaken by the surge of feeling that flooded her.

But Drew stood on tiptoe, offering pliant lips. "I think I'd like more, please."

The very things Zoe was most self-conscious about—those breasts, those hips, that profusion of curls at the juncture of her thighs—were the things Drew luxuriated in. And every feature she thought inadequate in herself was a marvel to Zoe. The trimness of her waist. The sculpted ribs. Her high, round breasts.

Lying on a mattress in the corner of an attic room, surrounded by stacks of books, they held one another in wavering candlelight, Zoe tracing the subtle curves of Drew's body, Drew nestling into the lushness of Zoe. And it was Malachi who transformed the moment from cuddling sweetness to electric intensity. Taking one of Zoe's nipples into her mouth, drawing it into tautness with her teeth, closing eager fingers around its mate. Feeling warmth pour through and out of her. Knowing she'd found her rightful place in the universe.

"Jesus God!" Compton cried. "This can't be your first time!"

"I swear it. Show me what comes next."

Which was Zoe's mouth on every molecule of Drew's flesh. Zoe's tongue tantalizing every opening. Zoe's strong hands lifting her hips. Zoe's deft fingers finding a home inside her. Zoe tweaking every nerve ending until Drew's climax went on forever.

She recovered slowly, then sat astride Compton, giving voice to words she'd never imagined speaking: "Do you feel how wet I am? That's how much I want you still. That's how wet I'll make you."

But too late. Because Zoe was already melting, and Drew's hands slipped effortlessly over every secret part of that voluptuous body. And her tongue had to taste it. And her lips had to explore. And when Zoe came—moaning, shuddering in her arms—Malachi was astonished to find herself coming again. Writhing, bucking, weeping from joy.

It wasn't so much that they knew instinctively how to please one another. It was that they knew how to ask, how to listen. No one had guessed that big, bold Zoe needed to be cradled gently, caressed softly, cherished. No one had suspected that Drew hungered for raw passion, yearned to consume and be consumed. No one understood how eager she was to shed that fraudulent aura of fragility.

In the middle of the night, she'd whispered, "Do you believe in love at first sight?"

"Never before," Zoe answered, pulling her close, "but you make it easy to believe."

"Ditto."

At dawn, reluctant to separate, the women promised to meet

for lunch. What they actually meant was they never wanted to let one another go. Yet by eight, Zoe had left to commune with her beloved machines and Drew was cutting across campus to change clothes before tackling the dreaded algebra test.

To Malachi's everlasting mortification, the remainder of that day hadn't unfolded as she and Zoe planned. Which was entirely her fault—she'd screwed things up almost beyond repair. When the women finally reunited, Drew learned exactly how much pain she'd inflicted. Because as she listened to Zoe describe every awful second since they'd said good-bye with almost cinematic detail, Drew felt she'd witnessed the damage firsthand.

That bleak night, red-eyed and distraught, Zoe had joined a longtime friend at a favored pizza place. She was pretending to scarf down her share of a supreme with extra cheese, but Rick wasn't dumb. "You're awfully quiet, Compton—even for you," he said.

Unable to hold back any longer, Zoe told him about the McGovern rally, about meeting someone incredible, then taking her home.

"Who?"

"You wouldn't know her—she's in early ed. Name's Drew Malachi."

"A sweet, petite natural blonde? I met her when the Kappa Sigs painted classrooms at the lab school—and she's memorable, to say the least. I can't believe you got into her pants! How the hell did you manage that?"

Compton laughed through her grief. "I have charms of which you know naught." Then she'd gritted her teeth and confessed the rest: "Malachi ditched me mere hours later."

"Come again?"

"We were supposed to get together for lunch—"

"And?"

"I got to the Student Union early…" Zoe's voice had trailed off while she silently reviewed her devastating afternoon. She'd been ravenous when she arrived, but not for any offering on the steam tables. At noon, heart pounding with excitement, she'd stared fixedly at the entrance. But forty terrifying minutes later, she was dashing inside the cafeteria, scanning the crowd for that singular fall of platinum hair. Finally she'd had to accept the obvious. Clearing her throat, Zoe said, "I got there early and stayed late, but the woman was a no-show."

"Hell, Compton! You should have known it was too good to be true—just one more straight coed having the regulation lezzie fling before graduation."

"She's not like that, man!"

"As if you'd know right off the bat."

"I do know...it was different...special..."

"Christ, Zoe! A woman like that wouldn't have the slightest clue about your work...or your after-hours predilections."

Zoe flashed back to that timeless interlude with Drew. To tingling thighs and spicy scents. To wet, wet fingers tracing indelible lines on her body, her heart, her mind. "I'll give you half credit on that one, Rick."

He unleashed a salacious grin. "Which half?"

"Watch yourself, old pal...before you're a former friend."

"Whoa! She dumps you, but I'm chopped liver?"

"She'll be back."

"In your dreams, sucker."

"I can feel it," Zoe insisted. "Something must have freaked her out. But she'll work through it."

Rick shook his head. "You're delusional, babe. Give it up."

Compton tore into her pizza to keep from tearing into Rick. One thing was certain: Malachi would have to make an effort to find her. They wouldn't meet accidentally. The campus was too huge, their worlds too separate. And Zoe was way too proud to go looking for her.

Although Drew allowed three hellish days to pass without making contact, Zoe had been unable to take Rick's advice. She simply couldn't stop believing Malachi would return. To complicate matters, she'd said, she couldn't eat, couldn't sleep.

So she did what she always did in distress—she buried herself in programming, debugging every bit of code she could lay her hands on. Then she volunteered her services to all comers, introducing a clutch of clueless undergrads to the mysteries of the flow chart. And her instincts were sound. Malachi had finally phoned, sounding frantic.

"I'm so, so sorry, Zoe. Will you please see me? Will you let me explain?"

"If you promise not to touch me while we talk."

"I promise," Drew agreed, but slowly—so slowly—that Compton had felt a spark of hope.

They'd met at a coffee shop off campus, where again Drew removed that hat, her gloves, her jacket. Then she'd lowered her gaze. "I'm such a coward!"

"Because you bailed on me?"

"Because I didn't tell you why."

"You had your fun and now you're done?"

Stormy eyes flashed in a pallid face. "You don't believe that!"

"Is there another interpretation?" Asked in a voice like shattered glass.

"How about this: I tried, but failed, to choose my career over you?"

"Meaning?"

"As my roommate pointed out, Zoe, lesbians aren't exactly top pick to teach preschoolers."

"You told your roommate about us?"

Drew nodded, a hint of defiance in her posture. Even though that ugly exchange had cycled relentlessly through her mind for three bewildering days, she wouldn't share the details. She'd made the mistake of confiding in Pam when she was still adrift in a dreamy haze conjured by her sensuous encounter with Zoe. To her friend, who was shocked that she'd slept with a butch like Compton on first meeting, Drew said only, "I didn't see the point of waiting when it felt so right."

"Have you lost your mind?" Pam had thundered. "You're a child development major! Who lets dykes work with little kids?"

"But—"

"But nothing! You can't throw away four years of hard work for someone you have nothing in common with!"

Drew had flushed with delicious memories. "Not exactly nothing..."

Pam flung up one palm. "Please! No details! I have a weak stomach."

"It wasn't ugly, damn it! It wasn't disgusting!"

"I'm not the only one who'd see it that way!"

"Well, fuck you!"

"You'll never come close!" Pam retorted, scooping up her French grammar, slamming the door...

Tired of the long pause, the suspense, Zoe rapped a spoon against a coffee cup, snapping Drew back to reality. "So I'm guessing your roommate disapproves?"

"In spades. It was horrible! Pam and I have lived together since freshman year, but she acted like I'd morphed into some kind of monster overnight."

"A helpful preview of what we're up against if we decide to pursue this thing."

"Not if, Zoe—as! Please say 'as'!"

Compton's shoulders relaxed at last and she allowed a grin to escape. "Okay, Drew. As we pursue this thing. What happened next?"

"I took an algebra test, which I'm pretty sure I failed. Then I reported to the lab school, where various events reminded me exactly how much I like kids, how good I am at my job. Then when I was headed to meet you at the Student Union, I remembered what Pam said. And I knew she was right—no way could I afford to fall in love with a woman."

"But you have," Zoe said triumphantly.

Drew smiled back. "Strange, but true. Still, no one who knew that would waste time interviewing me for a preschool position."

"So you panicked?"

"I panicked. I blew off my afternoon seminar and holed up in the dorm. Eating stale crackers, feeling like a rat in a trap. Crying immoderately—which didn't go unnoticed. For a long, abysmal time, I couldn't see a way forward."

"But now?"

Drew had slapped her forehead theatrically. "In a moment of rare clarity, Zoe, it finally occurred to me that I'm smart. Really, really smart. I can find other work—meaningful work—a job where it doesn't matter who I love. Because I already know I belong with you."

Compton stretched across the table to squeeze Drew's hands. "But I think you should continue on the path you chose. Any preschool director would be thrilled to have you on staff—and a fool to let you go."

"That happens, though, Zoe. All the time. You know it."

"Well, in the inconceivable case that you were fired, I'd be able to support both of us. Before long, computers will be everywhere, essential to absolutely everything, and people like me will be making big bucks. Mark my words."

Drew shrank from the sudden vision of herself as a kept woman. "No go, Zoe. I'll need employment of my own—to keep me out of trouble, if nothing else."

A silence fell between them, lengthening ominously, before Zoe made herself say, "I suppose there's always the closet…"

"I'd never ask you to live a lie—you're not the type."

"And you are?"

"I told you…I'll look for a different job."

Zoe laughed—a deep, magnificent, captivating laugh. "I'd bet my slide rule you're on track to graduate summa."

"So what?"

"So I'd rather live in the closet than see you give up something you excel at, a profession you love."

"It would be worth it to be with you."

"Here's an alternate scenario, Drew: we live the life we

choose. We're never dishonest about our relationship if asked. But we never volunteer private information."

"A sort of quasi closet?"

"Yeah."

"Could you stand that?"

"More easily than losing you."

Drew had picked up her hat, her gloves then, and stood. "Take me home, Compton."

In daylight, Zoe's apartment was stark and bare. But the bedroom was orderly and those soft sheets were tucked tight around the mattress, almost military in their precision. "It would be a shame to mess with such perfection," Drew teased.

Compton had snagged one wrist, pulled her down. "We can always make it again."

"But that would mean we'd have to get up…"

Some untracked number of hours sped by and darkness descended. Lounging on tangled linens in the moon's soft glow, Zoe said quietly, "I think we just passed our first big test."

"What's that?"

"We proved we can push through fear, find solutions to the insanity outside ourselves."

"Big deal," Drew had said dismissively. "I'm more interested in another kind of test."

"Such as?"

"Whether we can set a record for the most orgasms in the shortest period of time."

"Challenge accepted," Zoe said, bending to an enticing breast. "Better notify Guinness that Compton's on the case."

They'd been partners ever since. It hadn't always been easy—two such different personalities sharing that cramped little closet. Over the decades there were misunderstandings and arguments, hurt feelings and doubts. All trumped by trust and respect. By politics and passion. By overlapping values and beliefs. By parents' illnesses, parents' passings. By the doors each opened into worlds the other had only glimpsed. By a million midnight conversations and morning kisses and forty times their birthdays, anniversaries, Christmases, and new years. Until time wove them together into a serene, grateful, inseparable symbiosis. DrewandZoe. ZoeandDrew...

A discreet knock on the restroom door brought Malachi out of her reverie. Tossing her paper towel, she returned to work, to the stacks and stacks of files on her desk, to the endless decisions that defined the executive role in a child care center. But in calm moments that morning, she thought again about her partner. Wished it were the weekend instead of another dreary Monday. Wished she were just coming back to consciousness in Zoe's tender embrace. A thousand-thousand events would take place before Saturday rolled around again. But damn, the two of them were lucky! They'd run headlong at love when they were young and green and they'd never regretted it, never looked back.

LET ME HELP YOU PACK

Rebekah Weatherspoon

I'm in a huff when I walk back to my sorority house. The last day of class before vacation always has that weird rushed feeling, like even our professors can't wait to get the heck out of here. I'm ready to go too, but not without an explanation from my sociology professor about the absurd grade he gave me on my midterm paper. I nailed the proposed question, my footnotes were in perfect order, and the document itself was 100 percent error free.

I want to ask him why the low grade, since his notes to "expand" and "elaborate" make no sense to me, but he's out the door before I can even get my things together and make it down the lecture hall stairs. I rush after him into the hallway, but Professor Lutz is long gone. I'll find him when I get back for sure. Or maybe I'll email him. Either way, I want answers. I need to know on what planet I deserved this grade.

In the meantime, I have to pack. In less than two hours we're leaving town, and I haven't even checked to see if all of the clothes I want to bring on our trip are clean. I'm usually more organized than this, but last night after I finished studying for my Islamic history midterm, my girlfriend decided to show up in my room. Literally just showed up. She used to be undead, but now she's just a mortal with powers posing as a college student so we can still be together. She goes to classes and everything just so her presence in my life makes sense to my sorority sisters, who have no idea who she really is.

Alpha Beta Omega is really a nest, home to five immortal vampires that my sorority sisters and I feed, for the greater good. That's our motto. My girlfriend used to be one of them, a vampire who fed on the girls under our room, but she sacrificed herself for me, only to be reborn somewhat mortal with a lot of the vampire perks. Like the ability to vanish through walls. My roommate was crashing down the hall with a few of the other girls, so I had the room to myself. Yes, we screwed until the wee hours of the morning, which has a lot to do with how cranky and over-caffeinated I am right now, but I am not too keyed up or pissed off to know that this grade is bull crap. I almost run right into my roommate, Portia, as I storm back into the Alpha Beta Omega sorority house.

"Bridgette's upstairs," she says over the noise. The TV is on and there's music coming from the kitchen. All kinds of shouting. It's always like this when we're about to leave. "Came to say bye or something."

"Thanks!" That makes me feel a little better. I'd seen her four hours ago, but I want to see my girlfriend again. I pick my way around the luggage that's already piled up near the door and around the stairs and make my way up to my room on the second floor and find her sitting on my bed playing with my tablet. My body instantly reacts to her as I close the door behind me, shutting out the noise. We're blood bound to each other in a way now; we both serve the same vampire, and the feedings and the sex we share with Moreland only make us closer. It only makes me want her more.

The weather's still a little chilly, so she's in jeans and a Maryland University sweatshirt—unlike last night, when she appeared in my room in much less. She's never been a fan of clothes, not as a vampire and not now.

She smiles at me, that pitying smile because she knows I'm upset. "What's wrong?"

"B-plus. Read that and tell me that's not an A paper." I still have the pages gripped in my hand, flat, though; I don't want to crumple up my work or it won't sit smoothly in my file cabinet. I shove it in her face.

She laughs as she sets down my tablet. "No."

"What?" I wasn't expecting that. I know I get worked up about my grades, but she usually indulges me because she knows how important it is that I get As across the board. "Why no?"

"No, 'cause I'm not reading it."

"Why not?"

"'Cause you know and I know a B-plus will not screw up your grade in this class. I mean, we can pull out your assignment spreadsheet." Yes, I have one of those. "I'm pretty sure a B-plus on this and the next three papers will still only bump your average down to a ninety-eight. Still an A, baby."

"I just don't get these notes, and he didn't even stick around so I could ask him about it."

"Of course he didn't. It's Spring Break, baby! Come here." She opens her arms for me. I'm still grumpy, but I set my paper on my desk and take a seat on her lap. In her human form, she's small like me, barely five feet tall, but she still has her superhuman strength, so balancing my weight on her thighs is easy. She strokes my back and kisses my face. This doesn't do anything to improve my mood. I'm cranky for a lot of reasons today.

"You and I also know that the limo bus will be here in two hours to take you to the airport."

"I know. I don't want to go."

"Yes, you do."

"You're right. I do. But don't want to go without you." Things are tricky. The girls can't know who Bridgette really is. They can't know that she used to be their beloved Miyoko, affectionately known as Tokyo. She was amazing as an immortal. Fun, sexual, down to party twenty-four seven, and so, so loving. It has been a few months, and her girls have already been redistributed to other vampires in the house, but they still miss her and talk about her all the time.

Hiding her true identity was her choice in the beginning. She died in such a brutal way and died for a girl who wasn't even her bound feeder. Explaining the how of her reappearance would pose too many questions, and yes, there was the bit where I was afraid that the girls would blame me for taking away their vampire. The fact that she is both very alive and very well and that I am keeping her to myself in her new form will only make things worse. All of this is a complicated secret, but as time goes by we realize it really is for the best. We've both been through so much, and living as Bridgette—a name she's also taken on for me—gives Tokyo a real fresh start. It gives the two of us a do-over.

But that do-over comes with conditions, like if she wants to join Alpha Beta Omega and live in the house again full-time, she has to wait until the fall. That means she can't come on vacation with us. Most of the girls in the house are sleeping with other girls in the house, so they don't care about leaving friends and lovers behind for almost two weeks. Even though my roommate has a boyfriend, she sleeps with girls in the house all the time, so she'll have a blast on vacation. I am the only member of ABO in a truly monogamous relationship, and I have to leave my girlfriend behind.

She'll pop up randomly in the middle of the night because, as we determined over Christmas break, we can only go forty-eight hours without our body parts connecting intimately. Ten days will be way too long, but she has to wait until the right moments so I can sneak away from the group.

I lean into her. "I haven't even packed yet, and I need to shower."

Her lips are so close to my mine, but she doesn't kiss me. She talks close to my eyes. "I wanted to give you a proper good-bye. How can I help you get ready?"

Goose bumps spring up and my voice squeaks a bit when I speak. "Convince Ginger to let you come."

"You know she won't. Next year, I promise. Now let me help. What do you need?"

I let out a deep breath, then I reach into my back pocket, pull out my phone, and bring up my list.

Her laugh blows a wisp of air against my cheek. Everything about her still smells the same, sweet and citrus. "You made a packing list," she says, shaking her head. "Of course you did."

"I just wanted to be prepared."

"Why don't you get in the shower and I'll get started on helping you pack. Okay?"

"Okay," I whine, but it takes me a few minutes to get up. She starts kissing me before I can. And I'm useless when she starts kissing me. Thoroughly trained and seasoned dominatrix with a hundred years' sexual experience, fifty more as an undead, all boiled down into this reborn college student who made me hers. I'm lost with her tongue moving against mine, caught up in the way her hand is moving along my back and how her other hand is rubbing my thighs. I have to get in the shower.

"I'll be right back," I say when I manage to pull away from her.

It's so hard, especially when she looks at me with those deep brown eyes, because no one's ever looked at me like that. No one ever sees me the way she does. This is going to be a long ten days. I shake off the lust boiling inside me and climb off her lap. As soon as I step back into the hall I'm swarmed by the chaos. Music blasting from at least five different rooms, girls running up and down the hall searching for this, grabbing that, doing a little bit of pregaming, which to me seems pointless because who wants to be wasted on a plane.

"Hey, Jill! You want a shot?" Skylar asks me as I pass her room. I have to pass. There's a shower open and I snag it. When I hop back out Aleeka is waiting. I get out of her way, grab my toiletries out of my cubby, and carry them with me back down to the hall.

I find Bridgette standing over my full suitcase. I blink twice, looking at my things all neatly folded, then up to her face. Then a little lower. She's taken off her sweatshirt and all she's wearing underneath is a thin white shirt that is most definitely see-through. She's not wearing a bra. The fabric molds to her heavy breasts, and the tips of her light brown nipples poke at the shirt, inviting me to come investigate them a little further, but I can't get over what's happening with my suitcase.

I walk closer, water still dripping down my legs, and look at her handiwork. "You packed for me?"

"Yeah. Still got the super speed and that photographic memory. Plus I've been on this trip like sixteen times. I covered your list and some extras. Twelve perfect outfits including shoes and evening wear for your trip to St. Maarten." She taps her temple. "I know what all your clothes look like and I remember seeing your bikinis in the back of your closet. They were in—"

"In the Target bag. Right." I shouldn't be shocked. She is magic, and packing isn't exactly a superhuman skill, but... "I was only gone like ten minutes max. Whatever. Thank you."

"You're welcome. Here, give me that." She plucks my toothbrush and my toothpaste out of my hand and drops them into a plastic baggie. "Where do you want this?" she asks. This is another reason I love her. She's not very organized. She doesn't have to be with her memory, but she knows how anal and organized I am. No way I would just throw that stuff on top of my neatly folded clothes.

"Side pocket."

She shoves it into place and slides that pouch closed. Then she holds out her hand for me. "And that's not all." I clasp my finger with hers and follow her over to my desk. She's pulled my video library up on my tablet.

I lean back a little as her arms come around my waist.

"Downloaded three movies for you, plenty to get you

through the flight since I know you can't sleep on planes. Those should finish loading in a second. That way you can watch them even if the Wi-Fi isn't working. And I downloaded four books for you to read, for pleasure."

I opened my book app and there they were; four titles from two of my favorite horror authors that I have been dying to read.

"I almost deleted your textbooks off that thing 'cause I don't think studying and sunbathing mix, but you know."

I glared at her over my shoulder. "I would have kill—"

"You would have killed me. I know. Just promise me you won't study the whole time."

I pull her closer, wrapping my arms around hers, pressing my butt into her crotch. "I won't study at all if you come."

"Nice try. Do you need anything else?"

"No, I don't think so. I just need to get dressed."

"True, but I bought you some time." She's right. Even if I dress slowly and take a while to dry my hair, thanks to her we have an hour to kill. I turn around, and right away I see the impression my wet hair has made on the situation.

"Your shirt got damp," I say, licking my lips.

She looks down, probably following my gaze to the white fabric that might as well be clear. I can see the tiny bumps around her nipples, the fabric is so thin.

"Only a little," she says. "It can stand to be a little wetter. Why don't you use your mouth?"

I'm bad at dirty talk. I never know what to say, but she's so good at it. And she's good at giving instructions. I lean over a little and take one of her nipples into my mouth through the cotton of her shirt. I feel it harden against my tongue as I lick and suck at the tender skin. I know the shirt is adding a kind of friction she likes. I can smell the fragrance of the laundry detergent Moreland uses down at her place, but Bridgette's scent is there too, sweet and citrus.

"Up on the desk," she nearly pants. I do as she asks, but not before she can peel the towel from my body. I sit on the cold wood and take the terry cloth back as she hands it to me. "Dry your hair." More instructions for me to follow. I gently wring my curls dry, watching her as she goes for the big bottle of lotion Portia and I share. She's already wrapped up my travel-sized bottle and packed it away with my things.

I almost question what she's doing, but I know she remembers. I'm uptight about a lot of things, like how dry my skin gets when I've been out of the shower for more than five minutes. I wrap my hair in my towel, then brace myself, hands back on my desk. She steps between my legs and kisses me, so softly on my lips that I sigh. She breaks away for the short seconds it takes for her to gently rub the sweet-smelling lotion over my cheeks and down my neck. She's kissing me again as she moves lower to my shoulders. Lower to my breasts. She teases me, going back for more and more lotion so she can make my nipples nice and slippery smooth as she squeezes them. I moan into her mouth. She knows when I can't take any more. She moves down to my stomach and sides.

She gives me a chance to breathe as she gently massages the cream into my feet and calves. By the time she makes her way back up to my thighs, I know I've created a nice wet spot on my desk.

"Get down and bend over." I hop off the table top, and when I turn around I hesitate long enough for her to step closer to see what I'm looking at. The spot's not as big as I thought it would be, but it's there, sticky and shiny on the dark wood. I feel like my inner thighs are coated with my juices at this point.

"Did you make that mess?" she asks.

I just nod. I think I'm too turned on to speak.

"Excuse me." With a gentle nudge she moves me to the side, then leans over. With a lazy drag she licks the small spot up. I actually groan out loud at the sight.

She doesn't look me in the eye when she turns around. I know she's having trouble. There are still vampire instincts in her. She still associates so much of our sex, any sex, with blood, but she can't have it anymore. Like any human it would make her sick. Still, I know if things were different, this would be the moment when she would take me and bite me.

I run my fingers down her arm until our palms touch. "Do you still want me to bend over?" I ask. Maybe she needs something else. She looks at me again. Really looks at me, and I know that she knows that I love her.

She smiles. "Yeah. I still have to get your back."

I ease into position, grateful the wood has held some of my body heat as I press my nipples against the hard surface. The towel almost slips off my hair as I rest my cheek down, but I don't bother to fix it. Her hands are on me again, on my shoulders this time. She smooths the lotion around, gently working at my muscles and every bit of my restraint. I want her now, but I'm also so bad at saying the words out loud. Moaning will have to do.

"You want it?" she asks me.

A simple yes is all I can manage.

I hear the light clinking of her zipper as it comes down and then I feel her heat against the back of my thighs. But that only lasts long enough for her to lean over me and give my shoulder a little bite. I'm so accustomed to the feedings too, I come a little, a shiver rippling down my whole body until my pussy clenches and really aches. Then her mouth is on me, all over me. She's spreading me, using her fingers and tongue. Licking my pussy and my ass as she pushes into me.

I'm gonna come for sure. I know it, I'm so easy, but it's not what I want. Not exactly like this. And she knows. She doesn't have to read my mind. My eyes are still squeezed shut, my whole body trembling when she spins me around and picks me up. She sits us down in my desk chair with ease. I'm straddling her bare lap when I open my eyes. I've lost my towel for good. Her pants are suddenly missing from the equation, but she's still wearing that shirt.

I reach between us now, down between both our thighs, and

find her sweet center. She's so wet and so hot, pulsing against my fingers. It's nothing for me to spread my legs a little wider, nothing for her to hold me so I can lean back just enough to make room for her fingers to push into my slit. I thank her strength and her ability to hold on to me, even the sturdiness of the chair. My shameless grinding nearly turns into bouncing as one orgasm and another and another roll over me. I can't take any more, but I'm not done with her yet.

I slide closer, gripping the back of her neck as I press her lips to mine. I can't say what I want so I show her. She comes, a loud "Fuck" against my lips, and then she comes again and I'm positive the sensation ripples through us both. I want her, still.

The loud bang on my door make me freeze.

"Hey, Jill! You in there?" Hollis yells as she tries the knob. Bridgette must have locked it. My sisters know nothing of privacy.

"Uh, getting dressed!"

"Flor ordered pizza and subs if you want a bite before we go." Just the mention of food makes my stomach growl.

I look down at my love. She kisses my chin. "You should eat. You're going to be traveling all night."

"You're right.— Yeah, I'll be right down. I just have to finish packing."

"'Kay! We'll save you some grub."

Bridgette pulls my fingers to her mouth and licks each of them nice and slowly. I groan. Ten days is too long. "Just join the sorority now. I want you to come."

"Tomorrow night, I promise. As soon as the girls go to sleep."

"Fine, but I'm going to study the whole time. Maybe even do some extra credit to secure that A in my sociology class."

"Ugh, Professor Luz is going to give you an A. Will you please leave that man alone?" she says with a little laugh as she stands me up and sets me on the floor.

"Never."

HELL WEEK

MJ Williamz

S trip down to your undies," Sally Robinson said. She was the
pledge master for the class of Spring 2015. And she had been
brutal during the past week. It was Hell Week for the pledges, the
last long haul for them to prove themselves worthy of joining the
Phi Tau Gamma sorority.

Dawn Standish was tired of the head games. She had been
a good pledge, doing all that was required of her. She'd even
managed to keep a pleasant disposition during the first part of
Hell Week. But she was tired of it. She just wanted it to be over.
And now she was being told to strip to her underwear? She fought
the urge to flip Sally off and leave the sorority house. But she'd
come this far. She might as well see it through.

She took off her jeans and sweatshirt. It was November in
Northern California, and there was a chill in the air. They were
in a basement where the chill was amplified. Dawn was almost
scared to see what would come next.

One nice thing about her current state was that she could
look around and see all her voluptuous pledge sisters in their
thongs and bras. She felt the moisture pooling between her legs.
It was like being at a smorgasbord. She wanted to taste one of
everything. Well, one of almost everything, anyway.

"It's time for bed," Sally said. "Find your sleeping bag and
climb inside."

That was easy, Dawn thought. She was wary that there might be more coming. As she searched the pile of sleeping bags for hers, she heard a whirring sound and realized the air conditioner had just kicked on. She was freezing by the time she found her bag and laid it out on the floor. It was then the active members of the sorority wheeled some huge fans out of the storage area. Each fan stood taller than Dawn's height of five foot six. They turned the fans on, and the cold air caused goose bumps all over Dawn's body. She slid deeper in and pulled her sleeping bag closer around her. Still, she shivered. She wrapped her arms around herself to try to keep her body heat in.

Dawn heard her sisters shuffling sleeping bags and giggling. She poked her head out long enough to see girls climbing into sleeping bags to share. Her mind immediately went to the gutter. Her crotch was wet as she fantasized about what might be happening in those bags. She told herself to relax. Her gaydar hadn't picked up on any lesbians in her pledge class. She was certain some of the active members were, but no pledges. And no one knew she was, either. An out lesbian would not be accepted in a sorority such as Phi Tau Gamma.

She slunk down deeper in her bag and tried to block out the laughter that surrounded her. Her hormones were raging, and it wouldn't do to take care of them there.

"Dawn," someone whispered.

She poked her head out and saw the large breasts first. She looked up from them to see the beautiful face of Sharon Bryant.

"What?" Dawn said.

"Quick. Let me in. I'm freezing."

"What?" Dawn said again. The last thing she needed was to be that close to Sharon.

"We'll be warmer if we're together. Now, come on. Let me in."

Dawn unzipped her sleeping bag and braced herself against the cold air that washed over her.

"Hurry," she said. "You're letting all the cold air in."

Sharon climbed inside and Dawn reached around her to zip the bag. Sharon pressed against her while she did so. Dawn felt the swell of Sharon's breasts against hers and cringed. The temptation was almost too much. She had to be cool, to not let her arousal show, but it wouldn't be easy. Sharon was gorgeous, with her long, wavy blond hair that fell just beyond her shoulders and her emerald green eyes that sparkled even in the dark basement. And then there was her mouth. Her lips were full and quick to smile. Dawn had often wondered how it would feel to kiss them.

"Thanks for sharing," Sharon said.

"No problem. We'll stay warmer this way."

"Yeah, we will."

Dawn lay there uncomfortably. She couldn't figure out where to put her hands. She didn't trust herself. She wanted to run them over Sharon's curves, but knew better. She laid them at her side, but that was anything but comfortable.

"Are you okay?" Sharon said.

"Yeah. Why?"

"I don't know. You keep squirming."

"I'm trying to get comfortable," Dawn said.

"Here," Sharon said. "Put your arms around me."

She took Dawn's hands and wrapped them around her waist. Dawn fought to keep herself from squeezing Sharon's firm ass. She placed her hands flat on Sharon's back.

"You sure you're okay?" Sharon said again.

"Sure I'm sure," she lied. "Now, let's try to get some sleep."

Dawn doubted she'd be able to sleep. Between the press of Sharon's breasts and the warmth of her pelvis pressed into her, Dawn's mind was alert and her hormones were on overdrive.

"I'm not really tired," Sharon said.

Oh Christ, Dawn thought. The last thing she needed was for them both to be wide awake. She was hoping Sharon would fall asleep and she could eventually fall asleep listening to the sound of her breathing.

"Well, then, what are we going to do?" Dawn dared to ask.

"I don't know. What do you want to do?"

Dawn focused her attention outside of her sleeping bag. There were still hushed murmurs out there, but for the most part, it was silent.

"We need to keep it down, whatever we talk about. It sounds like most people are asleep now."

Dawn's nipples grew hard when she felt Sharon's hot breath in her ear.

"We don't need to talk, you know," Sharon said.

"What?"

"Ah, come on. I know you're family. Don't deny it."

"Shh. Come on. I don't know what you're talking about."

Dawn was terrified. What if this was some kind of joke to out her? But what if it wasn't? What if Sharon was truly offering Dwn her lush body to do with as she wanted? The temptation was starting to win out.

"Sure you do. Come on, Dawn. I've wanted you since the first time I saw you. Tell me you don't want me."

"Oh, shit." Dawn gulped.

"That's right," Sharon whispered in her ear. "Just relax and go with it."

Sharon ran her hand over Dawn's jawbone. She moved so her mouth was just above Dawn's. Dawn swallowed hard and stared at Sharon. She watched Sharon's eyes close as she lowered her mouth to Dawn's.

Their first kiss sent electric shocks coursing through Dawn's body. Her already wet briefs were now drenched. There was no turning back now. She had to have Sharon, and she was going to.

She pulled Sharon's face to hers and kissed her hard on the mouth. She ran her tongue over Sharon's lips until she parted them and allowed Dawn's tongue in to explore. Her mouth was warm and moist, just as she knew other parts would be.

She held her face in place and reveled in the simple act of

kissing her. She wanted to run her hands all over her body, to feel and explore, but she wanted to drag it out. She had to know it was what Sharon wanted. So she continued to kiss her. Their tongues danced over each other in a tango of lust.

Sharon broke the kiss and rested her forehead on Dawn's.

"Oh, dear God," she said. "You sure can kiss."

"Thanks," Dawn said. "Right back at you."

Dawn ran her hands up and down Sharon's back. She brought them to rest on her shapely ass.

"You'd better not have any plans of stopping now," Sharon said. "Because the fire's been lit. I'm ready for lift-off."

"You and me both."

Dawn pulled Sharon closer and ground into her pelvis. She could feel her own clit swelling and couldn't wait for relief. But first, she was going to love on Sharon. She was the most beautiful girl Dawn had ever been with, and she wanted her. She really wanted her.

She kissed down Sharon's neck to where her bra strap was, gently slipped the strap down, and nuzzled her.

"You smell so good," she said. She kissed her shoulder. "And your skin is so soft."

"You say the sweetest things."

"They're true."

"Aw. Thank you."

"Can we get this off?" Dawn tugged at Sharon's bra.

"Sure. Just unhook it for me, okay?"

"You got it."

Dawn was happy to oblige. She quickly got Sharon's bra off and pushed it down to the bottom of the sleeping bag.

"Just don't lose it," Sharon whispered.

"It can't go anywhere. We're in some pretty tight quarters."

Dawn lowered her hands until they covered Sharon's breasts. She drew in her breath at the feel of the full, firm mounds. She ran her thumbs over Sharon's nipples, and Sharon drew in a gasp.

"You okay?" Dawn whispered.

"Oh, yeah. That feels really good."

"Good."

Dawn slid lower in the sleeping bag until her face was even with Sharon's breasts. She continued to knead them as she took one nipple, then the other into her mouth. She ran her tongue over them and sucked them hard enough to feel them poking the roof of her mouth.

"You're making me crazy," Sharon said. "Damn, I need you."

"Yeah?" Dawn smiled. She needed Sharon just as badly, if not more.

Dawn slipped her hand down between Sharon's legs. The thong she wore did little to cover her wet center.

"Oh, shit. You're ready for me," Dawn said.

"Yeah, I am."

Sharon deftly stripped out of her thong and spread her legs as wide as they would go in the tight confines of the sleeping bag.

Dawn dragged her hand over every inch of Sharon's womanhood. She felt her clit protruding from under its hood before she plunged her fingers inside her tight pussy.

"Oh, God, yes. Give me more," Sharon said. She moved against Dawn and made Dawn even hornier.

Dawn slipped another finger inside and stroked her satin walls.

Sharon moved around and around on Dawn. Her cream was running down Dawn's wrist. Dawn couldn't wait to pull her fingers free and taste her. But for now, she just wanted to get her off. She sucked harder at her nipples and moved her fingers in and out at a faster rate.

Sharon dug her fingers into Dawn's shoulders, and Dawn knew she was close. She kept up her ministrations until Sharon buried her face in her shoulder to bury her scream. Dawn held her until the shudders subsided.

"Damn," Sharon finally said. "You were amazing."

Dawn finally withdrew her fingers and licked them clean. "You taste so damned good. I knew you would, though."

"I wish I could have felt your mouth on me," Sharon said.

"Maybe some other time, when we have more room."

"Yeah. Maybe."

Sharon pressed her hand to Dawn's briefs. "So, how are you doing?"

"I almost came with you. I need you desperately."

"Good. Because I love to bring a butch to her knees."

Dawn was taken aback. "Do I really come across as butch?"

"Only to me. No one else suspects a thing. Sure, they probably think you grew up a tomboy or some such, but I know a hot butch when I see one."

"Okay. You had me worried."

"Don't be. Now, relax and let me have my way with you."

Dawn didn't need to be told twice. She quickly stripped out of her sports bra and briefs and thought she'd self-combust as she felt Sharon's naked skin against hers.

"You've got the nicest tits," Sharon said.

"They're kind of small. Especially compared to yours."

"But I like small. Just a mouthful works for me."

Dawn was ready for her to take them in her mouth, but didn't say anything. The drawing out of things caused a pain that joined with the passion to create a whole new sensation.

Sharon ran her hands over Dawn's breasts and teased her nipples for a few minutes.

"Please," Dawn finally whispered. "Please suck on me."

Sharon smiled a sly smile. "Maybe I'm not ready."

"I'm going to come just thinking about you touching me, then."

"Oh, where's the fun in that?"

"I agree," Dawn said. "I'd much rather come with your help."

Sharon lowered her head and took one of Dawn's nipples in her mouth.

"Oh, dear God," Dawn said. She put her fist in her mouth to keep from saying anything else. She had no idea if anybody else was awake, but she didn't want to take any chances.

The white heat flowed through her body and formed a mass in her very core. She needed release in the worst sort of way. Her clit was throbbing. She didn't think she'd ever been that swollen before.

Sharon finally slipped her hand down to where Dawn's legs met. Dawn spread her legs to the best of her ability and welcomed Sharon inside. She was amazed at the ease with which Sharon entered her.

"You're so wet," Sharon whispered.

"What can I say? You turn me on."

"Oh, I like the sound of that."

Sharon moved her fingers inside Dawn, running them against all sides of her.

"Holy shit," Dawn said. "You're going to make me come so fast."

"Good. Come for me, baby."

"Touch my clit, Sharon," she pleaded.

"Happily."

One touch from Sharon, and Dawn felt the mass inside her start to break loose. She closed her eyes while her whole body quaked as the orgasm tore through her.

"Oh, my God," she said when she finally caught her breath. "That was so fucking awesome."

"You were so ready for me. That's what I call hot."

"I needed you. That's for sure."

"So now what?" Sharon said.

"We try to get dressed without getting out of this bag."

"No. I mean after. When Hell Week is over. Can we do this again?"

"I suppose so," Dawn said. "But we'll have to be very careful."

"Screw 'em. Once we're initiated, they can't kick us out."

"True. Well, either way, I'd love to continue seeing you."

"Good answer," Sharon said. She kissed Dawn full on the lips. "Very good answer."

THE WHIRLPOOL

Stevie Mikayne

The water looked too deep for a hot tub. Swirling streams shot across the surface, making the sunken pool resemble a whitewater rafting expedition more than a relaxing dip. But Zandra was determined to try it. When she'd come away to college, that was her first promise to herself: to get naked in the change room like a normal person.

Back in the dorm, her prim cousin and her entourage of giggling friends were preening for some dance. She preferred to stay out of their way. There was something about their dyed-blond hair, their long, lacquered nails, and the flawless lines of their shapely eyebrows that made her feel like squirming.

They knew.

Or they thought they knew something about her, and they always raked their scowls over her with a faint—almost imperceptible—rolling of the eyes. Tittering. Mentioning a manicure or a trip to the hairdresser, or a *boyfriend*.

She didn't have a nice haircut or a single dress in her closet. Or a boyfriend.

Zandra eyed the deck from the shelter of her locker door as she peeled off her clothes and drew the thin college-issued towel around her. It tickled her bare skin like rough hands. For a moment, she just stood still, gathering up her nerve.

She was going to get naked in that whirlpool. She was going

to conquer the fear of her imperfect body with imperfect desires. She was going to strip and plunge and dare someone to walk in and see her naked breasts bobbing along the surface.

Other girls did it all the time. At the pool at the university, girls got out of the water and strode into the change room, stripping off their bathing suits and standing naked in the showers. She'd eyed them discreetly, wondering what gave them the confidence to stand under streaming water, eyes closed, not giving a shit if anyone was looking at their powerful thighs, their heavy breasts. She wanted to be like them. She wanted to reach out and touch them.

The whirlpool was at the back, set seamlessly into the tile, like a sinkhole. In the dark, you could take three steps off the deck and just fall in.

Quiet surrounded her. The swim team was doing laps until ten p.m., the rhythmic kicking of their synchronized legs audible even through the cinderblock walls. The change room was deserted.

Taking a deep breath, Zandra lowered her herself into the water, her nudeness at once obscured by the streaming white jets. It was luscious. Warm streams enveloped her, and she sank lower in the water, just her nose and the top of her ears peeking above the surface. She closed her eyes and basked in the thrill of the warm, loud stream and the thrum of water on all her tensest areas.

She sighed.

She was finally one of the girls in the change room…well… not really. They stood stark naked in the shower and she was covered by jets, but she was getting closer. She was nude in a public place. She felt a jet at her thigh, at her foot, at her shoulder. She leaned back against the side and let the water carry her. She floated at the surface of the hot tub, just as she imagined, her small breasts bobbing along the surface, her nipples peeking out on the top.

When she opened her eyes, someone was standing over her, an amused smirk on her face. Zandra sat up immediately.

Face inflamed, she clenched her jaw and berated herself for being so stupid. She was lucky it wasn't one of her cousin's friends.

"Do you know what I saw Zandra doing? Floating down in the whirlpool, stark naked. And do you know what? It turns out she isn't a man after all!"

But of course it wasn't one of them. It couldn't be one of them. They'd ruin their makeup and manicures in this humidity. She lifted her chin almost defiantly.

The mysterious girl smirked down at her again. Perhaps she was smug because she'd remembered her bathing suit. It was a thong, with triangles of cloth that barely covered her erect nipples—but it was still a bathing suit. Her cascading black curls made Zandra's own light ponytail look all the more like a drowned rat's tail, and to top it off, she had naturally kohl-black eyes.

She swallowed hard and met the young woman's inky gaze. She knew the water didn't cover everything—that flashes of nude still shone through the dark jet-streamed water—and yet something about that gaze made her feel less naked. Zandra wondered for a moment if this young woman—probably within a year or two of her own age—could possibly be a gypsy. She looked exactly like the exotic travelers she had always seen in pictures, and she imagined her in a sequined outfit, riding bareback on a tall white horse.

The stranger was regarding Zandra with equal curiosity, but as if from a distance—another time.

As the gypsy girl slipped into the water, she put her hands behind her back and pulled the string that held the scant bathing top together. Instantly, the material fell from her round, firm breasts and went skirting across the surface of the whirlpool, sucked under by the jets.

She leaned back against the side of the pool and let the water carry her, just as Zandra had done, tiny bubbles bursting on her dark nipples.

Zandra held tightly to the bars at the side of the whirlpool. She tried to avert her gaze from the young woman's arching breasts, but found that there was nowhere for her eyes to go. And really, that she had no desire to stop looking.

The dark-haired girl was fascinating.

After a moment, she righted herself, her deep black eyes meeting Zandra's.

"Eva," she said in a low voice.

For a second, Zandra wasn't sure if she was introducing herself or calling her by another woman's name.

She slid closer, carried by the jet stream, and now sat directly next to her. Before Zandra could decide whether or not to feel threatened, Eva leaned over and was kissing her on the mouth. Her lips were soft, and her tongue lightly flicked against Zandra's lips, leaving a sheen of strawberry gloss.

Just as suddenly as she had come, she pushed herself away, back to the other side of the whirlpool. Zandra blushed and sank under the waves, hiding her colored cheeks. No woman had ever done that to her before.

Why had she done that?

When she surfaced again, the gypsy girl was kneeling in front of her. She stared into her eyes, a faint crease in her forehead. Zandra smiled a little and the crease relaxed until her skin was once more a creamy, flawless surface. This time Zandra leaned in to kiss her.

Eva cupped the back of her head and pressed her full breasts into Zandra's small, erect nipples. The sensation was shocking.

They sank neck-deep into the luscious water, caressing and pushing and squeezing and licking until Zandra moaned out loud. The gypsy girl suddenly pushed her away, against the side of the hot tub.

Zandra was startled.

Eva was leaning against the other side of the tub, a full body length away.

Why had she gone so far?

Zandra was suddenly aware of a strange sensation between her legs. Something was stimulating her firmly and…*God.*

Eva's eyes glinted, dark and sensuous. A dare. And desire. It was her toes, caressing Zandra's clit.

Before she could think of what to do, she felt the girl's other foot on her stomach, gently pushing her back.

Slowly, Zandra leaned back against the side of the hot tub, letting the girl's foot guide her. The sensation was amazing. Trying not to think too hard, she let her legs relax. In the dark back corner of the whirlpool, Zandra opened her legs for a stranger's skilled toes.

Just like fingers, the girl's toes pressed and stroked, and pulled Zandra to the brink of orgasm. She moaned, immediately biting her lip to quiet herself. Waves coursed up from her groin to her stomach, and she was breathing hard and fast, gripping the side of the pool to keep herself still. She pressed her cheek into the cool tile as the pulsation between her legs went on, and she thought she would scream.

And then suddenly, the sensation was gone.

She opened her eyes to see Eva staring at her curiously, teasingly. Zandra's clit was throbbing—she had almost come. The stranger's toes were dangling in the water in front of her, her breasts arcing out of the water as she let the water carry her up. She was beautiful. Mysterious and elegant and serene.

And waiting. Waiting for an invitation.

Zandra tilted her head, inviting her back.

The girl half smiled and reached across the surface of the water, pulling Zandra toward her. Her erect nipples seared Zandra's back, and she kissed her neck—her teeth biting gently into her pale white skin.

Zandra felt a cry erupting from her mouth. She turned her head into the stranger's long, sleek neck and buried her mouth to muffle the sound of her climbing pleasure. Slender fingers reached across her chest and down to where her toes had left off, stroking and circling and caressing. Zandra felt heat wash over her in waves as she arched into the girl's soft, slippery body, moans echoing off the spa tiles.

BREAKING RULES

Salome Wilde

K iss me," Chiaki said, the wind and rain whipping around us in the dark afternoon sky.

I gripped the umbrella tightly, incapable of moving. At that moment, I couldn't decide if a storm was truly rushing in on us—me and this beautiful near stranger—or if the thrill inside just made it seem that way. Regardless, I was in the midst of an experience I'd never had or even dreamed of having, and wanting it more than anything in the world.

❖

It had been a gloomy, overcast Sunday. The sky was full of low rumbling, and I'd found it hard to get my ass out of bed. I managed it around eleven thirty, meaning I'd been working on a midterm paper for my world history class for only about an hour when a flash of lightning, followed by a terrific boom of thunder, knocked the power out. I swore and cursed the weather, but my procrastination was the real culprit. Shit like blackouts only happens when due dates loom. Unwisely yet predictably, I decided to yield to the moment and went in search of food. The fridge was mostly empty, so I settled for leftover fried rice, cold. With a little Chinese mustard, it was not entirely disgusting. Wind rattled the patio doors and whistled through cheap, badly fitted windows. It was just the accompaniment I needed on my full belly to lull me back to sleep. After snapping to after only a few minutes from another long roll of thunder, I decided to make coffee, but of course that wasn't an option. I couldn't even heat up the dregs from the previous morning. I showered quickly in the dark, contemplating a full-blown self-pity party. A reprieve came in the form of a knock at the door.

I wasn't expecting anyone, and my roommate Gina hadn't come home the night before. So I'd thrown on a rumpled T-shirt and sweats after the shower, my short damp hair sticking up at odd angles. I considered not answering. Odds were it was some annoying neighbor wanting to know if my power was out too or to borrow a flashlight I didn't own. It could otherwise be someone for Gina or even a determined door-to-door Christian. I was in the mood for none of the above, though I was even less in the mood for firming up my thesis about the ghetto of medieval Prague without being able to see what I'd typed out so far. When the knock repeated, I ran a hand through my hair with a grimace and answered the door.

Standing against the dark sky was a stranger. She looked about my age, darker and a little shorter than me, and more than a little windblown. Also cute, really cute. Her quirky smile lit up her face, and I couldn't help but give her a once-over: brown almond eyes and thick black hair with overgrown bangs; loose, faded jeans, tight gray T-shirt, worn Nikes. And in her slender hands were two Starbucks cups, smelling of espresso and spices.

"Sorry to bother you," she said.

"No problem," I answered. While I couldn't entirely rule out a religious salesman or one of Gina's many lovers, I was hopeful.

"I'm Chiaki. I live two doors down." She turned and motioned with a cup. The wind blew her hair into her eyes and she tried to whip it back.

Two doors down? Why had I never seen her?

Chiaki's expression shifted to concern as she looked up at the angry sky.

I felt like Queen of the Morons. "Oh, sorry," I muttered. "Come in." I stepped aside, grateful for the darkness that hid my self-conscious blush and the messy living room. I silently prayed she hadn't come to use the bathroom.

Chiaki walked in, still holding the cups. "Want one? Cinnamon dolce latte."

"Uh, thanks," I said, accepting the strange and unexpected gift, though I usually drank my coffee black. And I never spent the pittance I made as a student worker on Starbucks.

"I was making coffee when the power went out," Chiaki explained as I walked into the living room, tossed some crap off the sofa onto the junk-covered coffee table, and motioned for her to come over and sit down. "I can't study on a Sunday without coffee," she continued, echoing my thoughts precisely. "So I picked up a latte for me and one for Tim, that's my roommate. He was still asleep when I left, but I figured he'd appreciate it."

I nodded with some disappointment, figuring Tim was probably Chiaki's boyfriend, but also wondering where this story was going and how I'd ended up with his coffee.

Chiaki obliged. "When I got back, his car was gone and he'd locked the door behind him. The dick! He knows I lost my apartment key."

"Ah, so that's what brought you to my door," I concluded aloud. I was still unsure about their relationship, but the way she said "dick" had a nice, queer ring to it. I sipped the rich concoction and burned my tongue. "Shit."

"Yeah, it's hot." Chiaki took the lid off of her cup and blew. She seemed so at ease that I couldn't help but feel we must have met before. Had to be some reason she chose my place to come in out of the weather.

A silence that should have been uncomfortable followed. We slowly sipped our scalding drinks as the wind lashed the bushes out front, making them rasp against the double window. Chiaki glanced at my history textbook.

"Student, huh? Me too. Philosophy. You know, one of those

great career-makers." She rolled her eyes in a geeky way that wooed the nerd in me.

"Like history," I said with a laugh.

"I've thought about switching to art," she mused. "Less reading. Equally annoying to my parents."

"You any good at art?" I asked.

"I doodle." She pulled another endearing face. "And I like comics."

I gave her the eye. "DC or Marvel?"

She folded her legs and turned to face me directly. "Marvel, duh."

I smiled. "*X-Men*?"

"Hell, yeah. Fuckin' Magneto," Chiaki said.

"Awesome villain," I chimed in, though I was a Rogue fan. Chiaki frowned at me. "More like hero."

I shrugged. "You think?"

She nodded firmly. "So, Ms. History Major, are your parents as proud of you as mine are of me?"

I laughed. "Well, I get decent grades. Keep my scholarship. Obey the rules."

"I don't." She sipped again and eyed me closely over the edge of her cup.

I got butterflies. *Please let her be flirting.* Getting picked up by a stranger was one of my biggest and most unlikely fantasies, even if it never involved storms and lattes. "Don't what? Get good grades?"

She made a sound of derision that deflated my fantasy bubble fast. "Why history?"

I opened my mouth, prepared to utter the common platitudes: *Can't know where you're going if you don't know where you've been* and *Those who forget history are doomed to repeat it.* On the tip of my tongue was garbage about critical thinking and being a good citizen and *Maybe I'll teach.* But with Chiaki listening, I couldn't say any of it. "I don't know," is what I said. "Just a major."

"Right," she replied, putting down her cup. Then she picked up a pile of mail from the table and flipped through it quickly. I just goggled. "So, neighbor, are you Gina Winston or Christina Corey?"

"Christina," I said. "Christy."

Chiaki held out her hand. I shook it, smiling.

"Good. I like Christy, much better than Gina."

Before I could wallow in the first time anyone had ever preferred anything about me to everything about my ridiculously charismatic roomie, the rain began to fall. "Do you want to call your roommate?" I asked, even as I realized it was exactly the wrong question to continue moving toward the seduction I longed for.

"I suppose I should." Her voice was quieter now, less playful, more real. "You walked right by me in the laundry room last week, you know."

"I did?"

She nodded then shrugged it off. "You had a huge basket in your arms."

I honestly had no memory of it, but then, when I did laundry, it was only as a last option and always put me in a bad mood. "I hate laundry."

"Who doesn't," answered Chiaki, finishing her coffee and looking around for a trash can.

"I'll take it." I brought it into the kitchen and put it in the bin, along with my own, only half-finished. Way too sweet.

From the living room, Chiaki called to me. "Hey, Christy, what do you think of rain?"

"Rain?" I came back to stand beside her at the edge of the sofa.

She was gazing out the big window at the slow, steady fall. Her smile made her look young, even as her voice didn't. I badly wanted to reach out and touch her face. "Yeah, rain," she said. "I love it." She rose and headed for the door, waving me to her. "Come on."

"Out there?" Even as I balked at the rain, I enjoyed the view of her little waist and narrow hips in her baggy jeans.

She laughed. "You won't melt."

I shrugged, stopped asking stupid questions, and followed, pausing only to slip on my sneakers and grab an umbrella from the hall closet.

Once out the door, Chiaki headed directly for the little park across from the complex. I raised the little black canopy over us, Chiaki so close I could smell the cinnamon on her breath. As we crossed the empty street, I watched the swings swaying at the center of the park, and I commented that other, wiser people were snug in their nice warm homes. But I didn't really mean it. I felt a flutter in my guts at being alone, here, with Chiaki—a kind stranger who might possibly become more. We walked to a bench but didn't sit, the rain starting to fall in earnest. And then Chiaki made her request: "Kiss me."

"We should go," I found myself saying, the rain shifting to slash sideways across our bodies. My shirt rustled as the little metal carousel creaked and started to turn. I might have been creeped out by the abandoned playground coming to life in the wind if I hadn't been so paralyzed by Chiaki's words. A sheet of paper blew by. "It's getting bad," I fretted.

Chiaki rolled her eyes at me again, and I noticed a damp piece of her hair sticking to her cheek. I reached out and pulled it away, heart-poundingly grateful that she was ignoring my words. I swallowed hard, gazing at her mouth, listening to the rain pound the umbrella. I felt this wash of warmth over me, like if I didn't take Chiaki up on her offer I'd regret it forever. I'd never had a type, but suddenly she was it, 100 percent it. All I wanted to do was throw my arms around her and kiss her so long and hard we'd both be drenched and light-headed, so high we could blow away like soggy paper in the wet, warm storm. But I was frozen to the spot by fear and inexperience.

Chiaki cocked her head with a smirk. "You want to." Her eyebrows lifted, as though she'd never doubted herself for a single moment in this lifetime or any other. But I looked deeper and saw that her expression might also be a plea. My mom always told me that other people were as insecure as I was; I just needed to see it. And suddenly, I did. Chiaki wanted me to want to kiss her, to know I was as drawn to her and the excitement of the moment as much as she, miraculously, was drawn to me...or at least to this risk-taking adventure.

My throat closed and I couldn't speak as I saw just over Chiaki's head how the clouds blanketed the sky, low and menacing. A fluorescent street light flickered on to little effect. I shifted in my shoes, damp but not yet soaked. The only shelter in the park was my umbrella. Shelter I was making for me and a slender, boyish woman named Chiaki. The thought emboldened me.

I closed my eyes and tried to stop time as I listened again to the rain pelting the umbrella. Beneath my lids, past intimacies mocked me: awkward high school groping, drunken college fumbling, and the ghastly one-nighter with the married server at Chili's. I fought back a groan of mortification, though no one but me was remembering. When I opened my eyes again—a second or a lifetime later—Chiaki was still standing beside me, studying my face. I searched hers for impatience or resignation as a droplet found its way down the back of my shirt and I shuddered.

"Christy," murmured Chiaki, a wealth of emotion in two short syllables. She put an arm around me. I fumbled with the umbrella as she whispered hotly into my cold ear. "Kiss me."

I basked in the warmth and the short, urgent words. I felt my pussy clench as I faced the desire for excitement and pleasure in her parted lips. She truly wanted me.

"Fuck," I muttered, and crushed my mouth to hers, pulse racing in absurd worry that, despite all evidence to the contrary, she would reject me or I'd wake up to find this magical moment a dream. Her lips were cool against mine, and then warm as she opened to me and I let my tongue ease in to taste her. The pressure of our soft, hot mouths gave me chills as I took the initiative to deepen the embrace. With our bodies pressed together, Chiaki made a low sound of excitement, and I couldn't help but echo it.

Though the wind and rain generously kept from growing into a storm, I was surprised when Chiaki pulled away and tossed the umbrella down. I bit my lip as she pulled me to the swings. The long chains hanging from the metal A-frame groaned as she led me to sit and climbed onto my lap, facing me. I steadied myself with my feet. Because she was smaller than me, her weight felt good, solid on my thighs. We kissed again, more hungrily now, and I wrapped my arms tightly around her. This was actually happening. I was having something—whatever it was—that showed I was desirable and even a risk-taker. I loved it as much as the tiny pain when Chiaki nipped my bottom lip and then dove back in to probe my mouth, curiosity leading to a sweet intensity that made the wet weather a stimulating counterpoint to the heat growing between us.

My hands grew as eager as my mouth for more. I reached down to squeeze her little round ass and she ground into me. I devoured her moan, but soon I was so dizzy I had to release a hand to hold the swing chain, afraid of falling. The wind picked up further, whipping rain through our hair, and I wondered whether we shouldn't head back to my place. Just as quickly, however, I recognized the danger in the thought. The power might be back on, forcing me to consider that paper I was putting off. Gina might be home, or Chiaki's Tim. And even if none of these were true, the magic that helped me to shed my inhibitions and take a chance with Chiaki might vanish if we found shelter. The icy thoughts chilled me more than any storm could.

"You okay?" asked Chiaki, voice thick.

I paused. My throat closed. I was going to ruin everything. I couldn't seem to help it. I was cold and afraid and there was a hot woman sitting in my lap who might as well be a stranger and the rain was pouring down and I could hear my father tell me I was wasting my time in college if I wasn't going to make something of myself. "I'm sorry," I said, and felt Chiaki's weight lift from me like my soul leaving my body.

"Hey, Christy," Chiaki said before her hand wrapped mine on the chain I was holding so tightly it hurt. "It's cool, you know. Everything's cool. We can just hang out, or we can go back home and try again another time...if you want."

Those last three words felt like heartbreak, but I opened my eyes to find Chiaki smiling down at me in the rain. I tipped my face up and she kissed me gently. Her sincerity and patience spoke of experience and confidence that helped me wrestle my self-defeating brain from its morbid uncertainty. I blinked against the downpour, taking in just how lucky I was to have met this woman on this day when the power so kindly went out. I released my death grip on the swing and took her hand. Determined to be heedless of the weather and whatever came next, I walked us to a bench, half-shielded from the deluge by a spreading maple tree. Chiaki followed along silently.

I sat us down on the bench and held her close with one arm while I let the other stroke her thigh, then slip up to feel her small belly beneath her wet shirt. I was simultaneously petrified and determined, lost in my need to make this fantasy come true. We kissed again and Chiaki slid into my lap, arching against me as she placed a hand over mine. She pushed my fingers up beneath her sports bra and I squeezed her breast gently.

Chiaki reached to slip her bra up over both breasts. Then she reached behind my head to weave her fingers through my wet, messy hair and pull my mouth to her neck. I licked and kissed her hairline as I let my fingers roam over the warm, damp skin beneath her shirt. I squeezed her belly, tickled her ribs, and kneaded her breasts until she gave a long, deep sigh. "Chiaki," I said, tasting her name and her flesh. Cupping her breasts, I rubbed a thumb across each nipple and made her moan again.

Releasing my head, Chiaki sat up and impatiently yanked off both her shirt and bra. I looked around hastily, unable not to worry about being seen. But soon she was arching in my arms again, still turned away and shivering as the rain trickled over her. I reached out to smooth over her soft shoulders and down her arms. She turned to face me for a moment, eyes glittering in the semi-dark. I held her breasts again and pinched each nipple. She pushed forward into my hands and ground her ass into my lap.

As she grabbed one of my hands and put it between her legs, I mumbled, "I've never done anything like this." I felt like an idiot, though I continued to grip and squeeze her breast with one hand and the denim that covered her pussy with the other.

"Everybody's gotta have a first time," Chiaki answered, rocking into my grip.

I guessed she thought I meant in the rain, or outside, where we could be caught. And I did mean that, but more too. I'd never wanted someone like this—not drunk, not cheating, not just for kicks. I didn't know Chiaki at all. But I wanted to. Every bit of her.

Chiaki looked at me, a hard, searching look, and then stood before me. Suddenly, she reached out to pull my shirt over my head. And I let her.

"Voilà!" she said.

I sat there in my old racer-back bra, getting wet. I felt entirely foolish. I grinned.

Chiaki licked her wet lips. "You want to show me those tits, Christy. You really do."

I nodded and felt my face flush. "And you really want me to."

Chiaki laughed and nodded back.

"Right," I said, and whipped off my bra, releasing the weight of my entirely average breasts. I was grateful for the dark that hid the beet-red blush I knew had spread across my face.

"Nice," appraised Chiaki, reaching out greedy hands to weigh and fondle them. "Yum," she added. She punctuated her appreciation with a noisy kiss to each hardening nipple, and then another. And then she began to suck.

When my mouth dropped open to tell her I couldn't handle being on display like this a moment longer—even if it was only her and me in the rain—she pulled her mouth away and plopped back into my lap, then crushed our bodies together in a wet, warm embrace. Tits-to-tits. She rubbed and wriggled against me, arms holding me tight. It was simultaneously childlike and deeply adult, sensual and ticklish and utterly ridiculous.

"Mmm, you feel good," Chiaki enthused.

"So do you," I echoed.

I reached up to take her face in my hands and we kissed again, topless and exposed in the rain, two strangers who weren't strangers anymore.

"Shit." Chiaki's startled exclamation as she peered over my shoulder made me turn around and look, too. I kept her body pressed to mine as we both saw dozens of lights come on in the apartments across the street. The sky was still dark and the rain was still falling, but reality had returned, and I couldn't push it away.

My heart raced as I eased Chiaki from my lap and fumbled for my wet shirt. She let me, grabbing her own top as well. We pulled and rolled them on with effort, each laughing at the other's predicament.

Bra in hand, I hunted down the umbrella and found it not far from where Chiaki had tossed it. I was soaked and the storm was letting up, but I still held it over me and returned to Chiaki. She stood beneath the little shelter and pressed close to me, wrapping her arms low around my waist and then pinching my ass.

I yelped. "What was that for?"

"Just needed to be sure I'm not dreaming."

"That's not the way it works." I laughed and kissed her deeply.

"We're big girls. We can make up our own rules."

"I like the way you make rules—and break them."

"Hey, I know a really good way to break the rules right now." Her eyes lit with mischief. "We get the spare key to my place from under the mat outside the back door and dry off—and other things—in my bed."

"Nice," I cooed. Then I grimaced as the truth caught up with me. "So when you brought me that coffee...?"

Chiaki winked. "My first rule is never to pass up a promising opportunity." She pulled away and ran ahead with a laugh, splashing in puddles as she went.

I chased her, smiling broadly, looking forward to all the rules we'd make and break together.

THE FIRST MOVE

Rose P. Lethe

When it all came down to it, Jasmine was too old to be behaving like this.

Not that she was *old*, really—at twenty-one, she knew she was technically quite young—but she certainly felt too old to be carrying on like a teenager with a crush. Flat-ironing her wavy and frizzy hair, applying a thick layer of dusky-pink lip gloss, shucking her usual full-support bras in favor of a black push-up, undoing an extra button on her shirt, and shimmying into her tightest striped pencil skirt—all to visit the campus's main library on a Friday evening in the middle of the summer session.

To be fair, she *did* need to work on her senior thesis, which was in a sad, poorly researched state after the course on romantic poets had kicked her ass last semester. A few hours in a quiet library with no television or Internet to distract her would probably do her a world of good, no matter what her initial motivation had been.

That motivation was three or four inches taller than Jasmine's 5'5", somewhere between twenty-five and thirty-five years old, lean, and long-limbed with olive-colored skin, chin-length brown hair, and black plastic-rimmed glasses. Jasmine had yet to identify an eye color; every time she got close enough, she was distracted by the eyelashes, which were long and thick like a model's. Her name was Meg, according to the name tag she wore on a lanyard around her neck, and she worked most afternoons and evenings at the library's reference desk.

Jasmine had been smitten for months. The way the woman carried herself, her spine always perfectly straight and her chin lifted, the air of cool confidence about her, how she never smiled any wider than a slight uptick of one lip—it made Jasmine's toes curl and her thighs clench. It made Jasmine want to go to her knees and worship her, kiss her hipbones, lick her cunt, beg her, call her Ma'am…or maybe even Daddy, if she would let her.

Although pining from afar felt juvenile and consequently mortifying, Jasmine couldn't seem to stop.

Which meant that just before five p.m. on a Friday, Jasmine was hauling her laptop, her thesis notes, and a stack of books and article printouts to the library for the sole purpose of catching a glimpse of Meg while she walked past the reference desk on her way to find a quiet desk space somewhere in the stacks.

When Jasmine arrived, Meg was there just as expected, frowning at the reference desk's computer and wearing a white long-sleeved button-up shirt tucked neatly into a pair of pressed gray pants. As always, she glanced up as Jasmine entered, although—to Jasmine's pleased surprise—this time she shot Jasmine an actual *smile*. Jasmine nearly tripped over her own feet, and her heart pounded faster.

"Hello!" Meg called.

Jasmine tried to smile winsomely back. "Hi!"

There was nothing to say then that wouldn't sound contrived, and Meg swiftly went back to her work. The spark of excitement fizzling like a faulty firework, Jasmine carried on her way, finding a deserted corner table near the history shelves. Although her pulse was throbbing in her ears, her stomach still emerging from its anxious coil, Jasmine spread her materials across the table, booted up her laptop, and tried to be productive.

She more or less succeeded. She paused occasionally to fiddle with her phone or nibble on a package of cashews, but nevertheless, she managed to annotate three articles and identify two other sources she needed to hunt down.

The library was quiet. A couple times, Jasmine heard movement somewhere nearby—the soft pad of shoes on the carpet approaching, stopping, and then retreating, the shuffling and thwacking of books on a shelf—but during the first hour and a half, no one came close enough to disturb her.

It served to highlight how ridiculous it was that she'd bothered to dress up. A two-second interaction, and the only person to appreciate her appearance now was herself—and even she wasn't really *appreciating* it. The waft of hairspray every time she turned her head was giving her a headache, her bare legs were cold in the frigid library, and looking down into her own cleavage was getting old.

Then a set of approaching footsteps didn't stop and retreat, but instead grew closer and louder until Jasmine lifted her head and spun around to find Meg walking toward her with a stack of books in her hands. When she caught Jasmine's gaze, she offered another smile—even brighter than the one before—and walked right up to Jasmine's table, where she set the books on the corner farthest from Jasmine's things.

"Oh. Hello again," Meg said. Since Jasmine had seen her, she'd untucked her shirt and rolled up the sleeves, revealing a pair of slender wiry forearms with a dusting of dark hair on the backs. She plucked a book off the top of the stack and carried it to one of the nearby shelves. "Sorry if I'm bothering you. I'll be done in a second."

Jasmine couldn't have shoved her work aside more quickly; some of her papers even skidded across the table and nearly flew off the edge. "No, I—it's fine. I need to take a break anyway."

Meg knelt to wedge the book in its place and stood again, sweeping her hands over her pants as though brushing off dirt. She returned to Jasmine's table, but instead of going straight to the stack of books, she stopped beside Jasmine's chair.

"I'm Meg, by the way. What are you working on? I see you here a lot."

Torn between gratification at being noticed and embarrassment at being so obvious, Jasmine felt her face heat. "I'm Jasmine. I'm, um, I'm doing research for my senior thesis."

"Nice to meet you, Jasmine. And you're studying—" Meg leaned over the table to poke at Jasmine's materials. The show of presumptuousness and invasiveness probably should have offended Jasmine. Instead, it made her heart beat a little faster. "Poetry?"

"Yes. Metaphysical poetry."

Meg gave a thoughtful "hmm" but stayed where she was, hovering over Jasmine like a teacher or a parent. Again, it should have been off-putting, but Jasmine's stomach began to coil itself all over again, this time in as much excitement as anxiety. "I was always more into Modernist poets, personally. Anything written before the 1900s bored me."

Jasmine stared dumbly at Meg's hand, taking note of her long slender fingers and trimmed clean nails. "Oh."

"That was years ago, though." Meg bent even lower, until her collarbone brushed Jasmine's shoulder. "I might think differently now. Especially if I had someone like you around to explain things to me."

Jasmine blinked, stunned at the flirtatious tone. But before she could respond, she was startled by Meg wincing and groaning as though pained.

"God, that was a lame come-on. Sorry."

Jasmine hoped she wasn't gaping. "You're…you're coming on to me?"

That almost never happened—not when the person was someone Jasmine actually wanted to hit on her, at least. Usually, she pined silently until whatever part of her brain was in charge of sexual attraction finally shrugged and moved on.

"Trying to. Doing a terrible job of it." Meg lowered her chin, shooting Jasmine a mischievous look over her glasses. Her eyes were brown, Jasmine noticed: brown with a ring of yellowish hazel around the pupils. "But in my defense, that shirt is seriously fucking distracting."

Glancing down, Jasmine realized that standing over her like that gave Meg a perfect view down her shirt, where her breasts were nearly spilling out of her bra. Her face went hot. Her first instinct was to cringe and cover herself, apologize profusely—because even though she'd meant to draw attention to her tits, she hadn't intended to go quite this far—but she didn't. Meg's playful expression gave her the courage to stretch backward slightly, arching her breasts up. The coquettish action drew a quiet groan from Meg's throat, and she swayed closer, practically draping herself over the back of Jasmine's chair.

"God, you're so fucking hot." Her voice was low, almost a growl. She turned her face into Jasmine's hair, nuzzling at the wispy strands around Jasmine's ear. "Is this all right? I didn't misread you, did I?"

Shaking her head, Jasmine raised her arms and wrapped them around Meg's neck, encouraging her to nuzzle even closer, to drag her nose along Jasmine's jaw. God, no, she hadn't misread anything. Jasmine was very, very happy with this turn of events, surprising though it was. She twisted her head to the side, lips parting invitingly, and Meg obliged, pressing their open mouths together.

Meg tasted faintly like spearmint. Jasmine probably tasted like lip gloss, and she hoped fervently that she wasn't smearing it all over both of their faces, although when Meg pulled back it didn't look as though any of the color had rubbed off onto her.

"Fuck," Meg breathed. She cupped Jasmine's breasts through her shirt and squeezed gently. "Can I?"

"Oh God yes." Jasmine didn't hesitate to pop open another two buttons so that Meg's hands could slip inside and follow the plunge of Jasmine's bra, which was a lacy black demi cup that made her tits look full and perky.

Meg sighed at the sight and then kissed Jasmine again while

she groped at them. Her thumb stroked back and forth over the cups until Jasmine's nipples began to harden. She pinched at them through the padded fabric, and the pressure, the friction, sent a tingle through Jasmine's groin. Her lower back arched, pressing her breasts more firmly into Meg's touch.

Meg broke away with a gasp. "I wanted you the moment I saw you." Finally—her legs had to have been getting tired, Jasmine thought—Meg knelt down to Jasmine's level and pressed a wet line of open-mouth kisses down the side of Jasmine's throat. "The way you always look at me. Like a tease. A shy little *minx*. I knew it was up to me to make the first move." Her fingers, skirting worshipfully up and down Jasmine's cleavage, finally plunged inside her bra and flicked her nipples, which were so tight and puckered now that they ached. Jasmine moaned softly and squeezed her thighs together, relishing the rising heat between them. "And I knew that when I did you'd be like this. Sweet, needy thing."

Meg's right hand abandoned Jasmine's breast in favor of skimming down her stomach and over her hips and pressing right where Jasmine's thighs were squeezed so tightly. In a second Jasmine was relaxing them and spreading them as wide as the stiff pencil skirt would allow.

"Look how badly you need it," Meg said. She hooked her chin over Jasmine's shoulder and stared down, watching Jasmine's breasts heave and her hips tilt up, trying to grind herself against Meg's palm.

"I do." Jasmine's mind had grown foggy with lust. "Please. Give it to me?"

Meg's answering groan was so long and deep that Jasmine swore she could feel it rumbling through her, as potent and devastating as an earthquake. "Come on then, sweetheart. Up we go."

Meg held her as though she meant to physically lift her, but she needn't have bothered; Jasmine was moving on her own.

She heaved herself unsteadily to her feet, gripping the edge of the table for balance. Then it seemed only natural to go one step further: to bend over, heedless of the haphazard spread of papers and books, and lay her shoulders and chest on the table, her head turned to one side.

"Good girl. That's perfect," Meg told her, and Jasmine shuddered, eyelashes fluttering.

There was a rush of cold air on the backs of her thighs as Meg lifted her skirt, bunching the fabric around her hips. Her panties, black to match her bra, were next. Meg dragged them down until they caught on Jasmine's knees, where she left them.

"Fuck," Meg said. "You're so wet. Look at you."

Jasmine couldn't look, obviously, but she could feel. She'd always been something of a gusher, and already she was slick to the very tops of her inner thighs. She felt exposed and wanton like this. It was a struggle to keep her hands on the table, to not reach down and touch herself.

She expected, *wanted*, to be immediately filled with one or two of Meg's long, slender fingers and then fucked until she was keening. So she was shocked when instead there came a puff of warm air against her ass and then the light brush of a tongue on her labia, licking at the smears of wetness there before dipping in and lapping at her cunt.

It was the sound of it more than the sensation that got to Jasmine: forced a breathy "uhhn" from her mouth and made her legs try to open wider, until her panties were stretched to the point of straining around her knees.

"Please," she said. "God, please." She reached behind herself and spread her ass cheeks, giving Meg more room to eat her.

It didn't occur to her until Meg's tongue ventured higher, flickering over her taint and then between her cheeks, that what she'd been begging for wasn't clear—and by that point she didn't care. Meg was already licking at her asshole: prodding at the little ring of muscle with the tip of her tongue until it was hot and wet and beginning to loosen. Because Jasmine had showered late that afternoon, she wasn't worried about cleanliness, but the feeling of her hole growing slick and open made her feel filthy.

She rocked into Meg's face, moaning, and nearly whined in protest when the motion made Meg stop instead of continue.

"Shh, I know." Meg stood, laying a quelling hand on the top of Jasmine's ass. "I'm sorry. I'd eat you for hours if I could, but we have to be quicker than that. Just because the library's been dead since you got here doesn't mean someone still couldn't come and interrupt."

It was as good as a trickle of ice-cold water down Jasmine's spine. She went rigid, scarcely even breathing. She'd forgotten where they were. She'd forgotten anyone could just walk right in and see her bent over a table getting her asshole licked. God, *how* could she have forgotten?

"Hey." Meg leaned forward, nearly climbing on the table on top of her so that she could sweep the sleek hair off the back of Jasmine's neck and nose at her nape. The weight of her, pressing down on Jasmine, made her mind go fuzzy again. "Still okay?"

Jasmine thought about being held down and fucked, pictured the burn of friction and the muscle cramps from the position she would have afterward, imagined Meg calling her a good girl again with her voice all sex-dark and deep.

"Yeah," she decided. What did it matter if someone walked in, anyway? Chances were that Jasmine would never see that person again. "Yeah, I'm fine."

"Good."

After another nuzzle to Jasmine's neck, Meg rose, and then she was behind Jasmine, running two fingers up and down her labia to get them wet before slipping them inside.

Jasmine's eyes went wide; her breathing stuttered. "Oh!" she cried, scratching at the table and crinkling her papers when Meg's fingers made a slow circular sweep of her inner walls, stretching her. "Oh God."

"Shh," Meg said, moving in another languid circle. "You're

so wet. I want you to soak my hand. I want my fingers to smell like you all day."

The position and the angle were so good. Jasmine was aware of not just how slippery and loose her cunt was, but her ass as well. Her asshole was still drenched with Meg's saliva, and when Meg swept her fingertips along the posterior wall of Jasmine's pussy, it felt almost like there was something in her *there* too. She imagined it, both holes stretched and full; her clit ached at the thought.

Jasmine couldn't resist propping herself up on one elbow so that she could drag the opposite hand downward: wrinkling book pages and shuffling papers aside until she was cupping her vulva, feeling the heat and throb of arousal between her thighs.

"That's it, sweetheart. Make yourself come," Meg said in a tender tone, followed swiftly by "Shh, shh, quiet," because Jasmine was nearly wailing, humping into the heel of her hand and rocking back onto Meg's fingers.

Jasmine dipped her fingertips past her labia, curling until she was stroking at her swollen clit, and she wailed again, and again, because it felt so good. There were showers of sparks inside her, lighting her up all the way to her toes.

She was taken aback, and then grateful when Meg leaned over her once more, this time to cover Jasmine's mouth with her free hand.

"There we go." Meg's voice was a breathless whisper, as soft and airy as a feather. Feeling dirty and slutty, Jasmine whimpered into her palm and shoved her hips up and down as hard as she could. "Oh fuck, just like that. Good girl. I want to feel you come."

In minutes, Jasmine was a mess of sweat and her own wetness. The silent room filled with the sounds of her muffled cries and the rhythmic squishing and squelching of her cunt as Meg fucked it. Pleasure rose like a fire, the flames flickering higher and higher, until finally Jasmine came with a sob, her pussy clenching around Meg's fingers.

Afterward, she lay shaking and panting, barely aware of anything except the little fluttering aftershocks in her cunt and the weak throb of her now-oversensitive clit. She scarcely even realized when Meg had let go and climbed off her until she heard an impatient grunt, followed by the noise of a zipper being yanked down.

Jasmine shook off the lingering postcoital haze in a hurry and heaved herself upright—clumsily, her hands and elbows slipping and skidding on her things—to find Meg bracing herself against the chair with her pants open and her right arm down the front of them. Her eyes were squeezed shut, her glasses crooked and smudged, and her chest heaving as she sucked in one quick breath after another.

"Let me help." Jasmine reached for her and framed Meg's slender hips with her hands. "Please."

Meg's eyes opened to slits. She looked dazed, drunk with pleasure. "It won't take long. Just—oh *fuck*."

Since Meg was loath to give up control completely, Jasmine settled on covering Meg's hand with her own so that she could feel the grind and roll of bone and muscle beneath Meg's skin as she rubbed her clit in jerky up-and-down motions. Eventually, her head dropped forward and she swayed into Jasmine's arms with a groan as she came.

Jasmine held her as she recovered, which didn't take long. Far too soon, Meg was drawing back so that she could rebutton her pants and smooth her shirt back down.

"That," she said, still breathing heavily as she straightened her glasses, "was amazing."

Jasmine stared, self-consciousness blooming in her like a stain. "Was it really?" She'd barely done anything, she realized now. She had bent over and taken it, and been too slow to give anything back.

Meg laughed, eyebrows arching. "*Yes*. Didn't you think so?"

"I," Jasmine began, but then Meg reached suddenly for

her panties, still tangled around her knees, and Jasmine was too startled to continue.

Instead, she watched dumbly as Meg gently, almost lovingly, eased them up her thighs and then rolled her skirt down over them. When that was finished, Meg turned her attention to Jasmine's shirt, redoing three of the buttons so that Jasmine's breasts were covered.

With a pleased hum, Meg cupped Jasmine's jaw and pressed their mouths together. Her lips tasted like sweat and musk. When Jasmine realized what it was—her own ass and cunt—she gasped into the kiss and fisted her hands in Meg's shirt.

She summoned enough nerve to break away and admit, "I had fantasies of, um…" But just as soon as she'd conjured it, her confidence faltered, and her cheeks grew hot.

You just bent yourself over a table and begged her to give it to you, she scolded herself. *Why are you getting shy again now?*

After a deep bracing breath, Jasmine made herself continue. "I had very, very detailed fantasies of going to my knees for you."

Meg arched an eyebrow, but looked pleased by the admission. "Did you?"

Jasmine's cheeks were still warm, as were the tops of her ears now, but she nodded. "Yes. And I didn't get to do that."

The corner of Meg's lip quirked up, forming the same confident not-quite-grin that had charmed Jasmine from the very beginning. "Well, there's always later."

Practice Makes Perfect

Sandy Lowe

Sylvie wanted to crawl under the covers and never come out. Ever. She kicked off her killer heels and flopped on her bed. Screw finals, screw vacation, screw everything. Finally, alone in her dorm room with the dusk light filtering weakly through the single, scrawny window, she buried her face in her pillow and cried.

She wasn't a pretty crier, she knew that. No delicately pink-rimmed eyes with tears sparkling on her lashes. She cried hard and fast, violent sobs beginning deep in her chest and bursting out. Tears a hot mess down cheeks grimy with damp foundation. Luckily, the only benefit of an ugly cry was that it would be over sooner, and the pressure that had lodged in her chest when she'd climbed out of the cab fifteen minutes earlier would be gone.

Over the worst, she turned to stare at the ceiling, the last of the tears sliding slowly down toward her ears. How could this have happened to her? *Her!* She was young and smart and not unattractive, right? She huffed. It was bullshit. It had to be bullshit.

Without warning the door banged open and Bennett teetered in, her slender frame hidden by the enormous stack of books balanced against her chest, all the way up to her nose.

"Um, a little help, please." Bennett's voice was muffled behind *Counseling: Principles and Practice.*

Sylvie grinned. Bennett always lifted her mood. She grabbed the top four books and dumped them on Bennett's desk, a mirror image of her own, in the left corner of the room. It was messier, though, piled high with file folders and small scraps of notepaper with unintelligible handwriting. Sylvie had no idea why Bennett didn't just take notes on her iPad like everyone else. She wouldn't be surprised to find an actual honest-to-God pencil lying around. "You are *such* a nerd. It's Friday night."

"Finals are kicking my ass." Bennett dropped the rest of the books and shoved her dark hair out of her eyes. "They're torture devices designed by sadistic professors who want to see the young suffer, because they're old and stodgy and probably never have anywhere to go on a Friday night."

Bennett turned and looked at Sylvie for the first time. "Wow, what happened to you?" She took a step closer. "You okay?"

"Yeah," she said. But this was Bennett. Her Bennett. Friends since freshman orientation, they shared almost everything, and Bennett was genuinely the nicest person she knew. That was annoying sometimes. She could never hide for long.

"I'm calling bullshit on that," Bennett said, and just like that, her tears started again.

Sylvie was too exhausted to care. "He said I was a terrible kisser."

"He? Oh, the guy. What's his name, Cameron? He is clearly certifiable. You're so smokin' hot I could grill sausages off your ass."

Sylvie choked out a laugh. "What did you say?" Bennett thought she was hot? Since when?

Bennett shrugged and walked into the teacup-sized bathroom they shared. Seconds later she walked out again with a damp white washcloth. "Okay, so the imagery needs some work, but you have to know you're gorgeous."

She sat Sylvie down on her bed and gently wiped her face. The cool cotton felt good on her flushed cheeks, and she closed her eyes and let Bennett work. It was nice to be taken care of for a minute.

"There," Bennett said, her voice soft, "better. Now spill. What happened with Cameron?"

"It's been three dates," Sylvie said, picking at a loose thread on the duvet. "I thought it was going great."

"And?"

"We were in the cab, and he asked if I wanted to go back to his room. He was pretty good about it, not pushy."

Bennett nodded.

"I said yes. I wanted to, you know, have sex. I *liked* him." She was still bitter about that. "Then he said, 'Yeah, I'd like that. But is it okay if we don't kiss?' I was like 'What the fuck? What does that even mean?'"

Bennett frowned.

"Then he said," Sylvie took a deep breath, "that he thought I was a great chick, but I was a terrible kisser." She stared at Bennett hopelessly.

Bennett looked thoughtful. "Well, *are* you a terrible kisser? I mean, it seems unlikely, you being so hot and all."

Sylvie squirmed. "I don't know! How am I supposed to know? I can't kiss myself. No one ever complained before."

Bennett nodded. "I guess you could ask him to show you how he likes it. I mean, if you really do want the guy."

Sylvie glared at her. "You are so *not* a girl sometimes, Ben. I never want to see him again. Not ever! The situation is, like, completely unfixable. I'm humiliated."

"Hey, I'm sorry." Bennett rubbed circles up and down Sylvie's back. "It'll be okay. He's probably just an asshole, and if he's right, well, you'll figure it out. Everyone does."

"Apparently not," Sylvie said. "You, for example, have girls falling all over you. Flirting and smiling and practically doing handstands to get you to kiss them."

Bennett cocked her head to the side, her expression

quizzical. "Are they wearing pants or skirts when they're doing handstands? Because that would seriously impact whether or not kissing happens."

Sylvie shoved her. "Not funny."

"Look…"

Bennett's fingers were tracing aimless patterns up and down her spine. Sylvie leaned into the touch. How could something so simple feel so good? She shivered. Bennett was just being a good friend. Comforting her. Not everyone's mind lived in the dirty gutter hers had called home ever since *that night*. Now she couldn't stop thinking about Bennett. Sexy naked Bennett.

"Maybe you just need to practice. It can't hurt. Find some willing guy and make out with him for four hours. I bet he'll come in his pants."

"No way." Sylvie shook her head, glad Bennett couldn't tell her mind was a million miles from any guy. "It's too embarrassing. What if I really am bad and he's too polite to tell me?"

Bennett squeezed the nape of her neck. She looked so serious, so intense, that Sylvie couldn't look away. "I'd tell you."

Her voice was intimate and Sylvie's breath caught in her throat. "You would?"

"Sorry, I didn't mean…I just meant that any decent person who cared about you would tell you. In general, you know. Not me exactly, not if you don't want…" She trailed off and took her hand away.

"Come on, admit it, you've been waiting for years for just the right opportunity to lay one on me, 'cause I'm, like, so gorgeous." Sylvie hoped it was true, but said it with a laugh just in case it wasn't.

Bennett flushed. "You look like a Victoria's Secret model, Syl, you're the stuff of fantasies. So yeah, I've thought about it. I'm only human."

Bennett fantasized about her? Had she *come* fantasizing about her? The thought made Sylvie's insides melt. This might be her only opportunity to find out.

"Well, I think it's a brilliant idea."

"It is?"

"Yes! You can give me lessons. I mean, if you want to. Do you want to?" At that moment, sitting on the bed with Bennett's thigh pressed against hers, the answer really mattered.

"God yes." Bennett reached up to tuck a stray curl behind her ear. "I've thought about kissing you a lot."

Sylvie was glad she was sitting down because the heat in Bennett's eyes surely would have knocked her on her ass. She grabbed Bennett's hands, excited, and not just because she needed the help. Kissing Bennett would be *hot*. "You'll tell me if I'm terrible and show me how to fix what's wrong. God knows, all your girlfriends can't stop moaning when you get all hot and heavy."

"You've *heard* me?" Bennett's eyes widened.

Sylvie felt her cheeks burn. "That night last March when I was supposed to stay with my parents, they canceled. But you didn't see me in bed in the dark when you stumbled in at three a.m. and, well, you guys were pretty into it. I didn't want to interrupt."

Sylvie remembered just how into it they were. She'd stared at the ceiling and listened to Bennett's soft commands for the girl to undress, to turn around, to bend over. She heard every moan, and she'd been wet. So wet. So *needy*. Her skin alive and tingling. She'd turned to watch them and she had to press her thighs together when the girl came, writhing in Bennett's lap and begging for *more, more, more*. Her long red hair tumbled down her back, and she arched her neck against Bennett's mouth when she came. The girl had slid silently to her knees and licked Bennett's clit. Bennett moaned, eyes closed, hips jerking. Sylvie slipped her hand into her pajamas and they came together, her heart beating wildly as she watched the pleasure play across Bennett's face.

Bennett looked horrified. "Fuck, Sylvie, I'm sorry. I didn't know."

"Hey, it's fine. Everyone does it. I got up early and studied in the library for a while. You never saw me." Sylvie tried to sound nonchalant but knew it wasn't working. She couldn't quite remember how to breathe.

"I wish you'd told me. I would have...I don't know, apologized or something."

"You don't have to apologize," Sylvie said. "I didn't mind. It was...nice."

"Nice?"

Sylvie rolled her eyes. "Okay, hot. Soak-my-panties hot."

Bennett grinned. *"Really?"* She shifted a little on the bed in a way that made Sylvie wonder if the jeans she was wearing were starting to get uncomfortable. Could she be turned on? It was time to turn up the heat and find out.

"Yes really. I came when you did. Watching you thrust into that girl's mouth."

Bennett was silent for a long minute, her fingers curled tightly into the duvet, her eyes a stormy sea. "Jesus, Sylvie." Bennett shifted again. Yup, definitely turned on.

If Sylvie was honest, it was the best orgasm she'd had in a long time. Maybe ever. She just didn't think too hard about the fact she'd had it watching her best friend get off. Or that thinking about it now, and every other time since, made her wet, started a slow pulse that was hard to ignore.

"It's my number one go-to masturbation fantasy actually." Sylvie was enjoying herself now she knew it made Bennett crazy to hear it. "Who knew I liked girl-on-girl so much."

Bennett breathed in sharply. "Fuck. That's hot. If I'd known, I'd have invited you to join us."

Sylvie remembered glancing back before she left that morning and watching them for a minute, Bennett's strong, tanned arms around the slender pale waist, the girl's chin crooked into Bennett's shoulder. And for an instant Sylvie imagined herself in the girl's place, saw herself wrapped up with Bennett, snuggled close, her thigh pressed between Bennett's legs. She'd left because she'd wanted so badly to stay and tried not to think about it again. She wasn't ready to face what it might mean.

"Come on." Sylvie needed to change the subject; thinking of a threesome made it hard to form a coherent sentence, and they had kissing lessons to get to. Her nipples had hardened under the red silk cocktail dress. "Please? Do me a favor."

"A favor," Bennett echoed. "You're sure?"

Sylvie slid as close as she could get, her thigh pressed tight to Bennett's. "I'm sure. Kiss me."

Bennett did. Softly. Gentle lips brushing Sylvie's so lightly she thought she imagined it. Sylvie tangled her fingers in Bennett's short hair and pressed closer. It felt so good. Sylvie needed more. She had wanted this for so long and now they were kissing, without it being weird or having to mean anything serious. She plunged her tongue into Bennett's mouth. She needed her. She was so caught up, it took her a second to realize that Bennett had eased back, her head tilted adorably to one side.

Sylvie narrowed her eyes. "What? Oh my God, I *am* terrible? I'm the world's most horrendous kisser!"

Bennett laughed. "No."

Sylvie pouted.

"No, really. You're just a little too enthusiastic right away. You need to ease in. You know, tease a little. It takes time and a little more finesse to start a fire burning."

Sylvie sulked. "I suck."

"No, you don't." Bennett pulled her closer, her lips an inch away. "We just need to practice." Then they were kissing again, a little firmer this time. Bennett teasing at the corners of her mouth, her hand cupped against the back of Sylvie's head to angle her in for a deeper kiss. Bennett knew exactly how to start her fire.

Sylvie was hot all over, heavy, dizzy. She felt so good. She liked the way Bennett handled her, totally in control of the situation. And because she was, Sylvie let go and just let it happen. When Bennett tugged at her bottom lip, she gasped and opened her mouth. Accepting the invitation, Bennett slipped her tongue inside. She explored Sylvie's mouth with long slow kisses, dipping, tasting, tugging and flicking with her tongue until it was all Sylvie could do not to crawl into her lap and beg to be fucked. She was so wet she didn't think she'd be able to hide it. The throbbing in her pussy kicked up a notch...or ten.

"Wait." Sylvie broke away, panting. "I can't. I need..." She wanted to come. She wanted to be alone so she could stroke her clit for the three seconds it would take her to explode. Then she wanted to do it again and again until finally she stopped thinking about Bennett's mouth moving lower.

"You're aroused." Bennett looked at her intently, her eyes somehow darker, sexier.

Sylvie dropped her gaze. Did she have to be so blunt about it? Did she have to say *aroused*? That word, it did things to her. It was so clinical. So sexy. So Bennett. "We should probably stop. I get it now. Slow and teasing. Wait to be invited, it's not a race. Blah, blah, blah."

"We haven't gotten to hard, demanding, intense kissing yet." Bennett eased back a little to take Sylvie in. "You sure you want to stop?"

Sylvie knew what Bennett saw. Her nipples had to be showing through the flimsy material of the dress, her legs were pressed tightly together, her blond hair a tousled mess that screamed *touch me*. Oh, they'd gotten intense already—the second Bennett had stuck her tongue in her mouth.

"When your partner is aroused, you can be as enthusiastic as you like. The more the better."

"That *wasn't* enthusiastic?" Sylvie was incredulous.

Bennett grinned. "Well, that was measured enthusiasm."

She didn't know what to say. She wanted Bennett to keep kissing her. More, she wanted to know what it was like when Bennett let go, lost some of that control. But if she kissed her again, she'd have to come, and that was embarrassing. They were just kissing. They were friends. Did she want more? Did Bennett? Could they have sex and go back to being friends?

Bennett's eyes were gentle, willing her to say something, and when she didn't Bennett cupped Sylvie's cheeks in her hands and brushed a thumb against her swollen lips. "If you say no again we'll stop, no questions asked. But I like that you're aroused. I like that kissing me makes you hot. I want to keep going. Okay?"

Sylvie nodded.

"Come here." Bennett positioned Sylvie so she was straddling her lap.

Sylvie groaned when she settled her ass on Bennett's knees. If she leaned forward an inch, she could rub her pussy against Bennett's leg. She trembled. She'd never been so turned on. Bennett sucked her lower lip into her mouth and bit it gently. Sylvie clutched Bennett to stay upright. She was going crazy. This was too much. Bennett was everywhere.

"Be good now," Bennett murmured. "You're so hot, baby. You need to wait."

"I can't, I have to…" She reached down only to have Bennett tug her hand away.

"Not yet. Soon. Kiss me now."

Sylvie did. Angling her mouth over Bennett's and kissing her deep. Months of trying not to think about that night, wanting her, not knowing if she should tell her, it all came flooding out in their kiss. Bennett pulled her closer, and Sylvie's breasts collided against her chest. She couldn't help but rub her pussy along Bennett's leg. She knew she wasn't supposed to but, God. It wasn't a fair fight. Her soaked panties were a delicious friction. She was tantalizingly, frustratingly close. Bennett plundered her mouth, hands in her hair, down her back, cupping the curve of her ass, pressing her tighter, harder. Fuck.

Bennett broke away, chest heaving, and pressed her forehead to Sylvie's. "Wow, Jesus. Just give me a minute."

"Why?" Sylvie whimpered. "Please, I can't stop." She slid her hands up under Bennett's T-shirt. "I want to touch you."

Bennett moaned. She shook her head but let it fall back as Sylvie swept her thumbs over hard nipples, cupping her breasts, loving the weight of them against her palms. Delicate curves on a muscular chest. "You feel so good. So soft and so hard."

Bennett pressed down on Sylvie's hips. "That's playing dirty."

She smiled. "I like dirty."

Bennett grabbed her around the waist and twisted so Sylvie was on her back, under her, surrounded by her. Her red dress was pushed up to expose slim thighs and a tiny patch of black lace masquerading as panties. "You like it dirty? You want it right now?" Bennett's voice was a growl in her ear.

"Yes, please now." Sylvie arched up to meet her, Bennett's weight wonderfully heavy. Blind with wanting, she wrapped her legs around Bennett's thighs. Closer, she needed to be closer.

Bennett closed her mouth over Sylvie's again, silencing the small whimpers vibrating in the back of her throat. Then Bennett's fingers were on her, cupping her over the lace. Sylvie surged against her palm and ground herself there. She was so close, about to come. A second later Bennett entered her, easing under the flimsy barrier and sliding inside with one smooth motion, pushing her knees up, going deeper. Fucking her. Hard.

"Oh God. Yes, fuck me. More. Please, I need…" She was completely, terrifyingly out of control.

When she pressed her thumb against Sylvie's clit everything splintered. Sylvie came so hard she thought she might have screamed. Waves of pleasure assaulted her as Bennett thrust and stroked and held her. Then Bennett was soothing her as she trembled and gasped against her shoulder.

"Oh my God." She lay weak as a noodle when it finally stopped.

Bennett eased out and brushed the hair out of Sylvie's eyes. "I don't think I'm in line for the top job yet, baby, but thanks."

Sylvie rolled her eyes and wiggled until Bennett slid off her and settled against her side.

"You okay?" Bennett asked.

"Oh, I think my kissing skills are greatly improved along

with just about everything else," Sylvie said. "Perhaps we should find out."

She edged down the bed until she was settled between Bennett's legs. The denim of Bennett's ancient Levi's was the only barrier between them. She tugged the zipper down and kissed the skin she'd revealed. Bennett was so soft here. Sylvie looked up. "What do you think? Am I getting better?"

Bennett swallowed hard. "A-plus," she said, her belly going to rock. "Are you sure? I mean, have you ever...?" She fumbled to finish the sentence.

"Kissed and licked and sucked a woman's clit until she comes?" Sylvie supplied helpfully.

Bennett blushed. "Well, yeah. That exactly, actually."

"Nope, but I have a really good teacher." Sylvie tugged the jeans down and off and halted abruptly. "Commando, seriously?"

Bennett looked a little sheepish. "There isn't a ton of room in those."

Sylvie made a mental note to give her crap about it later.

She'd never seen a woman up close before, and looking at Bennett, her breath caught in her throat. She was swollen and red, so wet it soaked her inner thighs. She was beautiful. She was kind of miraculous.

"You'll tell me if I'm not doing it right," Sylvie murmured as she dipped her head to kiss the top of Bennett's clit.

"Fuck." The muscles in Bennett's stomach flexed.

Sylvie swirled a fingertip in the wetness, dipping down inside and then back out to suck her finger clean. "Mmm, you taste good."

"Damn it." Bennett was propped up on her elbows watching her, her eyes so dark they were bottomless.

Sylvie gave her best wide-eyed innocent look. "Something you want?"

"I want you to suck me. Take my whole clit in your mouth and run your tongue all the way around it. Fast. Don't stop until I come."

Sylvie stared. Well, she *had* asked. And now she was wet all over again. "You're seriously sexy when you do that."

"What?"

"Give commands like that, be so specific."

"Then you'd better do as you're told. Now," she added in a warning tone when Sylvie didn't move.

She followed Bennett's command, cradling her clit against her lips and swirling her tongue around it. Bennett moaned. Her control finally snapped, and she pushed into Sylvie's mouth, threaded her fingers in Sylvie's hair, and pressed her deeper.

"Yes. That's it," she said.

Sylvie was in heaven. How had she lived for twenty-two years and never known the exquisite feel of a woman on her tongue? She slid her hands under Bennett's thighs and cupped her ass.

Bennett groaned. "Don't stop."

Sylvie didn't reply, unwilling to leave her pussy even for a second. She swirled her tongue around and around Bennett's clit and felt her get harder. She squeezed Bennett's ass and she jerked in response, her whole body stiffening.

"Sylvie baby, please."

Her name on Bennett's lips, the plea and the pleasure of it, was wonderful and giddy-making.

"Come with me." Bennett's voice was strangled, barely comprehensible. "I want to watch you come."

She whimpered, sending sweet vibrations up Bennett's clit, and slid her hand away to play with herself. She had never been so turned on making someone come before. It wouldn't take much to send her over the edge again, especially with Bennett thrusting into her mouth like that. God, that was sexy. She was so wet, her fingers slipping inside her pussy, thrusting in time to the pull of Bennett's hips. Palm bumping wildly against her clit, she rode endless waves of sensation. Her vision started to blur as the need to come overwhelmed her.

"Yes," Bennett said, her body taut, almost vibrating, waiting on the precipice. Waiting just for her. "That's it. Touch yourself. Come for me."

"I'm going to."

Bennett shattered, throwing her head back as she surrendered. She was so beautiful. Sylvie felt her clit pulse in her mouth and it was so fucking sexy she exploded too. Strong hands in her hair steadied her as she rocked against her fingers, whimpering.

Sylvie rested her cheek against Bennett's thigh and caught her breath. Waited for her heart to stop pounding and wondered why the hell it took them so long to admit they wanted each other.

"Best class ever." Sylvie crawled back up and into waiting arms. "I want to major in this. Finals would be a breeze."

"Consider yourself enrolled," Bennett said, and kissed her again.

ABOUT THE EDITORS

SANDY LOWE has a master's degree in publishing from the University of Sydney, Australia. She works as Senior Editor for Bold Strokes Books, publishing fiction that reflects the reveries and realities of LGBTQ lives.

STACIA SEAMAN has more than twenty years' experience in editing. Her background is in Slavic Languages and Literatures (M.A. University of Texas). After spending several years with a scholarly press, she moved into fiction editing, specializing in crime and romance as well as lesbian and gay fiction. She has published several essays and short stories.

Contributors

Lea Daley has two published novels. *Waiting for Harper Lee* received an Alice B. Readers certificate and was a 2014 GCLS finalist. *FutureDyke* was a 2015 Lambda Literary Award finalist and won a GCLS Award in 2015.

Rose P. Lethe is a corporate copyeditor, copywriter, and watcher of cat videos. After completing an MFA in creative writing, she found she could no longer stomach "serious literature" and has since turned to more enjoyable creative pursuits.

Stevie Mikayne writes fiction with a literary edge, combining her obsession with traditional literature with a love of dynamic characters and strong language. She graduated with an MA in creative writing from Lancaster University in the UK, and published her first two books, *Jellicle Girl* and *Weight of Earth*, shortly after. When she met a woman who could make the perfect cup of tea, create a window seat under the stairs, and build a library with a ladder, she knew she'd better marry her before someone else did. They live in Ottawa, Canada, with their young daughter.

Robyn Nyx is an avid shutterbug and lover of all things fast and physical. Her writing often reflects both of those passions.

She writes lesbian fiction when she isn't busy being the chief executive of two UK charities, working with victims of childhood sexual abuse and domestic violence.

MEGHAN O'BRIEN is the author of multiple lesbian romances and erotic novels, including *Infinite Loop*, *The Three*, *Thirteen Hours*, *Battle Scars*, *Wild*, *The Night Off*, and *The Muse*. She is also the author of a veritable cornucopia of dirty stories, published online and in various print anthologies.

RADCLYFFE has written over fifty romance and romantic intrigue novels, dozens of short stories, and, writing as L.L. Raand, a paranormal romance series, the Midnight Hunters. She is the president of Bold Strokes Books, one of the world's largest independent LGBTQ publishing companies.

JANELLE RESTON (janellereston.tumblr.com) got her start writing lesbian fiction while attending a women's college. She now lives in the Midwest with her partner.

AURORA REY grew up in south Louisiana and lives with her partner in Ithaca, New York. After a brief dalliance with biochemistry, she embraced her love of stories, completing bachelor's and master's degrees in English. She still loves spending time in the library. She may be contacted at aurorarey.com.

FIONA RILEY is a medical professional and part-time professor when she isn't bonding with her laptop over words. She went to college in Boston and never left, starting a small business that takes up all of her free time, much to the dismay of her ever-patient and lovely wife.

NELL STARK is an award-winning author of lesbian romance. In 2010, *everafter* (with Trinity Tam) won a GCLS Award in the paranormal category, and in 2013, *The Princess Affair* was a Lambda Literary Award finalist for romance. Nell's latest novel, *The Princess and the Prix*, came out in November 2015.

CARSEN TAITE's goal is to spin tales with plot lines as interesting as the cases she encountered in her career as a criminal defense lawyer. She is the award-winning author of numerous romantic suspense novels, including the Luca Bennett Bounty Hunter series and the Lone Star Law series.

ALI VALI is the author of the Devil series, which includes the soon-to-be-released *The Devil's Due*, and the Forces series. Her standalone novels are *Carly's Sound*, *Second Season*, *Calling the Dead*, *Blue Skies*, *Love Match*, *The Dragon Tree Legacy*, *The Romance Vote*, and *Beneath the Waves*.

ROBIN WATERGROVE writes at a messy desk in a neat room. She tries to capture life as it is, believing empathy to be a better medicine than escape. Robin lives in the Pacific Northwest and tells everyone it's rainy and gray so she can have the lovely weather all to herself.

REBEKAH WEATHERSPOON lives in Southern California, where she writes erotic romance, both paranormal and contemporary, new adult and adult. Her BDSM romance *At Her Feet* won the GCLS Award for erotic lesbian fiction. You can find Rebekah and her books at www.rebekahweatherspoon.com.

SALOME WILDE (salandtalerotica.com or @salomewilde on Twitter) has published dozens of stories across the gender and orientation spectrum, in genres from hard-boiled romance to kaiju exotica. She is editor of *Shakespearotica: Queering the Bard* and, with coeditor Talon Rihai, the forthcoming *Desire Behind Bars: Lesbian Prison Erotica*.

MJ WILLIAMZ is the author of seven novels, including GCLS Award winners *Initiation by Desire* and *Escapades*. She also has over thirty short stories published, mostly erotica, with a few romance and a couple of horror thrown in for good measure.

RION WOOLF loves all things water and all things erotic. Her story "Stay" appeared in the anthology *Shameless Behavior: Brazen Stories of Overcoming Shame*. "Stump Grinding" was published in the anthology *Dirty : Dirty*.

ALLISON WONDERLAND has contributed to over thirty arousing anthologies for Cleis and Ladylit and has also applied bold strokes to Bold Strokes' *Myth and Magic*. Besides being a Sapphic storyteller, she is a reader of stories Sapphics tell and enjoys everything from pulp fiction to historical fiction. Find out what else she's into and up to at aisforallison.blogspot.com.

Books Available From Bold Strokes Books

A Touch of Temptation by Julie Blair. Recent law school graduate Kate Dawson's ordained path to the perfect life gets thrown off course when handsome butch top Chris Brent initiates her to sexual pleasure. (978-1-62639-488-9)

Beneath the Waves by Ali Vali. Kai Merlin and Vivien Palmer love the water and the secrets trapped in the depths, but if Kai gives in to her feelings, it might come at a cost to her entire realm. (978-1-62639-609-8)

Girls on Campus, edited by Sandy Lowe and Stacia Seaman. College: four years when rules are made to be broken. This collection is required reading for anyone looking to earn an A in sex ed. (978-1-62639-733-0)

Heart of the Pack by Jenny Frame. Human Selena Miller falls for the domineering Caden Wolfgang, but will their love survive Selena learning the Wolfgangs are werewolves? (978-1-62639-566-4)

Miss Match by Fiona Riley. Matchmaker Samantha Monteiro makes the impossible possible for everyone but herself. Is mysterious dancer Lucinda Moss her perfect match? (978-1-62639-574-9)

Paladins of the Storm Lord by Barbara Ann Wright. Lieutenant Cordelia Ross must choose between duty and honor when a man with godlike powers forces her soldiers to provoke an alien threat. (978-1-62639-604-3)

Taking a Gamble by P.J. Trebelhorn. Storage auction buyer Cassidy Holmes and postal worker Erica Jacobs want different things out of life, but taking a gamble on love might prove lucky for them both. (978-1-62639-542-8)

The Copper Egg by Catherine Friend. Archeologist Claire Adams wants to find the buried treasure in Peru. Her ex, Sochi Castillo, wants to steal it. The last thing either of them wants is to still be in love. (978-1-62639-613-5)

Capsized by Julie Cannon. What happens when a woman turns your life completely upside down? (978-1-62639-479-7)

A Reunion to Remember by TJ Thomas. Reunited after a decade, Jo Adams and Rhonda Black must navigate a significant age difference, family dynamics, and their own desires and fears to explore an opportunity for love. (978-1-62639-534-3)

Built to Last by Aurora Rey. When Professor Olivia Bennett hires contractor Joss Bauer to restore her dilapidated farmhouse, she learns her heart, as much as her house, is in need of a renovation. (978-1-62639-552-7)

Girls With Guns by Ali Vali, Carsen Taite, and Michelle Grubb. Three stories by three talented crime writers—Carsen Taite, Ali Vali, and Michelle Grubb—each packing her own special brand of heat. (978-1-62639-585-5)

Heartscapes by MJ Williamz. Will Odette ever recover her memory, or is Jesse condemned to remember their love alone? (978-1-62639-532-9)

Murder on the Rocks by Clara Nipper. Detective Jill Rogers lives with two things on her mind: sex and murder. While an ice storm cripples Tulsa, two things stand in Jill's way: her lover and the DA. (978-1-62639-600-5)

Necromantia by Sheri Lewis Wohl. When seeing dead people is more than a movie tagline. (978-1-62639-611-1)

Salvation by I. Beacham. Claire's long-term partner now hates her, for all the wrong reasons, and she sees no future until she meets Regan, who challenges her to face the truth and find love. (978-1-62639-548-0)

Trigger by Jessica Webb. Dr. Kate Morrison races to discover how to defuse human bombs while learning to trust her increasingly strong feelings for the lead investigator, Sergeant Andy Wyles. (978-1-62639-669-2)

Wild Shores by Radclyffe. Can two women on opposite sides of an oil spill find a way to save both a wildlife sanctuary and their hearts? (978-1-62639-645-6)

Soul to Keep by Rebekah Weatherspoon. What won't a vampire do for love… (978-1-62639-616-6)